The Wondercurrent

Rella PenSword and The Red Notebooks, Volume 1

J.R. Parks

Published by ParksWrites, 2019.

This is a work of fiction. Any references to real events, real people, or real places are used fictitiously. Other names, characters, places, and events are products of the author's imagination, and any resemblance to actual events or places or persons, living or dead, is completely coincidental. Plucky Unicorn is an imprint of ParksWrites Publishing. www.parkswrites.com

Cover art by Tom McGrath

ISBN 978-1-7341746-5-6

To Kendra and our four little wonders -

AJ, EC, EM, and EJ.

"How easy is a bush supposed a bear!"

-William Shakespeare

Prologue: The Storykeeper of Ensea

WORD OF THE BREACH had spread quickly among the Storykeepers of Ensea. She had no choice. She had to report immediately. But abandoning Rella, her four-year-old daughter, was absolutely unthinkable. *Impossible*, she thought, over and over. *Impossible. There must be another way.*

Winter Deveraux-PenSword, a member of the Storykeeper's Alliance, had been called away before but never for a mission that would require years away from her family. Could she endure that much time without seeing Rella, her only daughter? What if the mission required five or ten years? Was Julian prepared to take on the responsibility alone?

"Don't forget to play the shadows game," Winter whispered to her husband as he tiptoed behind her holding a thin, yellow candle.

"Of course," he replied, waving the candle to illuminate a wide shelf jammed full of ancient books.

"It's her favorite game," Winter said. "And it calms her...helps her to sleep...to alleviate the nightmares."

Julian lowered the flame from his face to conceal his worry. He didn't really know if he was capable of raising Rella on his own. Though he knew others, like J, would be nearby to help.

"I'll play it with her every single night," he replied. "Until we have you back with us...safe and sound."

Julian turned and looked back towards the corner of the room and then back at Winter.

"I know it's here," Winter insisted, as she continued plucking books from the shelves and piling them onto the dust-coated floor.

Julian rechecked the piles on the floor. He wanted to be certain that Winter didn't overlook it.

"Why do these books always seem to jump and slide around?" Winter grumbled, tracing the spines with her fingertips. "They're never in the correct place when I need them to be."

"Perhaps Rella's been *re-shelving* them?" Julian replied, laughing. He was trying to alleviate the dread they were both feeling in that moment.

Winter chuckled and thought of how much she would miss Rella's curiosity. Her daughter loved to explore the bookshelves, though she certainly didn't pay much attention to where the books were supposed to go when she returned them, if she returned them.

Julian moved the flame closer to the shelf. A dark attic wasn't an ideal place to store the books, but it was the safest place for the time being.

Storykeepers, like the Deveraux-PenSwords, usually never stayed anywhere for long, and certainly not long enough to worry about dust accumulation or mold damage. Ever since Rella was born, they tried to anchor down, to give their daughter a sense of home like their parents had given them.

If you've ever met a child who's had to move a lot from house to house, or if you're one of them, you know how tough that can be: always packing up and moving on.

Julian climbed up on a tall ladder and waved the flame in front of another stack of books. He was so close to the angled ceiling that he had to be extra careful not to touch it with the tip of the flame. The shelf was littered, disastrously, with unbound manuscripts. Some of the manuscripts dated as far back as the first eleventh century, nearly two thousand years before this story begins, and more than a thousand years after the second eleventh century. Or about a thousand years after you, dear reader, were born.

"I don't see it up here," Julian said, blowing a thick layer of dust off of the one with a velvety light-green cover.

"This would go much faster if we could just flip on a light," Winter muttered.

She fiddled with the silver bracelet attached to her wrist.

When Winter was nervous, she would calm herself by tracing her fingers lightly over the etchings on the bracelet, as if she were reading braille—a skill she had only mastered out of necessity after Rella was born. They weren't sure Rella would ever have clear vision, but she'd been showing progress.

One of the etchings on the bracelet, a quill pen, was the official insignia of the Storykeeper's Alliance. The other etchings on the outside of the bracelet resembled the letters of an ancient alphabet. Winter thought they might be the same letters in two languages, like the letters on the Rosetta Stone.

Ensea had forbidden the use of electricity at this time of night. It was not an option. Winter knew that. She was desperate. Flipping a switch, though, would have instantly triggered the surveillance drones, and she couldn't risk the safety of the inno-cents in the village.

Julian placed the half-melted candle on the edge of a nearby desk and listened for the hum of propellers.

"Do you hear something?" Winter whispered, twisting her head around to face her husband.

"Nothing," Julian replied, after a pause. He pointed directly at the shelf just across from the desk where he'd set the candle. "Look over there...to the right...up just a little."

As Winter turned to face the shelves, Julian lowered his hands in front of the candle flame and formed a heart by pressing his thumbs together and curling his fingers.

When she saw the dim outline of the heart, Winter stopped scanning the compressed row of book spines and stood in si-lence. The shadow of the heart floated across the bookshelf like a sweet perfume, and she turned to face her husband once more.

"I wish...I mean...couldn't you come with me?" she pleaded, misty-eyed.

"You know we can't do that to Rella. She's only recently been able to see without the implants. And thank goodness they're out. We have to wait. And we don't know if she even carries...you know," Julian lowered his voice and spoke quickly, "*the gift.*"

Winter looked into the darkened corner of the room where Rella was sleeping and whispered. "Or if she carries any other gifts..."

The couple turned back around, knelt down, and continued sorting through the pile of warped book covers and tattered manuscripts.

"Should we wake her?" Julian asked. "Maybe Rella..."

"Found it!" Winter said, smiling nervously as she picked up the hand-stitched notebook with the red cover. Julian stood up and picked up the candle and waited for Winter to speak.

As Winter slipped her Red Notebook into her bag, the quill pen insignia on her bracelet started to flicker. The blinking patterns were a signal from the other members of The Storykeeper's Alliance. They were now waiting outside.

"Do you want me to wake Rella?" Julian asked again.

The bracelet blinked even faster, creating a strobe effect, like a security alarm, throughout the room.

"I can't do it," Winter said, clutching and unclutching the strap on the satchel with her Red Notebook inside. "You take it!"

"I can't!" Julian replied. "The Alliance has called on you."

If her fears were true, and the Dreambridge had been breached, every child on Earth One, from Eastcon to Westcon, was at risk of losing access to the Dreamworlds. And once the Dreamworlds were lost, the children would eventually lose their ability to play, to make believe, to tell stories, to think up anything original at all. They would become nothing better than copycats, or worse, plagiarists.

But it can't be true, Winter thought as she glanced over at Rella, still sound asleep. *Why now?* Winter feared that she would miss a lot more than Rella's fifth or sixth birthdays.

Julian placed his hand gently on his wife's shoulder and stared directly into her eyes.

"You have to do this," he said, "Could we really let Rella, or any child, grow up in a world without stories, without imagination?"

Winter looked over at her daughter one more time. She was taking slow, even breaths, a sure sign that she was happily lost in a dream.

"I know," Winter said softly, "I know..."

Julian glanced down again toward the blinking bracelet and then at the shelves.

"Promise you won't let her forget me," Winter said as the blinking light illuminated a small stream of teardrops rushing over her cheeks. "Promise you won't let her forget me," she said again, reaching for her husband's hand.

"I promise," Julian replied, taking her hand and looking back into her eyes. "And if you aren't back...before too long...you know I'm coming after you. I'll search every world, every past and future, every dimension, and every dream...a hundred times over."

"I know," Winter whispered, drying her tears on his shoulder.

As the candle burned out, Julian gently placed his hand on his wife's lower back and guided her into the stairwell.

Startled by the echoes of footsteps on the stairwell, Rella rolled over, opened one eye, and cried out for her mother.

Chapter 1: Rella PenSword and the Dream Traveler

"I'VE HEARD *his* name before!" Rella exclaimed.

"Where?" the girl asked, pulling herself up onto the wide branch.

"In a book...," Rella piped as she danced along the limb, "an old one my father used to read to me. It had these beautiful etchings...crenellated castle walls and queens with gowns woven by fairies."

Rella stretched her arms and twirled like a helicopter seed. Despite hours of climbing through the vine-laced branches, all five times larger than the ones in the forests surrounding the village of Ensea, Rella felt alive, as if she'd hardly traveled a step.

She peered over at her new friend whose colorful, rustic clothing reminded her of some of the characters in her father's books, but she couldn't remember which ones. *Most likely*, she thought, *it was one of the books I wasn't supposed to be reading.* At the moment, she also couldn't remember how or if she had ever previously met this peculiarly dressed girl.

"Do you *ever* get tired?" the girl asked, adjusting a thin, sandy-blonde braid that wrapped around her head like a crown.

Rella didn't answer. She was trying to recall the exact sound of her father's voice when he read that villain's name aloud. He always used a deep, cartoonish vibrato. She practiced once in her head and then, facing out at the wide expanse, bellowed: "*Aaar-rrrrchiiiimaaaaago.*"

The girl jumped up, whirled around and shouted, "Where? Here?"

Rella laughed, but quieted quickly as she realized that the girl was serious.

"What is it?" the girl said.

As Rella thought of her father, she felt sadness, like a bubble, inflating inside her stomach. She pursed her lips and took a long, slow, deep breath.

Why, she thought, *is this girl asking me about a storybook villain called Archimago?*

If you, dear reader, are a native English speaker, and you were to pronounce the villain's name the way it is spelled, you might think it was arch-imago. And this might make you think of arches, like the curve on the inside of your foot, or something you might walk underneath in a fancy old church. It is, however, most commonly pronounced as ark-imago, like the sound at the end of the word park, or dark, or aardvark.

"Sometimes I get tired," Rella answered, "but usually only when I have to read the grammar books at school or when..."

Rella paused and wiped a small tear from the corner of her eye. She was trying not to think of her parents. She had not seen or heard from her mother in over three years. Her father, about six months.

"You seem worried," the girl said, turning her eyes away from Rella and scanning the swirling, dusty shadows in the cliffs below. Though they were very high up in the trees, the girl didn't seem the slightest bit worried about falling.

"What's really bothering you?" the girl asked.

Rella tried to form a response. She was used to blocking out the sadness bubbles of missing her parents, but something felt different here in this place. She felt safe, and freer, and, somehow, more hopeful.

"I was thinking about my family," Rella said, "and my village...you probably haven't heard of it."

"You mean Ensea?" the girl interrupted.

"Yes. You do know it! But I'm...," Rella said, pausing as she recalled the turmoil back home.

Rella rubbed a soft, velvety leaf between her fingers and looked far down into the chasm of colorful mists. For a split second, she thought she heard the melody of one of her favorite songs about a land beyond a rainbow playing the distance. She tried hard to remember how she and this new friend had first discovered this wild forest of impossibly tall trees.

"Tell me more about the knights in your father's story," the girl said, breaking the silence.

"Oh...yes, in the stories my father reads to me," Rella answered, "knights are always very strong and brave, and they wear gleaming armor."

Rella examined her new friend's strange and wonderful clothing more closely. There was an array of fabrics stitched and clasped together. She felt the urge to ask if it might possibly be some kind of magical armor.

The girl noticed that Rella was puzzling over her clothes and, as if reading her mind, smiled and spoke: "No. This isn't armor, if you were wondering."

"Oh...well...," Rella said, smiling, "I don't mean to sound odd, but your clothes sort of look like they could be from one of my father's storybooks. Did you make them yourself? Or did you get them from a magician? Are they enchanted?"

The girl flashed a wide smile but didn't say a word.

As Rella spoke the word *enchanted* aloud, a flashing light, resembling a comet, glimmered off in the distance. At the sudden burst of light, she jumped up and pointed, but the mysterious girl, who wasn't actually wearing armor, didn't see it because she had returned to watching the shadows sliding along the distant cliffs.

"Sometimes these knights ride magnificent horses," Rella continued, smiling brightly as she watched the trail of dust blazing in the sky and reshaping itself into a sword and then transforming just as quickly into the outline of a galloping horse carrying a female knight on its back.

The girl glanced up at Rella and followed Rella's gaze toward the skyline.

"And the best ones," Rella said, pointing at the galloping outline of the knight in the sky, "always follow the chivalric code."

Streaks of silver light wove themselves in and out of the colorful layers of paper-thin clouds.

Rella felt that she was somehow responsible for this majestic scene, like she was painting it herself, though she couldn't understand why she felt that way.

"Please say more about the chivalric code," the girl said, in a tone that reminded Rella of a teacher who already knows the answer but asks the question just to see if you do.

"Well...," Rella paused. "Well...it means that a knight must have faith, integrity, humility, generosity...and, of course, courage."

Rella loved thinking about the origins of old words like *chivalric.* Old words gave her comfort. They reminded her that the ancient days weren't, perhaps, quite as distant as she sometimes felt they were.

"Was the chivalric code only for boys?" the girl asked, as she pulled a small, clear vial from her pocket and swiped it through the orange and white puff of particles passing over her head.

"No, no," Rella replied, watching curiously as her new friend collected the dusty substance and tucked the vial into a pouch tied to her intricately woven belt.

Rella tried to count all of the different colored strips of fabric included in the belt, but lost track once she reached thirty-seven.

"Some people," Rella continued, "once thought the code of chivalry was only meant for young male squires, but my father says that anyone could choose to practice chivalry."

"What else can you tell me about this code?" the girl asked, pulling another vial from the pouch and filling it.

"Well, in this old book...," Rella continued, "there was a story of a female knight who was brave, elegant, and smart...she was called...Brit...Oh...I can't remember. I don't know why I can't remember it."

Rella rubbed her forehead as if it might help her recall the name. She felt a terrible ache.

"I've heard the story at least a thousand times," she said, now rubbing her eyes.

As the shooting stars faded out above, Rella started to feel a strange sensation on her skin, and, though her eyes were open, she felt like she was opening them a second time.

Chapter 2: Rella's Dreamscape

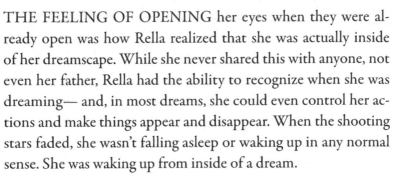

THE FEELING OF OPENING her eyes when they were already open was how Rella realized that she was actually inside of her dreamscape. While she never shared this with anyone, not even her father, Rella had the ability to recognize when she was dreaming— and, in most dreams, she could even control her actions and make things appear and disappear. When the shooting stars faded, she wasn't falling asleep or waking up in any normal sense. She was waking up from inside of a dream.

"Rella!" the girl shouted. "Are you ok? Stay with me Rella!"

She could hear her new friend but she was still in the process of regaining consciousness.

Dream recognition, for Rella, was a gift that came in handy, especially during nightmares. Rella knew that the monsters in the nightmares couldn't actually hurt her, but they often seemed more real within her dreams than the real-life monsters, like the genetically-modified drone-bird hybrids that often swooped overhead as she walked to and from Ensea Elementary School.

"Rella!" the girl shouted, moving closer to her. "Stay with me, Rella!"

When Rella was in her waking-dream state, she could simply imagine that the monster was a bunny and it would immediately change form. 'Bunny!' she'd think to herself and, almost immediately, the monster would become a bunny. Or she could just jump off of a cliff and the falling feeling would wake her. Once she escaped, she'd find herself comfortably snuggled beneath her favorite green quilt.

Rella looked at the girl. "I'm here!" Rella said, "I'm awake now!"

"Fantastic! I thought I was losing you!" the girl said, looking down at the corner of a book poking out of Rella's satchel. "Do you have your father's book with you?"

"No," Rella said, reflexively tucking the book back into the satchel, as she often did when she was transporting books to and from the secret libraries in Ensea.

Now that she was aware that she was dreaming, she was on alert for intruders.

"Oh...I just thought...where do you keep the book?" the girl asked, trying not to scare Rella, who was still orienting herself inside of the dreamscape.

Rella spoke quickly, "It's locked away in my family's private library. You have to climb a hidden staircase behind a bookshelf in our attic to get there." She wondered if she should have shared that information. It wasn't smart to offer trust so quickly, especially since this girl had only just appeared inside her dreamscape.

"Why do they have a hidden tunnel to get to the library? Books shouldn't be hidden," the girl said.

"Well, in my village, at least since I was about four, the government created new laws about who can own what books, especially storybooks, not to mention philosophical or religious books."

Rella watched to see if the girl knew what she was talking about. She was trying to decide if the girl was a creation of her own mind or if she was something else.

"That sounds terrible. No storybooks at all?" the girl said, shuddering.

"Some families still have them," Rella said, watching the girl closely. "But they have to be very careful about where they store them."

Rella reached her hand back into her satchel and pressed her fingers against a book. She sensed that the girl was trustworthy, but the way the girl constantly avoided her eyes and kept staring into the shadows made her stomach churn with worry.

Rella tried hard to recall if this girl, with mysterious, patched clothing and beautifully braided hair, was someone she knew from real life or from a book. She couldn't place the girl at all. She wasn't an elf, or a princess, or a witch, or any other film or video game character she knew. And she did not act like any of the boys or girls from Ensea Elementary. She seemed like a real person, but also a little older, sort of like someone who had traveled to a lot of distant places. Rella thought about the kids from her school who had lived in five or six villages before they had even turned six.

"In your father's book...was *he*, Archimago, a hero or a villain?"

"How do you know about...about?" Rella replied.

"About him?" the girl asked. "You and I were discussing him before...you know...before you woke up?" the girl said.

Rella laughed at the way the girl hesitated when she said "woke up" because she knew that she had not actually woken up yet. The girl seemed to understand as well.

Even if she was just someone her own imagination was inventing, Rella really liked talking to this girl. "Archimago was the worst villain," Rella said, "a deceiver, a thief, and a shapeshifter...he could conjure false images out of the air...and he could do it *at will!*"

Rella waited for the girl's reaction, but the girl's attention had returned to the dark forests and the shadows in the distant landscape.

Rella sensed that the girl wanted to say something, but she was still trying to recall if this girl had ever visited any of her previous dreams. If this girl was a dream traveler, something her father had talked about a few times, Rella had no idea how to confirm it. She had never met one and she didn't know if dream travelers were supposed to reveal themselves to the dreamers. The thought of meeting a dream traveler, though, at least a kind one, was thrilling.

Rella continued watching the layers of color in the sky and across the valleys below.

As she lost herself in distant thoughts of home, Rella placed her hand in her pocket and fished out a small stone. As she pulled the stone from her pocket, she nearly dropped it, but it seemed to jump back into her hand on its own. The stone then began glowing.

Rella didn't question its magical power, since she knew she was in a dream and luminous stones often appeared in her pockets when she was dreaming. She set the stone on the edge of a branch hanging over her head. The light from the stone cast a shadow onto a cluster of blue and yellow leaves hanging, like banners, nearby.

Rella contorted her fingers in front of the light from the stone and created a series of shadow puppets: birds, spiders, and wiggly creatures of her own imagination. She raised and lowered her hand to make it appear as though a phantom was flying over the leaves.

The girl was examining a crack on the trunk of the tree where some of the bark had been peeled off.

Rella continued to play the shadows game. When she was very small, her mother often played shadow puppets on the wall before bedtime and Rella had continued the tradition with her father, even years after her mother disappeared.

"My mother taught me this one!" Rella said, trying to get her friend's attention. She continued transforming her hands into different creatures: butterflies, wolves, and, her favorite, a dog-man-knight she had named Sir Miles Barkius.

Though it was a very impressive puppet show, the other girl still didn't notice. A message of some kind had appeared on the piece of tree bark in the girl's hands and, Rella noticed, the girl started to tremble. She was spelling out a word: s-h-a-d-o-w-s-p-l-i-t-t-e-r. *Shadowsplitter*.

Rella continued wriggling her fingers in front of the beam and imitated her father's cartoonish, evil accent: "And he delighted most...in making children believe the most devilish lies about their dearest friends. And about their families. And worst of all...about themselves." Rella hunched her back, lifted her hands like a pair of claws and turned around, casting a malicious but playful smile at the dream traveler.

"I know what you are!" Rella said, still using her cartoonish evil voice.

The girl looked curiously at Rella but was so deep in thought that she didn't understand what Rella was saying.

"I said...I know who you are!" Rella repeated, with a more playful tone of voice.

Rella had figured out that the girl was a dream traveler because the girl didn't resemble anyone she'd ever met or read about in a book, and also because she couldn't get the girl to join in on the puppet show. If the girl with the braids was just a figure created by her own imagination, she would have played along. Yet, Rella had absolutely no control over this girl's actions. The girl nodded and smiled.

"You got me!" she said, relaxing.

But, then, as quick as a fox, she locked her eyes onto Rella's.

"Your father's book," she said, pointing toward the distant shadows, "describes *him* exactly...although one of the others who first told me his name was Archimago also told me that *he* was the one who came up with the name...and that he was never actually given a name at all."

"You mean his parents never thought to give him a name?" Rella asked, trying to understand why the girl was suddenly so afraid.

The idea of a nameless man who stole the names of other characters from ancient books intrigued Rella. She loved to invent all kinds of names for herself and her imaginary characters, whether in her drawings or at the playground at school.

A raging thunder blast resounded overhead. The two girls turned their eyes toward the smoke-shrouded island.

"Do you think they could be the same person?" Rella asked, still gazing out over The Dark Waters.

The mysterious girl gritted her teeth. She seemed paralyzed.

This is not an ordinary dream, Rella thought. *Something is very wrong. I think it's time to wake up.*

The winds picked up and the tree began to shake. The luminous stone she had been using to make her shadow-puppets fell off of the branch and sailed down to the forest floor.

Rella stared into the depths and thought about jumping, but she was overcome with fear. A jump, if this was a dream, should have woken her up, but she felt like this girl needed her help. She also felt that there was a chance that this girl knew something about her missing parents.

"Follow me," the girl said, leaping onto a nearby branch and then grabbing a large vine.

Rella quickly followed.

"Where are we going?" Rella shouted, as she leapt across the branches.

The girl was already too far ahead to hear her.

Like acrobats, they swung through the branches for at least half an hour, though it felt longer.

Just as they reached a safe landing, the storm quieted down.

Rella felt exhausted and hungry.

While you might think that a person wouldn't get hungry in a dream, that was not the case for Rella. However, because she was aware that she was dreaming, she just imagined a pair of juicy pears and, almost instantly, they appeared on the branch above her. She plucked both of them and offered one to her friend.

The girl thanked her and they both savored their meal in silence. As they ate, Rella continued admiring the girl's intricately woven clothing. It was hand-sewn and the colors perfectly matched many of the surrounding plants and flowers.

"Well, it looks like I still have some control of this dream," Rella said to her friend, conjuring and plucking another fruit, a peach this time. She began feeling calmer and nourished.

The two companions were still as high up in the branches as before, but they had traveled closer to the banks of a sparkling river, known as The Wondercurrent.

"This place surrounding us," the mysterious girl said, "is a reflection of my home world, Hleo."

Rella looked around. She was enraptured by most of it, but the damaged parts also worried her.

"It is beautiful," Rella said. "At least most of it..."

"Would you be interested in visiting it for real?" the girl asked.

The view of Archimago's island was clearer from their new perch, and some of the luminous stones had reappeared next to The Wondercurrent, twinkling from a hundred feet below.

Rella wasn't sure how to answer.

"I think so...but what about that island? Is that part of your world?"

The girl knew that she'd have to explain it now, but she didn't want to frighten Rella.

Rella could see that the girl was trying to figure out how to explain something, so she tried to calm and distract her with one of her favorite games, where she would ask her friends what superhero name they would pick for themselves.

"What name would you pick?" Rella asked, wiping more pear juice from her lips and dropping the seed into the river below.

"Name? For *him*? For the nameless man?" the girl replied, her eyes still locked on the distant island.

Rella reached out and put her hand on her friend's shoulder.

"No, not for *him*...for yourself. If you were the hero, like Brit...oh, wait, now I've got it, yes, Britomart, like the female knight from the book?

"I never imagined picking a new name," the girl said.

Rella tried to remember if she had even learned her new friend's name, so that she might be able to suggest a pretend name. *How could I have forgotten this girl's name?* Rella wondered. She felt embarrassed whenever she forgot someone's name, especially someone she liked.

The tree swayed, knocking Rella onto her bottom. As Rella began to slide toward the edge of the branch, the girl reached down and grabbed her hand.

"It takes some time to get used to my world," she said, "Now...about that name of yours?"

"PenSword!" Rella shouted, as though she were releasing the name from a trap.

The girl pulled Rella back up onto her feet and listened as Rella said it again with gusto: "PenSword! Rella PenSword! And if you write it down you have to capitalize the S, so people don't mispronounce it."

The girl looked into Rella's eyes. They sparkled like the surface of a lake at midnight. She tested out the pronunciation in her mind: *Pens-word...Pen-Sword.* She loved the mysterious flexibility of Rella's language.

"That's quite a flashy name," the girl said.

Rella ducked as another crash of thunder burst out of the sky.

"Why PenSword?" the girl asked.

Another crack of thunder rang out over the horizon and both girls jumped. Rella looked around for a vine to swing on, in case the branch dropped out from beneath them. The girl put her hand on Rella's shoulder and offered a reassuring smile as she whispered: "Dream, remember?"

They weren't in any immediate danger, Rella supposed. But this situation felt so different from any other dream. It was like she was reading the final chapter of a book before she had even read the first one.

Rella paced back and forth over the wide surface of the branch. The girl's question struck her as odd. *Why PenSword?* After all, that actually was her family's last name. But, in her dream, she somehow forgot this fact. Like the meaning of the word itself was different. The words were the same, but they had a different feeling in dreams. It was similar to the differences between colors at home and here. Blue in her dreams wasn't exactly the same as blue back home.

Suddenly, she started to imagine her Uncle J's blue two-door sedan driving across the limb. She didn't know why she was thinking of his car in the middle of this dream.

"Be careful!" the girl shouted. The girl's change in tone caught Rella off guard. They were still over two hundred feet off the ground, and one hard gust could have carried them away like dandelion seeds.

"I don't want you to wake up yet, I've got something important to tell you," the girl said.

"There's an expression my father used to use," Rella answered, speaking more quickly, "One that we are forbidden by law to speak aloud: 'The pen is mightier than the sword.'"

"I like that. What does it mean? Does it have something to do with the knights, spelled with a K that you don't pronounce?" the girl asked, thinking about the oddities of Rella's language.

"Maybe. It might go back that far. All I know is that it refers to the power of using writing...stories and poetry and logic...in order to bring about change...and to settle disputes...without *murdering* people."

The way that Rella's tone flattened out at the word *murder* concerned her friend. Rella had too much understanding of the word murder.

"In one of your other dreams, you said that you were more of a painter than a poet," the girl replied.

"Oh. Well..I'd like to be a poet. But I'm only seven," Rella replied, "but you can include art...like sketching and making comics and illustrations as mighty things formed with pens."

"PenSword," the girl repeated. "I really do love your name."

Rella PenSword smiled and slashed at a passing puffball of red dust.

"Take that!" Rella shouted.

"Maybe," the girl said, laughing as she watched Rella battle the cloud of particles. "Yes, I think it would be good for me to find a new name too!"

Rella gestured as though she were polishing the dust off of an imaginary sword. She then reached over and adjusted her satchel. Aside from the strange fabric patch sewn into it, the satchel in this dream resembled the one she wore in real life, one that had once belonged to her mother, Winter Deveraux-PenSword.

As she thought of her mother, Rella felt a warm breeze blow across her back. She listened closely as it rustled through the leaves above and below her, shaking a few of them loose and carrying them like scraps of paper up over the cliffs and into the undulating valley below. She always believed that her dreams provided clues about what happened to her mother.

Rella opened her satchel and pulled out the scroll. She had never seen this scroll in any of the other dreams, but she loved the way the soft, metallic fabric felt against the skin of her palms.

"Did you give this to me?" Rella asked the girl.

"No, but it looks like it's something from...yes, it's got to be from my world," the girl replied. The wind picked up and the sky darkened.

"Are you certain a storm isn't about to blow through again?" Rella asked, lifting the rolled-up scroll with both hands above her head like she was about to strike something. She continued, "To tell you the truth, I feel like I'm not fully in control of this dream...so I apologize if something happens...to you."

"I think we're ok for now," the girl said. "I'm a pretty good builder."

"What do you mean?" Rella asked.

"I'll tell you more later," the girl said. "Let's just say...I do a lot more than just travel through dreams...and we are safe."

Rella knew that girl was trying to calm her, so she didn't push for answers at the moment. She figured she'd be waking up soon anyway. None of her dreams ever lasted *this* long.

The girl continued, "It wouldn't be safe to climb down right now, and Thalas, my guardian, will be arriving soon to carry us off."

At the mention of Thalas, Rella became even more curious.

"What...who...is Thalas?" Rella asked, brushing her bangs out of her eyes, "Is she a unicorn...a dragon?"

Rella hoped that the suggestion of the dragon might actually bring on a dragon, like she had done with the pears and the peaches earlier. She had usually only been able to conjure distant lights or small items, never a dragon, but she thought, with the way this dream was spinning out of control, this would be as good a time as any to try.

"You'll have to wait and see," the girl replied, smiling like you do when you're hiding a birthday present from your best friend.

They both turned and peered up in the opposite direction of the dark water, toward the clash of colorful clouds swirling over the northern cliffs.

Rella spotted the silhouette of the soaring, hawkish beast in the distance.

She quickly slipped the scroll back into her satchel. She sensed that she was supposed to be more careful with the scroll, though she had no idea what it was for.

"Would Rella Pen*Sword* also wear a cape?" the girl asked.

With the cliffs and mountains spread out behind her, Rella continued to act out the part of Rella PenSword.

She placed a hand over her heart and lowered herself on one knee.

"What is this gesture?" the girl asked. "It makes me feel...oh, what's the word...*noble*, as though I'm a great queen."

With her head bowed, Rella, still pretending to be Rella PenSword, extended her hand to her new friend. Her friend, resting her back against the trunk, reached out and took the steady hand firmly into her own.

"Allow me to introduce myself: I am Rella PenSword...Defender of..."

Rella looked around, trying to remember if she had ever learned the name of this world.

"What's this place called?" she said, stifling a laugh, and continuing to grip her friend's hand.

"It has many names. Some who speak your language have called it the sheltering wood, or Shelterwood. In an older tongue, perhaps from olden days, my lady...I mean, Miss...Sir...Lady... PenSword, it was also called Hleo."

The name Hleo landed softly on Rella's ears. *If this is only a dream*, Rella thought, *I don't ever want to leave.*

As Rella looked into her friend's eyes, she spotted a blue and yellow leaf, the size of a bath towel, drifting down from the limbs above.

Rella let go of her friend's hand, jumped up and grabbed ahold of the leaf. She punched a large hole in the top and put it on, pretending it was a cape. It reached just below her knees.

She twirled around twice, shaking dust from the leaves and causing a small cloud to form around her. Another warm breeze blew through the branches, sweeping more dust into the air.

As the dust cleared, Rella reappeared, like a magician, out of thin air.

Her friend, who was still worried and serious, couldn't resist Rella's theatrics any longer and joined the game, pretending to be the damsel in distress.

"Oh..brave lady knight...help me!" the girl said, feigning terror. She hadn't played pretend with anyone, in Hleo or in any dream journey, in a very long time, but Rella's game was one she knew well. "My kidnappers will be back any minute. Please!" the girl cried out.

As the two friends played their game, a dark, twisted shadow began drift from the coast of Archimago's island.

"My lady...I am Rella PenSword, Defender and Protector of...Hello," she shouted, looking directly at her friend.

"We are so glad you've arrived...now, please, they're coming!" the girl exclaimed, as though Rella had just come to save her entire village.

The shadow rose higher and hovered near the distant shore, but the girls didn't see it, as they were still facing the cliffs.

As the word 'Hello' echoed repeatedly off of the nearby cliffs, both girls thought someone was actually shouting back. Rella shouted again.

"Hello, Hello, Great people of..."

Rella paused and waited for the cliff to respond.

"Hello."

Rella thought she heard two voices at once, like the cliff responding but also like someone was standing behind her, whispering.

Was it her Uncle trying to wake her? When the dream voices and the outside voices clashed, she knew she was about to return to the physical world of Earth One.

No, not yet, Rella thought.

She wasn't sure if her friend, the dream traveler, could hear the doubled-voices.

"Not Hello. Hleo," the girl replied, breaking out of her role as the damsel and laughing so hard she had to bend over to catch her breath. "The middle is pronounced like 'lay,' as in 'lay an egg.' Huh-lay-oh. But you have to pronounce that H-part really fast. *Hleo*. Say it with me.."

"Hleo" the two girls sang in unison, stretching out the vowels.

Rella pulled the glowing scroll from her satchel and stabbed the air as she danced around, battling the small cloud of dust. She continued speaking with her friend, asking questions about Hleo, Thalas, and the guardians. She still felt odd that she couldn't remember ever seeing the scroll before, although she seemed to know it was there when she pulled it out of the satchel.

But that was how dreams worked, even if you had Rella's special talent for waking up in your dreams. You remember and recognize some details, but you might not know how you acquired a certain object here or there.

"What does this nameless man, who calls himself Archimago, want? Why is he out to destroy Hleo?" Rella asked, as she sliced at the air, redirecting the drifting puffs of particles.

"He wants us *all* to forget..."

"To forget what?"

Rella circled the puff as it drifted above her like a balloon. And then, from below, she thrust the scroll into it. It slowly split in two and then swirled back together directly in front of Rella.

Neither girl noticed that the shadow from the shore had now begun winding its way up The Wondercurrent.

The girl's tone grew more serious: "To forget the beauty and the power of language...and the truth of the stories...to steal our dreams."

"Well...I hope Archimago is ready to meet...Rella PenSword!" Rella exclaimed.

As she spoke his name, the giant shadow continued to seep into and out of the river, coating it with black velvet.

"Well...there are actually other foes Rella might have to battle first."

"Like who?"

"Well...there's a boy, known as The Architect. He is Archimago's most loyal servant...and these two girls...one is called Prisma, but we don't know much about them...if they're even human or if they're from Earth One...or somewhere else entirely..."

"Well...let's not waste any more time then!" Rella shouted.

"Yes," her friend said, "You are just the dreamer we need!"

"But which stories is he trying to destroy?" Rella asked.

Rella thrust the scroll toward the little cloud in front of her one final time and jumped back, landing on one foot. She lost her balance and dropped the scroll. The girl dove and caught it.

"The happy ones, mostly," the girl grunted, raising herself back up onto her knees and holding the scroll up. "And the ones that would have the power to make us all wise and noble..."

Rella took the scroll back from her friend and removed her leaf-cape.

The girl had just repeated one of the last phrases Rella had ever heard her father, Julian, speak before he left to find her mother.

Rella's father's recent words were still fresh on her mind.

Rella, I've got to find your mother because she needs my help. We will stop the ones who want us all to forget. We will not forget. The stories and the words must be kept alive.

The two girls, now huddled next to each other, and still high up in the tree, looked out at the dark water and the mists around Archimago's island.

"How do we stop him?" Rella whispered, as she began to notice the darkness overtaking The Wondercurrent.

Cold thunder rolled through the clouds overhead.

"I don't know," the girl replied, as the branch below their feet started to crack.

Rella looked down. They were hovering above the blackening river.

"But we can stop him, right?" Rella asked.

"With your help, yes!" the girl said as she looked into Rella's eyes.

Rella looked down just as the branch broke free of the trunk. She reached out, but her hands passed right through the girl's body. The girl had become a hologram.

Chapter 3: Departing Ensea

RELLA OFTEN MET CHARACTERS from her father's stories in her dreams, especially since he had gone missing. This last dream, where she learned of a villain called Archimago who was trying to destroy the enchanted land of Hleo, had terrified her beyond words. It was even more terrifying than her dreams about the seven-eyed frogs that slept on gravestones and the ones with the bald buzzards with clawed feet that kept trying slash through her bedroom walls.

She could get over her dreams about weird, clawed creatures who wanted to take her away. But this dream, with the deep thoughts of her father, reminded her so much of what was actually going on when she was awake. Rella didn't think that dream feelings were supposed to be so similar to waking feelings. She recalled part of a line from a play her father liked to quote: "Dreams are toys." She couldn't remember the second half though.

Rella loaded the small box of personal possessions into the trunk. The large shadow of an airplane drifted over the driveway. Rella looked up at the plane and wished that she and her uncle could afford to just fly to their new home. She'd never been on a plane. She loved to watch them take off and land.

She looked back at the box of folded notes, sparkly pencils, and bookmarks, making sure everything she wanted to bring was included. Uncle J's car was small, and she had to be very selective about what she would bring on the journey.

As she stood by the car, she tried to recall more of the dream's details. All she kept picturing was this mysterious girl with golden braids in the branch of a tree. The girl kept trying to tell her all about a group of animals called guardians who were supposed to protect children like her. And she talked about how they had been captured and dragged off to a dark island. There was a luminous scroll in her, Rella's, satchel and also a molten, shadowy liquid which seemed to be drowning the orb-filled water itself, if water was something you could drown.

The new friend Rella had met in the dream, whose name she still couldn't recall, seemed so worried and lonely, but also helpful. Rella wished she could get back to help the dream traveler.

Rella had read books about dream travelers with her father, but she didn't ever imagine she'd meet one. There was an entire shelf in their library with books about some of the most famous and infamous dream travelers and how they influenced major wars and treaties. She knew there were stories about who gets chosen to be one and why, but this girl never had the chance to tell Rella why she had been chosen.

Rella tried to remember what usually happened to people who met dream travelers. Sometimes they would be searching for a child to fulfill a quest in a secret land. Children had to be careful, however, because dream travelers were sometimes trying to use children to escape those lands, and they would lure the children in so that they could take their place in their own worlds.

This girl, however, appeared to have no interest in leaving Hleo, her enchanting world of pale mists and sparkling waters. She was clearly set on protecting and defending it. *But why did she choose to visit me?* Rella thought as she watched her uncle go back into the house to retrieve more of his things.

Any time Rella was reading a story and had to stop right when a character was in the greatest danger, she always felt that she couldn't abandon them. Sometimes, though she had never admitted it to anyone except Ms. Ochoa, the former librarian (and one of the last pubic librarians in Ensea before the anti-book laws were instated), Rella even felt concerned when an evil character was on the verge of death. Sometimes, she even rooted for the bad ones, even though they never won.

Rella never wanted to see stories end, no matter who might win or lose. But she was usually happy when the good ones prevailed, as long as they had to truly struggle for their victories.

The moment in a story she could never, ever leave off was when an animal was caught in a trap or lost in a dark forest. She had to know they would make it home safely and, if she had to, she'd stay awake reading a book for an entire month to make sure that the animals were safe.

As she stared down at the trunk of the car, Rella promised herself that, if she met with this girl again, and the girl really was a dream traveler, she would do whatever she could to help rescue those animals and protect the land and the beautiful river.

"Rella," Uncle J shouted, "are you sure those are all the books you wanted to bring?"

Rella looked down at the open box of books she had just placed in the trunk of the car. She *wanted* to bring a lot more books with her, but the trunk was out of space. She knew the other books would be cared for because they had friends in the village, members of The Alliance, who promised to keep them safe in their own secret libraries.

There were reports that Ensea was on a list at the Ministry of Informatics, and that the Ministry would be sending a delegation to collect forbidden books within days, if not hours.

In recent weeks, whenever they were in public, Uncle J told Rella they were moving because he had just found a better job. She knew that this was just something he had to say to make sure no one in the town (who wasn't part of The Alliance) would inform the delegation from the dream killers, as they liked to call the members of the Ministry.

Her mother, she was often told, was actually involved with The Storykeeper's Alliance at the highest levels, which was why she had gone into hiding, and, then, was possibly captured. Rella sensed that there was more to it, but she couldn't explain why she felt this way.

As she stood by the trunk of the car, waiting on Uncle J, she thought about her dream again, and the memory of the sparkling lights and warm winds of Hleo passed through her body.

She looked back at the boxes of books and thought about trying to stuff one more book into her satchel, which was already overloaded.

No one knew for sure where Rella's mother had gone, except her father, but everyone tried to hold onto faith that she would eventually return. After her mother had been missing for about three years, a few weeks after Rella's seventh birthday, her father couldn't wait any longer and had to go searching for her.

He hating leaving Rella, and he wrote Rella a long letter, with details about protecting the memory of the words and stopping the ones who would make them all forget their past, and, of course, promising he would return.

Rella sometimes doubted she would ever see him again. She already had more secondhand memories of her mother than firsthand ones. Why would this be any different?

And this was how she ended up living with Uncle J, her mother's youngest brother. Uncle J was only twenty, and had little experience with raising a child, but he loved Rella dearly and he had sworn to protect her with his life. He was also an important member of The Storykeeper's Alliance, so he would have protected Rella even if she was not his dear sister's only daughter.

Rella had no knowledge of her Uncle's specific assignment with the Alliance, but she had heard people refer to him as a Scribe, which must have had something to do with writing things down or keeping and recording information, since that was what scribes did.

Uncle J had been teaching Rella to how to make sketches since she was three (she was seven now) and, to cheer her up over the past few months, he would often sketch pictures of her as a superhero, which is how she actually came up with her own secret name, which she had never spoken aloud, except in dreams: Rella PenSword.

Rella grabbed one more book from the trunk and squeezed it into her satchel.

"Are you sure you've got everything you want?" Uncle J asked, closing the front door of the house. This was the only place she had ever called home, and the only place she had any memory of her mother.

Uncle J walked over and tossed one more book into the opened box in the trunk.

"I think you might have dropped this one," he said. "It was actually standing on its side in the hallway. Slippery thing. Every time I picked it up, it seemed to slide back out of my hands, which is why it took me so long to get out here."

Like all of the books they kept in the secret library, the cover on this one was blank, but Rella didn't recognize the texture. It was only slightly larger than her hand. Perhaps a hundred or so pages. Whatever material was used to make the cover, it was not something Rella had encountered before. It wasn't made of animal skins or synthetic fabrics.

Maybe this one is from Westcon, she thought. *If they can make those aerial shoes, I'm sure their book covers are going to be fancier too.*

The notebook was a natural shade of red. It made Rella think of the tinted maple leaves that covered their front lawn in late September. The smudges or scratches on the cover of a book was all Rella needed to identify the contents, but this one had no marks at all. It was so clean that Rella felt like the red had just been painted on. *If I touch it*, Rella thought, *I bet my finger will sink right into the smooth, liquid surface.* Given the strangeness of her recent dream, Rella decided not to risk getting pulled into the book, though she knew that was a silly idea.

Before she had the chance to pick it up, Uncle J shut the trunk and pulled Rella gently to his chest. She turned her face to the side and, with her head resting against him, took one final look at the house and the lawn. A few loose branches had fallen and a cluster of late-summer leaves tumbled by.

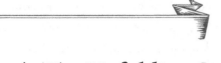

Chapter 4: The Unfolding Sphere

AS THEY DROVE OUT INTO the open countryside, Rella settled into the back seat. She wrapped herself up in her favorite green quilt (sewn by her great-great-grandmother Deveraux) and alternated between reading her favorite books and making sketches. When she grew tired of reading and sketching, Rella decided to make a tent out of the quilt. She lifted it over her head and tucked her legs up onto the seat.

The quilt was so thick that very little outside light came through. Certain seams, where the patches had come loose, allowed small slivers of light to fall into her lap, which created a wondrous play of shadow and light. By lifting and lowering her hands, Rella could control the direction of the slivers of light. She loved to play with the shadows.

She began moving twisting the fabric above her in various ways, watching the light cut into the shadows on her lap. One beam of light, however, seemed to be moving on its own. Rella concentrated on the beam. As she moved her hands, she whispered, "Where are you going, little light?" The beam flickered out and Rella redirected her attention to an oddly shaped circle that appeared on the blanket. It was black and round and thin. It seemed to be moving toward her, like a ball of shadow. Rella, transfixed, continued holding the quilt over her head and watched as the ball of shadows began to unfold itself, like a blooming flower.

And then...the brightest light Rella had ever seen spread out from within the blooming shadow. The light started white but burst into a million colors in an instant. It felt like her body was spreading or dissolving, like she had become water and was being poured into a stream.

Her instinct was to pull the quilt away, but she could no longer feel her arms.

Rella leapt backwards, crouched low, and shielded her face from the flying debris. As she emerged from the cave, a wall of pale blue mist pierced by fragments of wood and stone drifted toward her, like cold smoke blown from a giant's mouth. She narrowed her eyes and tried to sort the shapes and sounds soaring through her mind, the thrum of tumbling branches, the clamor of crumbling rocks, and the harsh howl of wind snaking in and out of the hollows.

Dim, red-gray sheets of sky blocked out the light. It could have been sunlight, or it may have been moonlight. Either way, Rella was certain that it wasn't Earthlight.

She surveyed the rumbling, shadowy landscape before her. Rocks continued flying over the distant wall. Much like the water droplets in the nearby cataracts, the large, colorful rocks were dropping at drastically different speeds. She tried to recall if she'd seen anything like this.

VR (Virtual Reality) would easily explain it, Rella thought. *A distraction trick or a glitch in a program was possible.* But then, she reasoned, some other factors in the environment did not fit that explanation either, because she was still feeling the dull ache in her right foot. If she was under sedation, or medical VR, she would not be feeling that pain.

Illuminations appeared all around her: the walls of caves, riverbeds, and even beneath tree bark. Trees as large as Redwoods scattered across the valley below toppled like children's block towers. This was not Earth One.

A crack. A whoosh. A crash.

In some places, where the trees fell the hardest, the soil seemed to bend like a rubber sheet. In other spots, the ground cracked open and gulped up the falling boulders.

Rella no longer felt like she was dissolving into a stream, but she still felt completely upside down.

Frantic for cover, she scurried beneath a stone archway. The arch, she thought, might have been part of a building or a palace gate once, although it didn't show the wear one would normally see in a ruined city—on Earth One or, although Rella had never been there, on Earth Two.

As she looked up, she noticed that the boulders were dangerously unbalanced. *Why haven't they fallen on me? Will they all drop at once? Are they coming down right now?* she thought, as the ground continued to rumble and warp.

Amidst the chaos, the steadiness of the stones should have been a comfort to Rella's unsteady mind. In this wild, crumbling landscape, however, the steadiness of the rocks merely increased her disorientation. She whispered aloud: "Why aren't they moving? Gravity seems to be working fine on me." She jumped up, curious to see if she might float (as if she were on the moon), and then she fell right back down.

She looked at her feet, which were firmly planted on the ground, and started thinking about the dreams again. Was this Hleo?

The girl with the braids and the rustic clothes (that were not armor), the strange animals, the villain Archimago. The words and the discussions from the dream started stitching themselves together in her mind.

Rella peered up at the arch and spread her arms out for balance. She felt gravitational flux all around her, like an invisible hand running rapidly over the un-seeable space and then slowly pulling everything back into these unnatural positions.

The invisible hand almost seemed to be playfully balancing the boulders above her head.

The ground beneath her started to shake again. Rella closed her eyes. She felt an invisible fabric descend upon her.

Rella blinked her eyes. She was back underneath the quilt. But how?

She slowly pulled the quilt off of her head. Uncle J had been driving for hours. *It was the same place as the last dream*, she thought, *only I can't remember falling asleep. Was I just dream traveling? Did I cross over? Mom? Dad?*

"You ok back there?" Uncle J asked, adjusting the volume on the stereo.

"Yes!" Rella had to think fast. "I was just...having a dream."

"About what?" Uncle J asked.

"Well...there was this earthquake and this sparkling waterfall with all these colors. And this huge, floating arch..." Rella replied. She felt safe giving him a few details.

"I haven't heard you describe that dream before. Did you see the seven-eyed frogs on the gravestones again?" Uncle J asked, chuckling.

"No. This was...different than those dreams," Rella said in a confused tone.

"How so?" Uncle J replied, sincerely interested and trying to make sense of her confused tone of voice.

"I can't say. More real, more colorful, more feeling...," Rella said, pausing.

"You should sketch it!" Uncle J said, adjusting a dial on the dashboard.

Rella looked down at the sketchbook in her lap. As she stared at the drawing, she started to remember. She had been sketching something from the previous night's dream when she covered up with the quilt.

"Good idea. But I forgot my colored pencils at home," Rella replied, trying to figure out if the drawing or the quilt had anything to do with her journey to the other world. Her father had read her plenty of books about kids who made journeys to other worlds by climbing into cupboards and getting on magical ships, but covering up with an old quilt seemed an unlikely object for interworld travel.

"Don't sweat it. We'll pick some up at our next stop. You've got your charcoal ones, right?" Uncle J asked.

"Yes, I always have them," Rella replied, assuring him that she wouldn't have forgotten the pencils he gave her for her birthday.

Rella shook off the thought of the shadow and the quilt for the moment, picked up her notepad, and examined the sketch she had been making of the waterfall and the trees.

Was I really in Hleo? she wondered. *In the dream,* she thought, *I was up in the trees and I don't remember seeing the sparkling waterfall, or all of the glowing lights everywhere.*

She began thinking of the guardians and her friend again. *Why did this dream have so much more...physical feeling?* She tried to think about the books with the dream travelers again. One of the legends explained that, once you met a dream traveler, it was possible that you, too, could be given the ability to become one, at least temporarily. You wouldn't know whether you were inside of your own dream or someone else's, though, until you met the traveler who chose you to join in on a quest. Most of the time, in the books, the quests were simple and fun, like finding a mysterious flower or solving a riddle to unlock a secret door. She sensed that this quest would not be so simple.

Rella looked out the window and up into the clouds passing overhead. She was already missing home.

Chapter 5: Quinn Finds the Scroll

THIS IS TOO GOOD TO be true, Quinn thought, as he unrolled the scroll. *How could Archimago's servants have let this fall into the water? And what are the chances the scroll would wash up here, a hundred yards from my workshop?*

For the past few months, ever since he had surfaced in Hleo, Quinn had been working in secrecy beneath a fort made of thick branches and covered with pink, yellow, blue and green leaves salvaged from the dying trees near the shore. It was nearly impossible to climb through the layers of intertwined branches leading to the fort, though they provided excellent protection. The only good way to get to the shoreline quickly was to tunnel underground. But this was extremely risky, since the soil was always shifting and sometimes mysteriously pulled objects deeper into its underground tunnel systems.

Quinn wasn't sure if he should attempt to read the scroll without the eye protection Eurie had given him. Ever since he and Eurie had discovered the enchanted inks on the parchments and in the tree bark, he knew that reading anything in Hleo was a major risk. Infected words could warp your mind like a virus. They could even take over your thoughts.

Quinn continued scanning the shoreline. *Whatever is on the scroll*, he thought, *has to be part of Archimago's plans. This is what we've been waiting for. The Storykeepers wrote it down. They said it would happen. It's time to get this message to Rella.*

Quinn pulled the eye paste out of his pocket and swiped it over his eyelids. Eurie had developed these 'liquid glasses' by grinding up one of the transparent stones near the banks of The Wondercurrent and mixing it with other materials she had found in the forest. As far as he could tell, there were no long term effects.

Quinn tried to decipher the images on the scroll through the liquid coating, but he couldn't see any correlation between the symbols and building or battle plans, which he was quite good at reading. They didn't seem to be plans for a new city, or, though he didn't want to think of it, plans for a prison for the Guardians. The thought of being imprisoned on Archimago's island terrified Quinn more than anything.

In one of Quinn's recent dream-travel meetings with Rella, she had appeared with a stack of parchments she had collected in the forest, all coated in enchanted inks. When Quinn asked her about them, she said that she'd read them all, but she couldn't fully explain how all of the symbols and messages were connected. She said she had a strong feeling that they were telling a story, but pieces of the story were missing.

In the dream, Rella told Quinn that it was like someone was trying to write a message to her in all of her languages at once but they couldn't get the sentences to connect. She said that the true meaning seemed to be right below the surface, but she just couldn't get it worked out on her own.

During that conversation, he also noticed the soft, metallic scroll sticking out of her satchel. He didn't remember asking her anything about it, but he knew, at that moment in the dreamspace encounter, that he was being prepared for this moment here in Hleo.

The next immediate step was to get the real scroll and a message back up The Wondercurrent and put it in the secret compartment in the wall of the cave. Once Rella arrived, she would be able to examine it and help complete the mission.

As he tried to decide how he would get the scroll up to the cave, Quinn tried to recall his last conversation with Eurie. She had mentioned something about Rella's arrival and he wanted to make sure he had the details correct.

"You went back to see her, Eurie?"

"Yes, I wanted to see if she was ready to come through."

"When are you going to tell me how you do it?"

"Do what?"

"Travel so easily back and forth?"

"Listen Quinn…I don't know if we have time to go through it now."

"Come on, Eurie, just tell me something!"

"Ok. Well. You remember telling me about your parents' hidden library. And about the old manuscripts and the notebooks they kept in the apartment in Westcon. Well… certain of these old books belong to very specific people."

"So you are transporting yourself through books, Eurie?"

"Not exactly, but it does involve the books. And you have to have read the same books or at least have heard the same stories as the person you're visiting. Does that make sense?"

"Kind of. So it's not really the books that transport you…it's not like a magical door you just walk through?"

"Not in the way you might be used to thinking about magic…"

Quinn, looking back down at the actual scroll, repeated Eurie's words aloud: "Not in the way you might be used to thinking about magic."

The last time Quinn had run into Eurie in Hleo, they also discussed the appearance of Rella's scroll in the dreamspace. They both agreed that it meant that Rella was already being prepared by another one of the Storykeepers. However, Eurie told Quinn that she didn't have time to explain to Rella exactly why she was being called in to help in the fight to save Hleo.

Quinn thought that was an odd thing to leave out, but he also assumed that Eurie didn't want to frighten Rella away either. From his observations of Rella, she didn't really appear ready to go on any dangerous missions or fight in any battles.

But, as you know, reader, people aren't always the same in their dreams as they are in real life. We often have very different skills, abilities, and even wishes. This was certainly the case with Rella.

Quinn glanced over the scroll in his hands but decided not to risk looking at it for too long. He didn't know how long Eurie's protective solution would last.

As he considered the fastest way to get the message up to Rella's entry point, he knew his legs wouldn't get it there fast enough.

Also, his new ship was only halfway completed, and, even if it did work, he wasn't ready to try and navigate up The Wondercurrent. He needed a swift messenger. A guardian.

Before leaving the shore in search of the guardian-messenger, Quinn composed a detailed note for Rella and fastened it to the scroll. Using a bright, silvery-green ink he had created from his own mixture of plant extracts, he scrawled the message on a fragment of silk leaf and wrapped it around the outside of the scroll. As he wrapped the note around the scroll, it started glowing, much like the signaling devices used by the Storykeepers of Earth One.

Quinn hiked a few miles north along the banks of The Wondercurrent before he started to feel weak. *A quick nap always helps a soldier,* he thought. He couldn't actually remember the last time he'd slept. As he looked around, he noticed a number of discolored, cracked tree trunks, a clear sign that the Shadowsplitters had recently passed through the area.

Despite his exhaustion, he decided to forego the nap and pressed on. The specialized military training he had received in Westcon's school for young soldiers had taught him how to overcome extreme tiredness, but he was certain that they had not covered fighting the servants of evil magicians and dark wizards, or whatever this Archimago was. He wished he'd had more time to talk with Eurie before this Rella PenSword business started happening.

Quinn examined the battered tree trunks and checked the lower branches for any signs of movement. While it was foolish to think that a guardian would be able to find a surfacing point here, Quinn knew he wouldn't make it much further north without better supplies, and a companion or two. He was not keen on solo missions.

The luminous scroll continued to blink. He pulled it back out of his pack and thought about opening it and trying to read it again.

I've still got the paste on my eyes, he thought. *Maybe...if I ask it the right questions, there will be a map that might show me*

which areas haven't been attacked yet. If these are Archimago's at-
tack plans, then they have to be meant for The Architect.

Quinn had never seen the boy known as The Architect up
close, but he had seen him out on his ship off shore. It had heavily
barred cages and they were often full of captured guardians, including an arctic fox and a panther.

Quinn unrolled the scroll. He knew it was a risk. If the letters
were enchanted by Archimago, and the solution stopped working, his memory could become fractured and his mind repro-
grammed. He would become one of Archimago's automatons.
He'd seen a few kids who had been stripped of their memory already. They would just walk through the forest asking who they
were, what had happened to them, and if Quinn could help them
find their way home.

While Archimago was clearly trying to put his plans in place,
he had not been able to fully infiltrate Hleo, which meant that,
if they could get Rella's help, there was still a chance they could
stop him.

Quinn decided not to take the risk and rolled the scroll back
up. He rewrapped the silk leaf around it and slid it back into his
pack.

All of a sudden, a cloud of red and white dust snaked around
a nearby trunk. A cold wind rushed across Quinn's face and the
ground quickly expanded and then contracted beneath his feet.
A large animal began emerging at the trunk of a nearby tree. The
animal's legs were forming directly out of the exposed roots.

Quinn had never seen one surface quite like this. He considered how rare it was at this time to see any guardians appearing
at all. Did the scroll have something to do with this?

Quinn tried to get the creature's attention by holding up two branches and crossing and uncrossing them five times to signal that he was in need of help.

After the legs emerged, a body appeared, though still encased in a coating that matched the bark of the tree. The animal continued to move forward and split off from the wood. Quinn then realized that it was not just any large animal, but a full-grown tiger. The proportions were exactly like other tigers he'd seen back home. Quinn was certain that this was a tiger from Earth One.

The one thing that threw him off a bit, though, was the fur. Instead of orange and black or white and black, the tiger's fur glinted and reflected a brilliant array of colors.

Eurie had mentioned something about another tiger who had once come to Hleo with a similar coat. She called it 'the chameleon's fur.' It was meant to blend in specifically with the surroundings of Hleo.

This tiger, known as Menagerie, was in fact a direct descendant of one of Hleo's first guardians, also called Menagerie, who arrived during one of the dark ages of Earth One, nearly a thousand years before Quinn's very recent arrival.

The new Menagerie, Quinn knew, took a major risk to enter here in this area of The Wondercurrent, so it must have sensed the urgency. Quinn couldn't figure out how Archimago's servants had missed this tree when they were closing the portals.

As he examined the tree, he remembered something Eurie had told him about how she had been testing a new mixture of leaf extracts and dry-water from The Wondercurrent. Quinn had attempted to put his hands into the Wondercurrnt a few times, and, although it felt like water as it ran past his fingers, it never actually left them wet when he pulled them out, which is where Eurie got the idea of calling it dry-water. Quinn's best guess at the phenomenon was that there was something in the atmosphere or in the chemical properties of the water that kept it from being absorbed.

The mixture Eurie created didn't last more than a few days, but it could be painted on a tree to make it appear as though it had already been damaged to block any new entries. This tree must have been one of the ones Eurie was using for a test, because Archimago's clan never made a mistake, which puzzled Quinn all the more as he thought about the appearance of the scroll.

Menagerie had now separated fully from the tree, and, as she prowled forward, Quinn's heartrate tripled and sputtered like a toy that was wound too tightly.

He locked eyes with the stalking tiger and tried to guide her calmly towards his hand. He was now holding a small morsel he had pulled from his pack. This food, however, was not just for energy but was a medicine. It would help Menagerie adjust to some of the new environmental conditions in Hleo.

Menagerie took the morsel and lowered herself at Quinn's feet. Quinn's heart continued to race as he noticed the animal's wild, natural, comforting scent. He hadn't been close enough to catch the scent of any animals in a while. Her scent reminded him a little of Huxley, his golden retriever. When he was back home, Huxley always slept in his bed with him, even though his parents told him not to let her. She was one of the old, non-engineered breeds, so there were possible health risks having her around. Quinn didn't care though. He didn't want a dog made in a lab; he liked having a real one.

Menagerie's head was only slightly lower than his own, and Quinn was almost five feet tall. He wondered if she was actually this large back on Earth One, or if she had grown in the surfacing process. Quinn crouched down and looked curiously into Menagerie's eyes, brushing her fur with his palm.

He lifted the scroll in his free hand and briefly explained the risks of the mission and why he needed to get the scroll to Rella as quickly as possible.

"I need you to take this scroll to the cave...up to the cliffs. Near the top of the waterfall."

He pointed up to the source of The Wondercurrent. He hadn't ventured far enough above the falls to know exactly where the current originated, but he had planned to explore it as soon as he finished building his ship.

Menagerie nodded.

"Just follow the edge of the water toward those cliffs. Don't try to take any swimming breaks though, because I have no idea what might happen to you if you step into that current. Also, those glowing orbs, as far as I know, are not food or play toys. So don't try to eat one or play with it...if one happens to bounce up on shore."

Eurie had, in fact, been experimenting with some of the orbs, but she advised Quinn to leave the experiments to her. He respected her expertise in that area.

Menagerie nodded and almost seemed to be smiling, as though she had heard this lecture from her own mother and father before.

"Right before you reach the top of the falls," Quinn continued, slowing down to make sure that Menagerie took in every word, "you will see a cave on the right. It should be illuminated by a bluish light. It is the largest cave entrance in that area."

Menagerie nodded again and noted every single detail. Just like her ancestors had done in the past, she would help and protect the children of Hleo—with her life, if necessary.

Quinn rubbed her back, admiring and also puzzling over the transformations in her fur. For a half second, the fur seemed to absorb and mirror the deep brown tones of Quinn's own skin.

As he pulled his hand away, he saw that it had momentarily left a print on her back. Quinn looked at the back of his own hand and noticed that it had taken on the colorless shimmer of the chameleon's fur.

Quinn reached into his pack and pulled out a small stone dagger. Because there was no fire in Hleo, nothing could be forged the way it was done back on Earth One. He had always had an interest in metalwork, and all of the fascinating metals in Hleo would have been fun to play with as base materials for weapons. This dagger, which he had polished himself, shined well enough to show him his reflection. He examined his skin closely. His face was still brown and his hair hadn't changed a bit.

He put the dagger back into his pack and took a few steps back. It wasn't unheard of for a guardian to surface and begin going through some adaptations right away, but Quinn had not yet seen this type of adaptation.

It worried him a little that Menagerie's fur also seemed to be affecting him when he touched it, but he had more immediate problems to solve. The next time he saw Eurie, he would mention it. At the moment, however, he had to encourage Menagerie on her quest.

"Be sure that no one stops you, and you must not try to rescue anyone else on the way. There could be other children wandering, even some crying out for help, but The Sisters have been using these children as decoys. And they have been able manipulate your fellow guardians."

Quinn knew that he was overwhelming Menagerie, so he tried to communicate his confidence in her by keeping his eyes locked directly with hers.

"I know you may not know everything about what is happening here, but you answered the signal, so I believe you will fulfill your duty."

Quinn's military training taught him how to give confident orders when he needed to, though he never knew how the animal guardians would respond, since they were not really subordinates to humans. In Hleo, Quinn was discovering, the role of the animals was even greater and more important than that of humans.

Menagerie nodded firmly to show that she fully understood, and that she was ready to fulfill her duty.

"Once you reach the cave, locate a loose rock about ten feet inside. It is on the right. It will be dark in there, but you should be able to find it. Push the rock out of the way and slip this scroll into the hollow space. Then, slide the rock back into place. There may also appear to be a liquid dripping from the walls in various places. You are free to drink this liquid. It will restore some of your energy so you can make it back here and then... (Quinn didn't know what would happen then)...well, we'll worry about that later. But, remember, do not eat or drink anything else along the way. There are poisonous traps everywhere."

Quinn reached out and touched her now majestic gray and white shoulder. She was standing next to a large boulder.

"Understand?"

Menagerie nodded firmly again, narrowed her eyes, and then turned to face the falls in the distance. Quinn pulled a rope from his pack and wound it carefully around Menagerie's right front leg. As he wound the rope around her leg, he slipped the scroll into it securely so that it wouldn't fall out. In between the loops, Quinn could see the scroll glowing and he was tempted, once again, to pull it out and look it over. Before he could give in and untie the rope, Menagerie sprinted northward along the shore of The Wondercurrent. It would be a half day's journey at least, and that was only if there were no interruptions.

Quinn smiled as he watched her sprint away, still in awe at the way this tiger moved so weightlessly, although there was such a great weight of responsibility upon her.

Chapter 6: The Storm and the Invisible Hands

RELLA TRACED THE UNDERSIDE of the arch with her eyes and tried to steady herself on the waist-high boulder beside her. If the arch collapsed on top of her, and she somehow survived, she knew she would never get out, and no one, human or animal, or even any inter-dimensional alien she could imagine (since inter-dimensional aliens weren't actually a proven fact), no one would have any chance of finding her body, alive or dead—even if they did happen to find a direct pathway into this landscape...planet...dream...nuclear fish tank...or whatever this was.

Rella, when she last entered, had not even noticed the blinking waterfall or the silent river only a hundred yards away.

The cacophony of breaking branches pulverized her eardrums. She sat down at the foot of the floating arch and propped herself firmly against the stones. As she pressed her fingertips into the stone, it felt like a mix of foam and marble. She'd touch it in one spot and it would be hard. Another spot would be softer than melting marshmallows. As she continued kneading her fingers into a soft spot in the stone, a light wind slipped across the tip of her nose.

The archway overhead shifted and a few small rocks, about the size of her fist, dropped to the ground. Rella sprang up onto her feet and dove out from beneath the arch, scraping her elbows and knees and tearing a few holes in her clothes. Her muscles tensed up and she squeezed her eyelids like she was trying to extract the last drops of juice from an unripe orange. Beads of sweat rolled down over her cheeks.

Inside and out, her body was fighting to balance two extreme climates. She felt like she was passing through some physically twisted planet, where arctic and tropical regions existed in the same exact space at the same exact time. She had not yet considered, however, that some physically twisted planet might just as easily be passing through her.

And, then, the invisible hands she had sensed all around just moments earlier were gone. She was still figuring out how the portal process worked. She knew the quilt had something to do with it...and the unfolding shadow-ball...but she hadn't worked it out yet. She had no idea if or when she might end up back on Earth One again. She crawled back under the arch, which still seemed safer than sitting beneath the canopy of crumbling trees.

One more rumble, one more small gust of wind at the wrong angle, and I'll be flattened out thinner than a snake skin, Rella thought, looking up at the arch, which had not yet fallen, but still posed a threat. Her mom always said she was a bit of an exaggerator, that her mind perceived things more from a worst-case scenario vantage point. But, here, in Hleo, her worst exaggerations were all half-hearted understatements.

Rella kept her eyelids down to keep the smoky chards of debris from blinding her, and also because she was completely terrified of the aliens or monsters she knew must be nearby.

She forced a long, slow, deep breath into her lungs, but her insides continued fluctuating like a fever. In the distant sky, a trio of amoebic shapes floated by. They looked like painted shadows and they made Rella feel like she was being hunted.

One of the painted shadows stretched itself into a hoop and dropped down over one of the giant trees on the edge of a cliff. As the hoop lowered over the tree, all of the bright and beautiful colors disappeared. The tree turned to ash in an instant and the hoop then floated back up into the sky, hunting for its next victim.

"Just wake up...home...home now!" Rella yelled aloud to herself, taking her hands off of her weakened stomach and pinching her eyelids in an effort to wake herself.

She sat with her eyes closed for a few minutes, trying to make the ugliness go away. But it didn't work. She had no control over when she would go home.

As she opened her eyes, the painted shadows had begun to clear and the storm was receding, leaving only one recognizable sound: the scraping of critter claws through the underbrush. As she looked around, she noticed some inscriptions on the stone arch, but couldn't tell if they were Earth-One based letters or not.

Rella hoped the little animals nearby were safe and uninjured...unless, of course, they were the kind of creatures that might want to nibble on her toes or feast on a few of her bones. While she could appreciate the beauty of all creatures, including scorpions, snakes, and even buzzards, she preferred spending her time around furry cuddlers with very small teeth, like, very very small, itsy-bitsy baby kitten teeth.

Rella listened for any reptilian claws, any beastly moans, or conspiratorial whispers of alien spies in animal disguises. Yes, she could see all of that. She was a very creative listener.

The dark images of all of the most horrible creatures she had ever seen in her comic books flashed through her mind. She tried to block it out and think about the last, most beautiful thing she had seen: the butterfly wings at the Remembrance Day ceremony.

Another minute passed and she carefully opened one eyelid. Out across The Wondercurrent, past the shadowy webs of tree limbs, she focused her open eye toward the crest of the waterfall. The waterfall, though, had no clear top. It just climbed and climbed, or fell and fell, depending on your point of view.

Rella swabbed two fingers across her forehead and collected a glob of dusty, gray-blue paste. Instantly, tiny vibrations passed over and around her fingers, like invisible strings threading themselves into the secondary layers of skin.

Her arms were also eerily discolored. The paste accumulated like powdery snow over every inch of her exposed skin. Yet it didn't cling to her clothes, her shoes, or her satchel. If any of her school friends had seen her at that moment, they would have thought they had run into a wild blue swamp monster, and not a seven-year-old girl from Ensea.

She thought about diving directly into The Wondercurrent (she *was* a decent swimmer), or at least running over to the shore to scoop up some water to scrub off the paste, in case the paste was poisonous. Rella certainly didn't like these strange vibrations on her skin, but she had to be careful.

She also had to consider that an actual wild blue swamp monster, with wriggling tentacles, might reach up and pull her into the water. She thought seriously about climbing back to the cave, but...as she looked down at the scroll and the attached note, she did not want to run into...*him.*

Chapter 7: More Discoveries, New Questions

THE ARCHITECT, WHOM Rella had only just read about in Quinn's note, was bound to show up any second. She had to flee the area, but she was worried about what she might find if she ventured too far into the falling forest, where the bulky branches reminded her of the twisted bones of an ancient race of giants.

She peered into the tapestry of shadows and tried to estimate the speed of the falling branches. She remembered playing a video game with her uncle once where they had to get a character across a wooden bridge while dodging flaming rocks that had been shot out of a nearby volcano. Unfortunately, she couldn't remember ever making it across the bridge without having to reset the game about twelve times. And she didn't suppose that there were any reset buttons here in this mysterious forest with the twinkling river.

If she didn't time her escape into the shadows precisely, she knew she would either end up a prisoner or be left pinned to the ground beneath one of the branches.

She took a deep breath and tried to muster the courage to run. But she couldn't move. The way the branches sliced so effortlessly into the soil, like spears dropping into marshmallows, baffled her. She didn't want to become a marshmallow, at least not one that had a spear running through it.

So much of this place seemed to be playful and harmless, but then, at the same time, so much felt like a threat.

Rella turned her attention back to the thick, gray-blue substance slathered over the back of her hand. She still couldn't pinpoint what, exactly, was so strange about its powdery texture. She brought her hand to her nose and sniffed. The particles floated up into her nostrils.

She felt herself dozing. The tension winding through her back and neck muscles, which she did not even realize had been there, suddenly loosened. She took another sniff, and then inhaled slowly. Her mouth watered and, though she knew it wasn't smart to do so, she stuck out her tongue and licked just a bit of it off of her palm.

The scent reminded her of hyacinth. It was natural, flowery, and sweet. *It would make a very good tea flavor*, she thought, suddenly wishing she had something warm or cool to drink. When she hiked the canyons back home on Earth One and kicked the dust up into her nose, it always felt and tasted dry and bitter. This, in turn, usually left her coughing for hours. Whatever elements coalesced to create this dusty substance, however, did not seem quite as natural to the environment here.

As unnatural as it seemed, however, in this enchanted world—and Rella was becoming more convinced that this was definitely an enchanted place and not a dream or a dream-within-a-dream at all—this substance did seem to have an effect on the surrounding environment. It attached to certain objects and surfaces quite easily, while completely avoiding others, like it knew where it was supposed to go.

Despite the overwhelming fear, Rella was glad to have found refreshment. She would take time later to figure out whether this blue powder was a mineral or a bacterium—or she'd find someone who could identify it accurately.

This brief refreshment, and the extended break from the storms, allowed Rella to think through the previous hours' chaos. She vaguely recalled sitting in the backseat of Uncle J's car, and then she remembered putting the quilt over her head, and the ball of shadows, and the blast of color...but then she was waking up inside of a softly lit cave near the edge of a towering, sparkling waterfall. It was taller than you would ever see on Earth One or Earth Two.

The waterfall, Rella noticed, didn't actually fall like Earth One water. The droplets moved at different speeds; and, as she peered through the mists, she realized that colorful flashing orbs, of many sizes, were weaving and splashing their way through the curtains of water. She took a few careful strides toward The Wondercurrent (she didn't know how she knew that was the name of the river, if it could be called a river).

As more branches and rocks flew her way, she dove beneath a giant arch made of fallen rocks. *Is this another part of the palace gates?* she wondered. From beneath the archway, she began recognizing more Earth One-like objects, but she was still unsure of whether this place was a real, physical landscape or if she was hallucinating. The brain fog was strong and she could not remember how she had actually ended up here, or how many hours or days it had been since she'd left home with Uncle J.

The rumble in her stomach told her it had been long enough to miss at least a couple meals. *I'm so hungry*, Rella thought. *I'm going to die if I don't get something to eat right away.*

The more she observed this foreign landscape—the silent things that should have made sounds, the smells that seemed to be mismatched to their substances (like the fruit flavored dust), and the lights that seemed to have no solar or electrical source—the less she actually recognized it as any natural ecosystem. It couldn't be real, at least as she understood the meaning of real.

A new word suddenly popped into Rella's head: Drealismic. She tried spelling the word in her head. Did it have one 'L' or two? She was not a great speller, and she had only just recently heard the word. It was such a fun word, though, that she really wanted to get the spelling right. *Drealismic*, she thought, and then spelled the word aloud in her head: *D-R-E-A-L-I-S-M-I-C*. *Definition: a world used to describe a world imagined or invented in a dream, but then made into a material entity through a combination of technological and bio-chemical processes.*

On Earth One, before Rella was born, some engineers in Westcon and elsewhere had been developing a computer system where they would read and render the images from a person's dream and then begin to build miniature models of those worlds with a combination of 3-D printers and, if a person was patient enough, they would use genetic and chemical engineering to create simulations of living, breathing creatures.

Rella didn't know if it was true or rumor, but she thought that this place in front of her would fit into that description, though she would have to have been shrunken down to microscopic size for her to have actually been put into a 'drealismic' landscape. The kids at school were always talking about wanting to have their own fish tank-sized dream worlds in their bedrooms. Rella wasn't sure. But, then, maybe her dreams were a little more complicated than those kids' dreams?

Just as she settled on the idea that she was now trapped in one of these synthetic dream worlds, she felt a little more steady and her thoughts cleared. Despite the renewed clarity, and hope that the true reality wasn't completely gone, the world around her felt inverted to most of her other senses, especially her sense of taste and sound.

Rella thought about what her father, Julian, might say if he was beside her. She knew. *Think with your ears, feel with your nose, and see with your feet, as well as your eyes. And wait for the answer. You'll feel it...right in your gut.*

"Those boulders should have crushed me," she whispered aloud, just to hear the sound of her own voice. To test her senses.

She thought, again, of her sensation of the invisible hand steadying the arch of boulders.

Things that were supposed to move fast as they fell from cliffs or trees, moved too slowly; things that were supposed to make noise when they crashed to the ground were quieter than cotton balls falling onto a carpet; and things that should have made me sneeze and cough soothed my throat and my stomach like the scent of mother's butter-slathered, blueberry muffins. It didn't make sense. But it wasn't altogether so bad either. Rella's stomach growled so loud that she jumped, thinking there might be a wild bear nearby.

As she continued imagining sinking her teeth into the soft tops of her mother's home-baked muffins, Rella finally decided to flee into the forest.

After only a few quick steps, she heard a crack...pop...crack...pop...crack echo from the surrounding mountain ledges. Rella's Earth-oriented eyes could not make sense of the warped angles on the mountains. *If someone laid that wall down flat on its side*, Rella thought, as she continued sprint-ing, *it would have resembled the bumpy skin of the ocean.*

From her view within the shadows of the trees at the base of the waterfall, the mountain wall looked like a sculpture craft-ed by an ancient goddess who thought it might be fun to freeze time, slice off a layer of the ocean, prop the slice up on its side, and then paint it all of her favorite shades of green, gray, and sil-ver.

She stopped to catch her breath. As she stood and observed the panorama, Rella sensed that true beauty had once flourished in this place, and she felt sad to see how it was falling to pieces.

Feeling very unlike a goddess, and faint, Rella leaned back against a gigantic tree root and tucked her knees into her chest, mimicking the position the school officials in Ensea taught her to do during the safety drills.

Rella waited for her teetering brain to steady itself once more. She thought again of the invisible hands, and, for a mo-ment, of her parents. Two small tears rolled down her cheek.

Rella picked up a small rock and a thin piece of tree bark, about the size of a sheet of notebook paper, and started outlining the events of the day to see if something was missing or out of or-der. She made a list:

I was in the car, and then I was in a cave.

I was in the car, sketching a picture, and then I was in a cave.

I was in the car, under Grandma's quilt, drawing a picture, and then I was in a glowing cave. And, when I got out of the cave, there was a sign, a broken sign, with missing letters that read: H-l-e-o.

No, the ceremony, a memorial, wings above a branch, floating, calm, a song....

She read over her list and tried to concentrate, but she also had to fight the constant fear of being blown away by the hard gusts of wind or being crushed by the falling boulders.

The tremors started up again. *Pop, crack, thud...thwack...crum, pop, thud, rumble.*

Rella started imagining the words that would accompany each sound if someone were writing them down. She didn't know why she felt so compelled to think about spelling words right now, but something about this world seemed to be trying to pull actual words out of her head. She looked down at the bark in her hands and the words she had written down appeared to move and rearrange themselves. It was like the tree bark was trying to learn how to spell or communicate with her.

She dropped the bark. She felt as if it had shocked her hands but then immediately bent over and picked it back up. The words she had etched into the wood had dissolved like midmorning snow. She tossed the bark back to the ground.

As she listened to the pops and cracks and thwacks all around her, Rella remembered the time that she accidentally stepped too far out onto a frozen pond and fell through ice. It was one of the last memories she had with both of her parents.

Her father and mother were standing only a few feet away, and, when she plunged in, they were right there to help calm her and pull her out. She could remember their calm and assured voices. "We've got you, Rella. Don't panic. We've got you." She also never forgot the popping and cracking made by that thin sheet of ice just before she fell through. Every time she heard a similar sound, her entire body would tense up and begin to shiver. The memory seeped like ice into her bones.

Here, now, in H-L-E-O, whatever this place was, she knew her father and mother would not be able to rescue her. As far as she could tell, there was no clear way up or out of this world. She no longer had the quilt, which she began to think might have something to do with her ability to move between the worlds. Or, perhaps, it was the ball of shadow. All she really knew was that this world had no exit signs, no moving stairways, no floating platforms, no wooden bridges across the sky, or even beams of light to carry her home.

Chapter 8: Prisma and Scarlett

"WE HAVE TO COLLECT as many of the blue ones as we can," Prisma ordered.

"Why the blue ones?" Scarlett asked.

"That's how he makes them," Prisma replied, sounding agitated.

"But what happens if we fall into the water?" Scarlett asked.

"Well," Prisma said, looking down into the current, and waiting to lower her net and grab another one of the blue orbs. "I don't really know what he does with them...but they seem to have the most power. He mixes them with some of the other materials he's got out on the island and then he sends them floating over to destroy...all of it!" Prisma let out a malicious laugh.

Prisma was delighted at how quickly the Shadowsplitters were tearing apart the environment of Hleo. When her master was happy, she was happy.

Scarlett didn't say a word. *It won't be long,* Scarlett thought, *before Archimago has weakened Hleo enough that he will be able to take control The Wondercurrent itself. I've got to figure this out soon.*

"Yes. I expect him to give us the signal to proceed soon, possibly today," Prisma said.

"Then what?" Scarlett said, trying to avoid eye contact with Prisma. Something about Prisma's eyes seemed artificial to Scarlett. They looked human, but they didn't always move or focus in a natural way. She also found it odd that Prisma never slept.

"Why don't you ever pay attention," Prisma shouted. "I can't believe he chose you to help me carry out this plan. You haven't earned the right, in my opinion," Prisma chided.

Scarlett swiped her net down into the pool, trying to capture one of the blue orbs, but she missed completely.

"Look!," Prisma ordered, "You have to lower it more slowly."

"Do you think they're alive?" Scarlett asked, watching Prisma grab another one. "Just look at the way they blink when you pull them out of the water. It's like they're screaming. Does that bother you?"

"Bother me?" Prisma asked. "Who cares if they're alive? Archimago must have them. I serve him and he rewards me."

Scarlett looked back into the water and watched more of the blinking orbs floating by. She wondered if the colors related to specific powers, or if they were all made of the same substance. The way the blue ones blinked gave her a strange feeling, like she should protect them. She couldn't help but think that some of them, though they looked alike, were actually living things.

"Scarlett! Are you listening?" Prisma asked.

"What?" Scarlett replied, annoyed, but trying to remain calm.

"When he sends the signal, which will come through the jewel in The Architect's sword, we are supposed to meet at the shore, right where this river touches The Dark Waters. He will send the army, the Shadowsplitters soon."

"And then?" Scarlett asked, acting like she cared.

"And then," Prisma replied, "I will direct them up the banks of the sparkling river. We will put out the light."

"Are you sure we...you...can control a whole army of them? What about those other children we've seen around here?"

"They can't stop us. Even if there were more than two of them, which there aren't, we're going to have an army. And there's no way to destroy them."

Scarlett repeated Prisma's words to herself.

Put out the light. No way to destroy them.

"Now, hold up that bag," Prisma commanded as she dropped another blinking blue orb into it.

"Are they alive?" Scarlett asked.

"Alive? What difference does that make?" Prisma replied.

Chapter 9: The Message and the Scroll

THE EARTHQUAKES RESUMED. They were even stronger than when Rella had first arrived. The cracking and crashing pounded her eardrums. She steadied herself, tightened her stomach, and pressed her palms firmly and fully over her ears. She had survived earthquakes before: coastal ones, mountain ones, and even the ones made from the explosions during the construction of the new airport in Ensea.

As the clouds of gray-blue dust drifted like fog all around her, she could not fathom how she would survive this one. Her entire body felt numb, like she was sinking beneath ice.

"Mother? Father? Where are you?" Rella whispered. She looked up into the clouds. She knew that she couldn't be heard, but she was trying to find courage, like all the strong, brave people in the stories her father read to her before he went away.

She stood up and attempted to push the thick cloud of gray-blue dust away from her body. She was not going to give up. Nor was she planning to sit around and hope those invisible hands were actually real and might come back and rescue her.

As the fog reached her face, she began salivating. The fog smelled so sweet, and, when it dissolved on her tongue, it tasted even sweeter than the blue dust she had licked off of her hand earlier.

She felt foolish for trying to stand up in the middle of an earthquake, but something in this savory dust restored her mind, even if it didn't do much to soothe her stomach. Rella knew that some force in the environment itself, despite the chaos all around her, was reaching out, attempting to nourish her.

Another explosive tremor knocked her flat onto her back, spilling some of the items in her satchel. When the back of her head hit the ground, she was surprised to find that the ground felt soft, like the surface of a giant mushroom, and not the hard surface of rocky soil, or a frozen pond. *How does ground go from being rocky and hard to soft like a mushroom in a split second?* Rella thought, relieved that it was so soft. She reached over and began collecting the items that had spilled out of the satchel, including a book that her father used to read to her quite often. She held the book to her chest and hugged it.

Her father's voice, like a memory but also somehow more than a memory, floated into her head. He was quoting from a poem in the book, but it made even less sense here in Hleo than it did back home. It was probably a translation of a saying in some old language her father had been studying. All she kept hearing was "othning omecs morf othning"

You see, dear reader, language can sometimes play tricks on you, and, if you're clever, you can play tricks on it, but, in this case, Rella couldn't seem to decipher the meaning of the phrase. If her father was, somehow, trying to speak to her, this wasn't going to be much help—at least not at this moment.

Knees knocking and palms sweating, Rella crawled into a thicket of blue and silver grass, where she thought she spotted some juicy berries that glowed like jewels.

For a moment, Rella wondered if she might have somehow shrunken down to the size of a ladybug, or maybe even a microscopic cell. She watched the colossal tree branches falling and sinking into the floor of the forest. And then a few more shadowy creatures scampered through the branches above her.

It was too dark to tell if they were some variation of an Earth One creature or something else entirely. Her instincts told her the creatures were not out to harm her and she trusted the feeling.

Rella peeked out through two of the tall, silver blades of grass and caught the eyes of one of the small critters. It seemed to be smiling at her.

She blinked and tried to refocus, but it was gone in half a flash.

To stifle a coughing fit—as the spongy, sweet, blue dust tickled its way down her throat—she pressed her nose and mouth firmly into her sleeve. She caught the cough somewhere in the middle of her throat.

Another creature hooted nearby. And another chirped.

But, soon, the silence closed in around her again. This time, though, it felt more like it was outside of her head than inside.

On Earth One, the boulders she saw tumbling down the mountain wall and down through the nearby trees would have echoed like basketballs in a bathroom. The silence was puzzling.

Despite the weight of the water coming down over the rushing falls, nothing splashed, swish-swashed, or even drip-drop-drip-drip-dropped. Even her last bedtime bath, like I imagine it was for your last bath, reader, was noisier than The Wondercurrent.

Water, especially thousands of gallons falling from the top of a mountain, is supposed to roar as it splashes into a river, isn't it? Rella wondered.

As she inhaled even more of the sweet blue fog, her concentration improved. She could hear her heart drumming rapidly inside her chest.

Now that she was adjusting to the air (or the air was adjusting to her), Rella looked up and saw her worst fear. It was *him*. From her low hiding spot in the thicket, she watched a tall, pale-faced boy in a cloak emerge from the cave. *The Architect*, she thought. *That's him! He's the one the girl from the dream told me about.*

Rella leapt up and dashed behind the broad trunk of a fallen tree. She watched him carefully rummaging through the fallen limbs. And then she spotted the jeweled sword. It was partially hidden beneath the cloak.

She hoped he was not as horrible as he looked from this distance. There was still a chance, she hoped, that he might just be misunderstood. *Maybe he isn't all bad*, she thought, foolishly.

Then again, Rella said to herself, *When has a tall, pale, bony boy in a dark cloak, carrying a sword, ever been on the good girl's side in a story?* She'd read a lot of stories. She knew the answer to that one. It was zero.

Rella watched the cloaked boy scour nearly every inch of the ground outside of the cave. She was relieved that she hadn't left any footprints or dropped anything that might lead him over to her. *Could this really be The Architect?* she wondered, starting to panic. *If so, as soon as he passes back through the entrance of that cave, he is going to realize that a girl from a faraway land, me, has taken his lost scroll, and he's going to chase me down, and, then...*

Rella shivered at the next thought that came into her head: *Will he use my bones as material for building some evil fortress? Is that why Quinn called him The Architect in the message?*

Of course, The Architect did not know she had the scroll, which she still had not even unrolled. She was, as children sometimes do, she was overthinking all of it, since this tall, bony boy could not possibly know of her identity.

As she looked back toward The Architect, she watched him disappear, once again, into the glowing light of the cave's entrance.

The only reason she had to believe that he might be dangerous was because of a note she had found on the outside of the scroll. To Rella, the script seemed familiar, but she couldn't place the language exactly. It seemed to have parts of all three of her primary Earth One languages combined, but also a hint of something else. An extra layer of coding. Somehow, though, she could read the words without any problem at all. Here, reader, is the message that had been scrawled in the green ink.

DEAR RELLA: IF YOU are reading this, you are no longer dreaming and you've fully surfaced in Hleo. I know Eurie wanted to explain it all, but I don't know if she had time. I'm sure you've guessed that we were both dream travelers, and, yes, we have been preparing to bring you in. We have so much more to explain, but, for now, whatever you do, don't let The Architect find this scroll— I think they are plans of some kind, but I don't really know.

I tried to read them, but I didn't want to risk having my memory wiped or being controlled by a hidden code. Some have said you have the gift, Rella. Though we don't understand it, we know that you're protected.

But beware. He's going to be searching for you. He's tall, but not as tall as an adult. He will be wearing a cloak and possibly carrying a dangerous sword.

If you can, go find Eurie. Eurie will know what to do.

If you cannot signal to Eurie, look for Alister, the bear who lives halfway in and halfway out of the trees. I can't be sure which tree he'll be in. He moves a lot. But I tried to signal to him that you'd be coming. He knows how to find us. You can't mistake his thunderous voice.

We believe in you, Rella. Welcome back. See you soon.

Your Friend,

Quinn.

As Rella finished reading the scroll, a small critter, something like a chipmunk, walked up to her. She looked down at the critter and spoke to it: "Quinn? Who is Quinn? And who is Eurie? What did he mean by *you*?" The critter gave her a puzzled look, turned its head, and then scampered away.

Rella vaguely recalled a boy named Quinn from school. It was a common name in Ensea, throughout Eastcon, and in Westcon. But Eurie? She was certain she'd never met anyone named Eurie. That sounded like a name for a mermaid or some other mythical character from one of her dad's books about ancient goddesses. She looked down at her satchel and thought about pulling out the book to search for the girl's name. Or maybe a name for an elf queen? Rella would have loved to meet an elf queen...but only if she was a very nice one.

Rella tried to concentrate. She thought about the unfolding sphere of shadows again. She thought about the explosion of colors that flowed into her eyes as she left the backseat of Uncle J's car.

Then she started to remember the dreams. The memories poured in, each one like a bucket of water. *Could Eurie be the girl who traveled in the trees with the guardian called Thalas? And Quinn, was he the boy from Westcon? The soldier who was working on a rescue ship to go and save the kidnapped guardians from...yes...*She remembered now. *Archimago's Island.*

Arriving in Hleo had felt, in part, like walking into all of her mother and father's storybooks and chemistry and astronomy lessons at once. Although this specific setting, among the fallen trees and the cave, did not quite match any particular realm.

She tried to recall any discussions with the dream travelers about the bear named Alister, who lived halfway inside of a tree. She had a vague memory of a boy in a cloak who was the devoted servant to a sinister, hollow-eyed man; but this boy she just saw didn't seem like someone devoted purely to evil and destruction. She hadn't really met a lot of real-life villains though.

Perhaps actual villains just look like ordinary people, Rella thought.

A phrase, in her father's voice, resounded again in her head: "Watch with your ears, listen with your nose, and think with your feet, as well as your eyes. Then wait for your heart to confirm."

If I've fallen into a storybook, Rella wondered, *why didn't Alister have a more mythical sounding name, like Eurie, which I just realized I have no idea how to pronounce. Is it your-E or year-E, or Yo-rye? And if Alister really lives halfway inside of a tree, would he really be a bear or more of a tree-bear?* She'd heard of half man-half horse creatures, but half tree-bears seemed a bit out of step with most of the traditions she knew.

Even if she did find this half-bear in a tree, she didn't know if she was looking for a live, carnivorous bear or just something called a bear because that was the closest thing to a bear Quinn, the boy who wrote the letter, could describe.

Rella listened for movement in the underbrush. She wondered if the little chipmunk might come back.

After a brief silence, her body started wavering again. She needed a cold drink of water. It was only a few leaps over to the edge of The Wondercurrent, but she had no idea if she should attempt to drink from it.

It didn't have any odd smells and, from what she could tell, there weren't any dead things floating in it. Yet she didn't want to dip her hand in there and lose it between the teeth of some invisible piranha, or have it singed or melted off by some chemical reaction.

She'd heard of a river once that contained all the dreams of all the children who ever lived. *Could this be that river?* Rella wondered.

When she dreamed of it, at times, it seemed pure and inviting. But there were darker dreams too, where the river smelled foul and seemed to bubble with ooze.

Since the cloaked boy had been in the cave for at least fifteen minutes, she thought about retreating again into the nearby forest to try and find a route to higher ground. This way she could gain an advantage if there was a fight. From the look of that sword hanging from his belt, she knew she'd need an advantage.

Thunder rolled and the distant skies cracked. The grassy plains on the far side of the dense, colorfully shaded forests trembled. More small animals, birds and lizards, scattered.

The ground beneath Rella's feet hardened and throbbed as a throng of gargantuan limbs fell soundlessly onto the forest floor.

As the entire landscape and shadows around her vibrated, she began to work out one of the puzzles of seeing in Hleo. It reminded her of when she was learning to see for the first time, after her surgery. About a year before her mother disappeared. Vision, in Hleo, required moving your eyes, or letting your eyes move, in rhythms and along curved lines of sight that didn't exist on Earth One. It was like constantly looking at abstract paintings.

As Rella started running toward the current, the white boulders she had been hiding beneath a few minutes earlier shifted and exploded, sending large chunks of rock ripping through the air. Some of them slammed into the surface of The Wondercurrent and skipped across. Yet, still, there was no sound on impact.

Rella sat with her back pressed against a large stone pillar. The ruins around the waterfall seemed ancient, but, at the same time, well preserved. *Maybe it was the climate that preserved them?* she thought. Despite their ancient-looking construction, Rella could see that they didn't have the usual wear on them that one might expect. She also noticed a small broken sign with unfamiliar letters carved into it. The letters appeared to be a combination of old Earth One languages like American English, Japanese, Cyrillic, and Arabic, although they were more likely a completely different language altogether.

She thought about the carving with the name of the land: *H-L-E-O* and the one beside the waterfall that was missing a few letters but Rella had figured out spelled: Wondercurrent.

She somehow already knew that word, but, seeing it written, at least partially on a sign, was reassuring. It certainly sounded like a river you'd want to swim and bathe and dream in.

Rella ducked and waited for another explosion.

Much more like dynamite, she thought, *than the movement of tectonic plates. But where's the smoke, the fire? The dynamite would have to be close by. Or was Hleo under attack from some other unnatural force?*

She thought about a friend from Ensea who was obsessed with stealth planes, warships, and conspiracies. She remembered how he'd once told her about a secret air force of invisible planes that carried invisible explosives. *Perhaps he wasn't just making that up?* Rella thought. *Maybe her friend had been visited by dream travelers too?*

Rella's father's book then came to mind, but she still couldn't picture the cover of the one with Archimago, the shape-shifter. *Was it gray or red?*

Rella wondered again if the environment here was actually trying to protect her. *Is it possible?* she thought. *Could this place be like one of those virtual reality hospitals in Westcon? Maybe I'm hooked up to some kind of machine with a VR mask?*

She smacked and pinched her own arms a few times, trying to wake herself up. She had heard about some of the new medical Virtual Reality on an audio program in her uncle's car. The doctors would put a mask over your head that would then attach itself to your skin and send signals through to your brain. And you'd be transported, for a while, to a fabulous new world.

Would anyone believe this? What would Uncle J say about all of this? Rella wondered.

And then, for the first time since she'd arrived in Hleo, she thought of Uncle J, and the exhaustion and sorrow of her last day at home, the moments before they left Ensea. It all rushed back to her. She felt the bubbles in her stomach begin to grow.

Rella had no idea how she would find Uncle J again, or if he was worried and out looking for her. *Can adults be transported here?* Rella wondered. *If so, would Uncle J be able to help her fight The Architect?*

Chapter 10: Sketching

IT WAS NEITHER SEVEN minutes nor seven days since Rella had surfaced in Hleo. It was actually closer to seven hours (Earth One time).

Just prior to arriving in this strange and beautiful new place, she was in the backseat of her Uncle J's car, tucked under her grandmother's hand-stitched green and white quilt, which she now suspected had a role in transporting her into Hleo. Rella was trying her best not to think of her parents' disappearance, and the strange feelings she was having during the secret ceremony in Ensea earlier that morning.

During her last few seconds on Earth One, Rella had been sketching a small pair of wings she had seen floating above the branch of an apple tree, which jutted out right over the ceremony leader's bowed head. *Did I make that sketch or did I just think about making it?* Rella wondered. She was confusing memories with dreams. Forward thoughts moved neither backwards nor forwards, and everything, here in Hleo, seemed to be turning inside out.

Everyone at the pre-dawn ceremony, she recalled, had gathered in a circle around the firelight and softy hummed the Remembrance Day song. They all had their eyes closed. Everyone except for Rella.

During the ceremony, her throat was too choked up with tears for the notes to come out and her eyes would not close no matter how hard she tried to squeeze them shut. That was when she was captivated by the appearance of the wings. She concentrated on their rhythmic movements. The twinkling outline seemed to be suspended on the water vapors drifting upon the morning air. To Rella, it felt like a pair of friendly eyes were looking back at her, telling her they knew the exact thoughts of all who were standing around that circle singing the sacred songs. It was like the winged being knew the reasons why all of these familiar faces from so many different places had gathered here to remember her missing parents, and other members of The Storykeeper's Alliance who had also gone missing.

But the wings, if she was remembering correctly, couldn't tell her anything about her parents or what happened to them, or if she would ever see them again. Rella tried to reach her hands out, to invite the creature to come closer, but the mysterious being simply vanished, leaving the world without even a puff of dust or wisp of smoke.

Rella's last memory of that morning in Ensea was standing and staring at that crowd of mourners, all singing the names of the lost.

The memorial song, I should tell you, dear reader, actually contained special codes with instructions for Uncle J. They told him exactly where to take Rella next. Rella didn't know the code, but she had paid enough attention at previous ceremonies to know that was part of the way that the Alliance communicated.

Rella listened closely, but couldn't pick up on the message. Her Uncle then placed a warm hand on her slumping shoulders.

As the memory faded, Rella focused back on her immediate surroundings. She would need to do some quick thinking. The sky in Hleo had darkened immensely since she had arrived, and soon, it would be a complete blackout up above.

Rella did not want to end up spending the night alone in this decaying forest and she needed to get a closer look at the scroll, and the note from Quinn. She still hadn't met Quinn in person, but somehow, he seemed to know more about her than almost anyone on Earth One.

Could he be one of the boys from my dreams? she thought, trying to remember if any of her dreams of Hleo involved a dream traveler named Quinn.

Every time she had those dreams, she always seemed to forget to learn people's names. In one of the dreams of Hleo, she had met this one boy who spoke with the accent of Westcon, though she was only guessing. Though young, he was dressed like a soldier. And he had a couple of handmade tools hanging from his belt. His skin was a bit darker than hers and he had a very stylish haircut.

As the clouds overhead thickened, Rella was doubly worried about getting lost and traveling around in circles. She peered into the thickening shadows of the forest and formed two escape plans.

Plan A: I'll climb the path next to the waterfall even higher to get a better overall view of the landscape, and then locate a village. If it works, then I'll create a signal by piling up some of the nearby luminous stones to create a beacon.

The climb was steep, though, and she worried about falling. From her already high vantage point, she hadn't seen any signs of a village, and, going higher probably wouldn't reveal a whole lot more. Though it was dark and misty, she did, for a second, think that she had seen the top of a tower of some kind, although it may have also just been the top of a mountain or one of the giant trees growing out of the top of a mountain.

Plan B: I could follow along The Wondercurrent, in case I have to jump in and swim across to make an escape. I could stay close to the ground, look for footprints or other paths, and then keep on the move while I figured out my next steps.

As she starting climbing down the falls, toward the more thickly wooded side of The Wondercurrent, Rella kept an eye out for The Architect. She still had no idea how she would cross the water, or if she could get near the shore without being seen.

The gray-blue sky turned into an iron red and darkened further.

Suddenly, the shadow of two giant wings swooped overhead. The breeze from the wings rippled across her face.

From the mouth of the nearby cave, a faint, blue glow pulsed like a warning signal. Rella wondered if the blinking in the cave had anything to do with the swooping shadows overhead. The blinking pattern seemed familiar, but she couldn't place the memory.

Rella hoped the signal was someone trying to help. But she also felt like running away.

But then where will I go? she thought.

As she stared into the mouth of the cave, it occurred to her that The Architect may have just been carrying some kind of light, perhaps a luminous stone, while making his way out of the cave. The shadows above, she reasoned, might just be drifting clouds.

Rella crept around the rock pile and toward the thickly wooded side of the bank. The trees were twenty times larger than any trees she had ever seen, and in a few places, where the bark seemed to have been chipped away, she saw faint gold and silver lines, like some kind of writing, though she could not get close enough to see if she could read it.

As she looked out at the flowing water, she saw something nestled behind a tall thicket of white grasses: The Architect's transport ship.

Until this moment, she was not sure if anything but natural objects existed in Hleo. The Architect's vessel, though, resembled the stealth fighter planes her friend back home would design on his Touchpad-4xi drawing computer. He would work on his designs all day long while he was in class, when he was supposed to be doing his math and reading.

Rella liked using old-fashioned pencils and paper to do her drawings, though she was always impressed with the way her friend maxed out the drawing program to create such vivid blueprints.

Rella remembered a specific promise her friend had made to her before she left Ensea. It was during the ceremony. He said he would send her an important message once she arrived at her new home with her Uncle J. She had no idea how he knew where they were going, but she trusted her friend. He kept his promises.

The Architect's boat, just like her friend's drawings, had jagged angles and corners everywhere, and a solid metal frame. It looked like it could hold at least four fully-grown adults, or maybe six kids. There was a large cage on a platform attached to the rear of the ship.

Even though it belonged to a villain, she really wanted to see it in action.

The blue light at the mouth of the cave glowed brighter. Rella knew that whoever or whatever was in the cave was getting closer to the exit. She had to make a move.

As she turned to run, she felt a magnetic force pulling her back around toward the blue light. She resisted it, but it didn't go away. She turned away from the cave, forcefully, and examined the nearby trees and boulders and the crumbling archways.

Everything still seemed to shift around, or, she thought, she just wasn't seeing it properly. *The tall, wide branches of the trees*, she thought, *would be an excellent place to hide, but what if something else is up there...what if there are bears?*

Quinn's letter did say that a bear in a tree would supposedly be willing to help her. *But what*, she thought, *what if there was more than just one bear in the tree? What other animals might also be hiding in those crackling branches?*

Rella rolled the scroll as tightly as she could and grasped it firmly in her hand as she sprinted off into the shadows. She slid between the wide, glowing trunks. She had no idea where she was going, but she needed to put as much distance as possible between herself, the cave, and The Architect's armored ship. The cage on the back of that ship, she figured, would easily hold her, and she had no interest in being locked up in it.

As Rella trekked deeper into the thick mists of the forest, she tried to keep from veering too far from The Wondercurrent, since she still hoped to cross it to get up to the lookout spot at the top of the waterfall.

Rella continued running until she was completely out of air. She looked back behind her and everything that had been whirling and whipping around was now completely still again. It was like the forest was following her, but when she turned around, it didn't want to be caught.

Rella shivered all over. A leaf, large enough to be a blanket, was lying on the forest floor. It had fallen from high above. Rella covered herself with the velvety leaf and sat down. A small critter, which looked just like the one she'd seen earlier, crawled up next to her. It was about the size of a chipmunk. It didn't say a word, but looked at Rella with curiosity.

"Hi, there!" Rella said. "Can I tell you a story?"

The chipmunk chirped back and nodded.

"When I was five, I snuck out of my house once," Rella said.

The chipmunk looked at her and shook his head with disapproval.

"You see...there was this old, abandoned storm drain...and I really wanted to see it."

The chipmunk nodded as though he understood.

"I had overheard the older kids in the neighborhood talking about this place called The Graffiti Halls. Some kids, they said, without anywhere else to live, used to hang out and spray-paint the insides of the old stone drain pipes. A lot of kids said they had been through the tunnels and had seen graffiti murals of magical forests, mythical birds, and terrifying monsters that looked like they were actually coming out of the curved walls of the drainpipes."

The chipmunk tried to stick his nose into Rella's satchel.

"Hey! Get out of there!" Rella said. "I don't have any food."

The chipmunk jumped back and curled up in her lap as if to encourage her to keep talking.

"Well, one boy even said these kids, the runaways with no families, were part of a gang of dark wizards and that the monsters could actually come out of the walls if you said the right spell... I didn't really believe that part of the story at first, but I had to see the artwork...plus, I wanted to have a magnificent tale to bring back to my dad...he always had the best stories. I wanted one of my own."

"And then what?" the chipmunk said.

Rella looked at him in disbelief. "Excuse me? Can you talk?"

The chipmunk nodded. Rella smiled back and continued.

"On that Saturday morning, when I ran away, I met up with my other sketch-artist friend to see the murals. The tunnels went much deeper than we realized, and, at one point, we got split up."

"I had my own flashlight, but the batteries died and I was left all alone. Just like I am right now. I heard voices approaching, and I had to lie down and wait in the dark until the gang passed by."

"Oh. That's terrible. Terrible," the chipmunk said, sneaking back into Rella's satchel. Rella grabbed him and pulled him back into her lap.

"The wizards never came through her tunnel though...I was so certain I'd heard footsteps and voices, but then the tunnel was just filled with an empty, eerie silence..."

"Oh. Strange. Strange," the chipmunk said, and then ran off into the dark.

"Wait!" Rella shouted, but the chipmunk was gone.

Could those kids, Rella thought, *have possibly come from this place?*

After examining the dimly lit forest floor, Rella knew she had distanced herself safely from The Architect. She knelt down, unrolled the scroll on the ground, and tried to examine it again. The area was so dark that she couldn't see anything on the scroll. She ran her hand across it, trying to activate it, but it didn't light up.

Shadows seemed to hover everywhere she moved, and there were no stars or moons visible in the sky. *How can a place like this have no visible stars or moons?* she thought. *There are giant trees, sparkling rivers and waterfalls, luminous grasses and plants everywhere. There has to be some kind of light source to energize it all.*

She carefully searched the shadows for any reflections of light. Even a tiny firefly might do, if she could catch one. The memory of the wings flashed through her mind again.

While fleeing from The Architect, she had seen a few flickers of light near the waterfall. *What were those things? Mutant fireflies?* she wondered, still very disoriented by the odd scale and shape and taste of her surroundings, like the twenty-foot tree limbs, the quilted textures on the leaves, the mushroom-like soil, and the sweet bluish powder floating everywhere.

She looked again in the direction of The Wondercurrent. As she slowed down to focus her mind, she realized that flickers of light were coming from hundreds of small, jelly-like orbs floating down the river. These lights provided, at least, a little comfort as she gazed out into the layers of darkness above.

How could so much moving water be so silent? she thought, wiggling her fingers in her ears again, thinking she had somehow suffered hearing damage.

Rella sat down to catch her breath and tried to concentrate on the dense, shadowy space around her. She could barely see the back of her hands. The bubbles inside her stomach caused her to double over in pain.

She pressed her dry palms together. A single, hot tear slipped out of the corner of her eye. She clutched her stomach, bowed her head, and closed her eyes tight. *Think, think, think, Rella. How did you get here? Why does this place look so strange, yet feel so familiar?*

After what felt like hours of trying to sort out all the images and impressions passing through her mind, she stopped and picked up the scroll. "Do something!" she shouted at the scroll. "Speak!"

As she did, a bluish light illuminated the thin, glassy, metallic scroll.

And then the image of The Architect flashed across the scroll. The warmth drained from her face. She was now as stiff as the white boulders piled beside the cave.

Rella waited for signs of movement. She listened closely for a footstep or a snapping twig. She kept imagining a devilish, hollow voice ordering her to "hand them over or pay with her life!"

Unlike the mythical graffiti wizards, whom she never saw, she knew The Architect was real, at least as real as she was at this moment. If the scroll in her hand contained some kind of evil blueprints or was itself some kind of super-weapon, she knew that he was coming for them.

Rella held her breath and waited.

The blinking blue light of the scroll faded out and she was swallowed up into the inky black silence of the night—in a place where she still wasn't sure a sun would ever rise.

If this is a distant planet of some kind, she thought, *it's possible I just arrived at the sunset of a night that could last for years.*

At this moment, she absolutely regretted her decision to listen to some old recordings of her mother's lectures on interstellar astronomy. It was nice to hear her mother's voice, even after all the years she was gone, but, sometimes, Rella knew just a little too much about speculative astronomy for her own good.

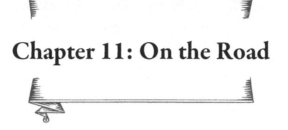

Chapter 11: On the Road

RELLA PULLED THE QUILT down and away from her face. *Have I been dreaming?* she thought. Her skin felt unusually warm, then cold, then warm again, like her body was trying to figure out how to regulate its temperature.

"What have you been doing under that blanket? It sounded like you were directing an intergalactic war movie!" Uncle J exclaimed.

Rella looked over at the light flooding in from the opened car door and then back at the quilt, now on her lap.

"Come on...let's grab a bite to eat!" Uncle J suggested, reaching down and helping her out of the car.

As she entered the Automa convenience store, she recognized it as one of the retro stores, the ones where they recreated the convenience stores of the early twentieth century (Earth One), before full automation. She wondered if Ensea, with the arrival of the new airport, would also be getting one more of these stores. Some people probably wouldn't like it, because it was from Westcon, but she thought they were fascinating. She loved the variety of products and the feeling of stepping across time periods but with all modern conveniences.

Rella could feel her stomach rumbling. She thought of the hungry, talking chipmunk in Hleo and wondered if he ever found something to eat.

Uncle J, she knew, didn't have a lot of money to spare, so she tried to find something inexpensive to eat. She walked by a heated display case. The salted, twisted pretzels made her stomach rumble even louder, but they cost twenty-five dollars apiece. The hot dogs were so shriveled that she wasn't even sure she would feed them to a starving possum.

Even if they only cost seven dollars, there was no way she'd ask Uncle J to buy one. Then she spotted a steaming, cheesy slice of pepperoni pizza. But it was fourteen dollars. *Too much*, she thought. *But I'm so hungry.*

Rella walked down a few aisles of dry packaged goods, including nacho chips, almond butter crackers, and tacky taffy. Another display case had been filled with an assortment of clear gummy candies that sparkled and lit up when you touched them. These candies were not typically placed in the retro Automa convenience stores, since they were a post-2150's product, but they must have sold well in this new territory. Rella wasn't so sure about eating candy that lit up like that.

Rella then turned to a girl standing by the case, eyeing the candy.

"What happens once you swallow it?" Rella asked.

The girl looked at her, but didn't seem to understand her.

"Do the chemicals dissolve into your stomach and give you luminous saliva?" Rella asked.

The girl just shrugged and walked away.

Despite her fear of the glowing candy, her mouth continued to water as she watched the colorful gummies blinking on and off in random patterns.

The blinking made Rella think immediately of The Wonder-current. She was still trying to figure out what pulled her back to Earth One.

She really wanted one of those candies. She couldn't stop staring. And then she began to daydream.

After a very long minute of imagining the taste of the color-ful gummies, Uncle J tapped lightly her on the shoulder to break her out of the trance.

"Ah!" Rella shouted as she leapt up off the ground. She could leap higher than most kids her age, so Uncle J had to jump back to avoid being knocked over.

He nearly dropped the warm, salted pretzel in his hand.

"I got a deal on it," he said. "The Automa cashier, the P.R.I.S.M.A., said it had been in the display for more than an hour, so it offered me half price." The way Uncle J talked about the Automa cashier as if it was a person made Rella laugh, since no actual humans had been employed in convenience stores since 2145. There were, of course, states and provinces where living people actually sold goods, but only in remote villages far off the main roadways.

Rella gave him a bear hug and grabbed the hot pretzel out of his hand. She took three quick bites, and then a very, very slow fourth one.

The blinking candies caught her eye again and she thought about the strange, glittery waterfall in Hleo.

She held Uncle J's hand as they walked out to the car. She wanted to go back to Hleo, but she also wanted to stay with Uncle J. She didn't really know if she had a choice.

Uncle J opened the door for her and helped her get situated in the middle of the back seat. He also pulled a cherry-flavored drink from behind his back, like an old-fashioned magician, and handed it to her.

As their car reentered the highway, Uncle J turned up the radio. A journalist was interviewing a *supposed* inter-Earths naturalist employed by the newly elected government of Westcon. The naturalist was explaining some recent advances in tree designs, and how these newly engineered trees would replace a lot of the ones starting to fall apart in the courtyards of the high rise buildings all over the capital city. Rella had never seen any of these engineered trees, but she'd heard kids at Ensea elementary claiming to have traveled to the capital of Westcon, where the trees were planted and then sprouted and grew hundreds of feet in a single week.

The naturalist mentioned that they required very little sunlight and were supposed to be as strong as steel. However, the naturalist pointed out, these trees had some defects.

Rella could tell that Uncle J was listening closely because he kept talking back to the radio out loud as though he was part of the conversation. He had shut off the actual talkback, two-way feature, which recorded your verbal comments, turned them into a code and then synthesized them into a live response on the audio broadcast.

In other words, you shouted out a thought and then the computer analyzed all possible arguments and responses and then played out the rest of your most likely thoughts for you as you listened.

Rella found this quite eerie and did not like listening to her Uncle J listening to a computer version of himself talking to himself.

Rella took a final sip of her cherry drink and licked the last grains of salt from her palms. She didn't really believe Uncle J had only paid twelve dollars for that pretzel, but she wouldn't dare let him know she didn't believe him. Perhaps the Alliance members had taken up a collection for them?

Rella loosened her seatbelt and reached down to the floor to pick up her sketchbook. It was dark outside, but there was enough light from the digital display on the dashboard that she could see her sketchbook clearly enough to continue working.

One of her clearest memories of her mom was the way she used to always compliment her on how well she could navigate in the dark. Rella couldn't remember those early years, before she got her full sight. But Rella's mom told her that every night since she could climb out of her bed, she would find her way out of her room and to her parents' bed without stepping on a single mislaid toy or running into a corner. Her mom once called her the shadow girl, which made Rella laugh, since she never pictured herself as any kind of superhero.

Rella didn't want to think more about her parents at the moment, or the sadness of the morning, so she put the sketch of the wings aside and tried to remember what was happening in Hleo before she ended up back in the car beneath her quilt. She wasn't ready, however, to put the quilt back over her head.

She picked her sketchbook back up and rapidly began sketching the entrance to the cave, the path from the cave to the river, and then, without lifting her pencil, followed the river upstream to the towering waterfall with the colored lights that seemed to bounce in mid-air as they dropped into the base of the falls.

She remembered the first sensations of the air on her skin: it wasn't really warm or cold; she remembered a hint of sweetness in the scent of the thick grass beneath her feet. Though it seemed impossible, she could swear the deafening rumble of the falling rocks and the bomb-like blasts were still ringing in her ears, even as she made the sketch.

As she shaded in part of the picture, one thing she couldn't recall was hearing any sound coming from The Wondercurrent. She was certain, actually, that the magnificent river made no sound at all.

How could a river so wide and active produce no sound? she thought. Then she remembered the blue light, the scroll, and The Architect.

She looked up toward the rearview mirror and caught Uncle J looking back at her.

"Are you ok, Rella?"

She stared up at his eyes in the mirror and tried to speak, but felt completely terrified as she recalled the bony, tall boy wearing the ancient cloak.

They need my help, she thought. *I've got to get back to them.* She tried to smile back at her Uncle and finally found her words: "I'm fine. That pretzel was amazing! Thanks Uncle J."

"No problem, Rella. Try to get a little rest. I'm going to drive us through the night."

Rella pulled the quilt over her head and tried to concentrate on returning to that impossible, mysterious place. She had no idea how she would avoid getting nabbed by The Architect, but they needed her.

As she sat beneath the blanket, she watched the picture in her lap begin to glow. Then, the ball of shadow appeared above the paper and unfolded itself again, bursting into a million sparks of color.

Chapter 12: The Luminous Stone

RELLA GRIPPED THE SCROLL so firmly her knuckles were throbbing. She tried not to breathe. She felt as if she had fallen into the deep end of a swimming pool.

She slowly turned around and noticed a small, glowing crystalline object on the ground about ten feet away. She couldn't see much else, but wasn't sure if she should walk over to the stone and investigate. *Who put this here? Can I lift it? Perhaps someone dropped it here for me to find?* she thought.

She didn't want to lose any more time and the light would help her navigate the thick foliage in the woods. Hopefully, this would lead her back to The Wondercurrent where she might find a bridge to cross so she could get to higher ground. She did consider heading back to the cave and climbing up alongside the waterfall, but the path looked a hundred times more difficult. The rocks also seemed to be loose and crumbling more quickly on her side of The Wondercurrent.

Rella lowered onto her stomach, pressed her face close to the sweet-scented grass and began crawling towards the stone. It was no bigger than an ice cube. It looked like a common machine-made Earth One crystal, but as far as Rella could remember from the few manuscripts she'd read and seen about magic crystals, they often attracted danger, as opposed to repelling it.

This was the first time Rella had considered the possibility that real magic might exist in this place (her mind was always turned towards natural causes first...the result of her mother's scientific influence), and she still figured it was more likely just another bio-luminous rock of some kind, just like the ones they had been engineering for years in the capital of Westcon.

She picked up a small branch and moved it toward the rock. *What if it electrocutes me or blows up?* she thought, as she prepared to tap the rock with the stick.

To avoid electric shock, she decided to throw the stick at the stone first. She tossed it toward the small light and waited.

No flashes of lightning.

No explosions.

She crept a little closer and decided to move the stone with the stick. She slid the tip of the branch underneath the edge of the rock and gently rolled it over.

A quick memory flashed through her mind. She was holding a stone just like this. She was up in a tree and she was making shadows.

The stone moved quite easily, leaving a soft indentation in the soil below. Before picking it up, she tried to guess whether it might feel hot or cold to the touch. She hadn't seen many signs of heat here yet, and no signs of fire at all, so she guessed it would be cold.

She held her hand just millimeters from the surface and realized that she was only half-correct. She felt neither extreme heat nor extreme cold. Just pure light.

Rella looked around once more to make sure no one was standing nearby and listened for the sound of footsteps or, perhaps, a chirp or a growl.

She swiped the rock off the ground, covered it with her fingers and dashed behind a tree trunk. Just in case any predators were standing nearby, she made a few scary animal sounds.

She barked, howled, growled, yapped, moaned, and hissed.

Then she listened for movement, but she didn't hear a single chirp.

While this bright stone would help her navigate through the night, she knew that it also made her a target. She opened her hand and examined the stone closely. It reminded her of a chunk of ice she once found on a hike with her parents on an abnormally warm winter day.

Ensea had been experiencing many weeks of cold storms with arctic wind chills. Then, out of nowhere, it warmed up to nearly fifty degrees and the sun was beaming like it was June and not January.

As they hiked around an ancient burial mound at a nearby park, they found hundreds of tiny, rocklike pieces of ice on the ground, half-melted but brightly illuminated by the winter sunlight. It was, as her father said, "a paradox of nature." The first time she heard her father say the word "paradox," she thought he said "pair of dots" and she wondered why he would describe things as pairs of dots. She eventually sorted it out. Whenever she used the word in his presence, though, she would still say "pair-a-dots" to make him laugh.

As she considered whether to travel any further that night, Rella decided it might be best to climb up into the trees overhead and hide out until sunrise.

She put the glowing stone into her vest pocket. It shined so brightly through the fabric that it worked as the perfect flashlight for climbing up into the thick branches. In some spots, the trees appeared to be woven together like fingers folded in prayer. Many of the limbs were even wider than any bed Rella had ever slept in.

After scuttling around the branches for a few minutes, Rella found a safe perch where she could spot anyone climbing up from below.

Rella didn't have a clear view of anything beyond the trees, but she hoped this meant nothing had a clear view of her either, since she couldn't rule out giant birds or possibly even dragons lurking nearby to swoop her up. This world didn't seem much like a dragon's world, though.

As she curled up in the branches, Rella wondered if her father really knew what he was doing reading her all those wild stories about little girls who got carried away from their homes by giant birds.

On the one hand, his stories did leave her terrified of being out in open spaces when she really shouldn't have been. But now, as she began to try and piece together what kind of story or world she must have fallen into, she knew these stories might have truly been preparing her for a very important mission. She just hoped she had the skill to survive.

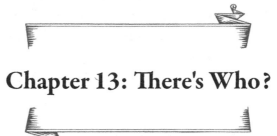

Chapter 13: There's Who?

RELLA LEANED BACK ON the thick branch and clutched the scroll. She then set the glowing stone on her chest and covered it up carefully with a leaf, so the creatures with nocturnal eyes couldn't find her. She assumed there were probably creatures nearby that could see her as clearly as if it were day, but she didn't want to attract extra attention.

A few quiet hours passed without incident, and just as Rella was drifting to sleep, a strong wind pressed down from above.

She instantly thought of the wings of a pterodactyl or a glider plane rushing over the treetops. She leapt up onto her feet on the branch and held out the stone, trying to catch a glimpse of whatever was approaching.

She heard something moving through the branches. It was moving quickly. Leaves rustled and twigs snapped. *Why didn't I grab some kind of protection?* Rella thought. *There were plenty of thick, strong branches below that I could have used as a staff.*

"Who's there?" Rella yelled. "Don't come any closer...or you'll be sorry!" she shouted in her best angry-fighter voice. She remembered a lesson from a video she once saw that said you were supposed to make as much noise as possible if you were in the presence of a bear.

And, since the only living things she knew of (at least from Quinn's note) that did live in trees here in Hleo were bears, she tried scaring the thing away.

"Hey. I'm not kidding. You are in danger. DANGER! Go away. Now!" Rella shouted.

The movement stopped.

Even though the note said the bear would help them, she didn't want to take any chances in case this bear, if it was a bear, was not the bear that was supposed to help her find the dream travelers.

The branches and leaves in front of her became illuminated by the same blue light she had seen earlier. She didn't know if she should turn around or try to jump down and escape. It was too far down to jump without risking breaking her legs, even though she was pretty skilled at dropping and landing safely from dangerous heights.

Without turning around, Rella shouted, "Is it you...are you...The Architect?"

The light blinked off and she was surrounded again in the inky cloud of shadows.

She waited for a response.

"If you're thinking of kidnapping me, I should warn you. My Uncle J is nearby and he will find you and break you into pieces."

Still no response.

The blue light seemed to come from the forest floor behind her, so she knew she had an advantage if The Architect was planning to climb up and grab her by the feet.

And then she heard another snap in the branches.

"There's who?" a girl's voice asked.

"Huh?" Rella replied. *Why is she speaking backwards?* Rella was relieved that it wasn't the menacing voice she expected to hear.

"The Sisters with you are?" the voice asked.

Why is this girl speaking so strangely? Rella wondered, though she thought it was interesting and it made her quite curious. *Does everyone here speak this way or is my brain just scrambled? Or is it her brain that's scrambled?*

"Them with not you're, so?" asked the voice.

Rella decided she probably shouldn't assume it was an actual person yet, since she couldn't see who was speaking. The tone seemed familiar though.

Rella tried to decipher the girl's words in her head. *"There's who? The Sister's with you are?"*

Then a word floated into Rella's mind. Palindrome.

"Racecar!" Rella yelled out.

"Racecar?" The voice replied.

No, wait, Rella thought. *She's not speaking words backwards, she's speaking sentences backwards.*

"Me after Repeat. My name is Rella."

"Rella is name my...oops...My... name... is... Rella," the voice replied, giggling a bit.

Rella giggled a little too, and then waited for another reply.

"My...name...is...Eurie," she said. Rella heard another twig snap. She must have been in the branches of a nearby tree.

Eurie, Rella thought. *Why does that voice sound so familiar?*

"So, are you with The Sisters?" Eurie shouted, her voice now closer and clearer than before. She was no longer reversing her words.

"No. I'm not with The Sisters. I don't have any sisters or brothers," Rella replied.

"Can I see you?" Eurie asked. Aside from a few glowing spots on some distant tree bark, black and blue-gray shadows buried everything around her. The sky, however, seemed to be lightening up a bit.

Rella looked down toward her clenched fist, where she had been hiding the glowing crystal. She opened her palm and held it near her face.

"You, it is you!" Eurie said. Rella could hear her moving through the branches nearby.

Suddenly the ground started to rumble and shake again. Rella slipped, dropping the crystal. Everything went black again and she hooked her arm around a branch just as she fell.

The earthquakes resumed.

Eurie swung herself up onto a sturdier branch. She had been in these trees during plenty of similar storms, and she knew which ones would hold.

"Rella. Rella. You are...Where are you?" Eurie shouted.

Rella looked down at the glowing crystal about thirty feet below. She knew she'd have to go down and retrieve it once the rumbling settled.

"I'm ok. But I'm going to climb down and get the stone. Are you ok?" Rella said.

"Yes. Way...coming...I'm coming your way." Eurie said, still trying to recalibrate her speech. She hadn't spoken any Earth One languages for a while and she'd been using the reversed speech as an extra precaution.

Rella launched herself through the branches and dropped back down to the forest floor. She kept her eyes focused on the stone. As she reached for the stone, she looked up and saw the shadowy outline of a girl about her size, but who seemed older.

The scroll, Rella thought. *I've lost the scroll.* Rella sat down on the ground.

"Are you ok?" Eurie asked, standing over her.

Rella's face was a blend of surprise and confusion.

"You look like you've lost something. Was it very important?" Eurie asked.

Rella then looked up toward the trees just as the scroll came floating down and landed directly on her forehead, which was still a little sticky from the blue dust.

"Is that your scroll?" Eurie asked.

Rella reached up and swiped the scroll off of the top of her own head.

They both started laughing again.

Eurie sat down beside Rella. Rella, still a bit unsure if Eurie *was* really Eurie, the dream traveler, quickly rolled the scroll and tucked it under her arm.

Now that they were seated together, Rella could see the girl from her dreams more clearly. She was a half a head taller than Rella, though she seemed even taller. Her hair was carefully and purposefully braided. Rella had never seen such intricate, beautiful braids. She wondered if it would be possible to do something similar with her own hair.

Eurie held her head and shoulders high, as though she was looking far beyond whatever was in front of her. Even as she looked into Rella's eyes, she seemed to be staring off into the distance, like she was thinking deeply about someone or someplace she missed.

Eurie's eyes fascinated Rella even more than the braids.

Her eyes were pale green with one small, curved line of silver along the outer edge of each pupil. The silver line reminded Rella of the final moments of a lunar eclipse.

"Questions, questions have you?...I mean, I'm sure you have a lot of questions," Eurie said.

Rella laughed a little again and shouted, "So many!"

"I see," Eurie said. "Actually, I knew that. I was just testing to see if you were actually you."

"What?" Rella said.

"Well, we've figured out that The Sisters, and any of Archimago's servants, always speak backwards, like they are reading something in a mirror. So, if they understand you when you speak backwards, you know it's not really a person from where you're from, which is Earth One or Earth Two?"

"Earth One," Rella answered. "And who is Quinn? Is he a person?" Rella asked, also wanting to know so much more about, as Quinn wrote, the one who calls himself Archimago, not to mention these Sisters, which, from the ugly way that Eurie said the word "Sisterssss," it was clear they were rotten lima-bean unlikeable.

"Quinn is a boy from your world, Westcon," Eurie said.

"And he already knows me?" Rella asked.

"Yes, he does," Eurie said, in a tone that suggested she was holding back something important, but also, perhaps, for good reason.

Rella proceeded with caution as she asked more questions.

"But I don't know him, do I?" Rella asked, leaning in and focusing. She didn't want to miss a detail.

"Well, that's sort of complicated. In a way you do, but... no... right now... here at this moment... no...you haven't met him yet," Eurie replied.

"Ok. That's a relief," Rella replied. "I thought I was supposed to know him, but I could only remember this one boy I met named Quinn who liked to kick stuff and hit his head on walls a lot...and it didn't seem like he would be the kind of boy who would leave me a mysterious scroll in a cave on a distant...whatever this place is...is it a planet?"

Rella waved her hands around, trying to gesture towards all of the nearby and distant objects and natural formations. She basically replayed every gesture of confusion, terror, and surprise she had made since arriving in Hleo. Without saying a word, and in under ten seconds, Rella managed to communicate every question she had.

"So that's where he left it!" Eurie said, not answering Rella's question. "He must have gone back on Samara's path. Of course, The Architect wouldn't find him that way! Of course!"

The ground started trembling.

What is Samara's path? Rella wondered.

"Is there somewhere safer...we...could....go?" Rella asked between the rumbles.

"Ye..eh...eh...eh...es," Eurie replied between the rumbles.

Eurie then motioned her to follow and they made their way out of the trees along a soft path that appeared out of nowhere.

As they came out of the thicker patch forest, Rella saw that they were now further away from the river.

They stood quietly together for a moment and then Eurie began to sing.

The notes rang out clearly, like wind chimes, and the tones expressed a combination of sorrow, peace, and joy. It felt like listening to chimes and cellos all in once voice.

Rella then felt a strong wind pressing down from above and sensed the wings hovering above her. Eurie grabbed Rella's hand and pulled her along through the dark and up onto a gigantic creature covered in soft, metallic plumage.

"Her name is Thalas!" Eurie yelled as they took flight.

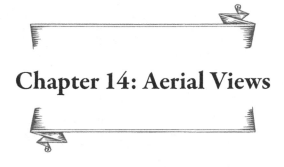

Chapter 14: Aerial Views

RELLA HAD NEVER BEEN on a roller coaster, but she was certain that this ride topped them all. Eurie showed Rella how to weave her fingers and her feet into Thalas's feathers so she would not lose her grip, even if they flipped upside down—which happened repeatedly.

As they soared into and through dark mists and pale clouds, Rella tried to make out the vast landscape of hills, mountains, and sparkling waterfalls below. She'd seen one of the waterfalls already, and she knew, from all the other books she'd read about fantastic worlds, that there had to be many more.

Thalas took another sharp dive and the wind rushed over Rella's cheeks and forehead, blowing her hair in every possible direction—and even some impossible ones. Eurie screamed with delight and Rella followed her new friend's lead, screaming loud enough to wake an entire village.

She took a deep breath and gazed out over the landscape.

And then she spotted something terrible: a humanoid shadow was sliding over the treetops. She felt herself slipping off of Thalas's back.

"Help me, Eurie! I'm losing my grip!" Rella shouted, still eyeing the shadow.

"It's ok!" Eurie shouted, "If you keep your hands beneath Thalas's feathers, she will hold onto you. I don't know how she does it, but her feathers seem to have a...what's a good translation...a magnetic power..."

Rella exclaimed, "No...it's not working."

Eurie reached over and grabbed Rella's hand.

"Look down there," Rella said, pointing. "Eurie, look...is that a person? It looks like a human shadow."

The wind carried such a variety of dusts and mists, it was difficult for Rella to talk without catching some of it in her teeth. She cleared her throat.

"Is that a flapping cape?" Rella asked.

"Where?" Eurie replied.

"Yes, there, over the treetops," Rella said, as Thalas took another sharp dive to avoid a red and green swirl of mists.

Eurie knew what Rella had spotted. It was a Shadowsplitter.

"Rella," Eurie said, "keep your eyes on it and let me know if it gets any closer. I'll try to steer us up through the clouds and get out of its view."

"Can they actually see us?" Rella asked.

"Not exactly...I don't really know," Eurie answered as she began to chant something in a language and a melody Rella didn't recognize, though she felt like she could understand something in the tone.

They started flying so fast that everything blurred together into wide streaks of color.

As Thalas continued to accelerate, Rella tightened her grip on the metallic feathers, even though she didn't have to, and tucked her head against the creature's body.

She felt like crying and laughing at the same time. At this moment, the crying won out. Tears began to flow. As Rella started crying, the clasp on her satchel unfastened itself and the scroll, like a child sneaking out of a bedroom window, slipped out and dropped down into the forest below.

Thalas continued soaring through the clouds until Eurie sensed that the Shadowsplitter below had lost track of them.

"Can The Architect find us up here?" Rella asked, remembering the metallic black vessel she had seen by the shore. She was wondering if the shadow-thing was actually connected to The Architect, and if he had any way to fly after them.

"Oh no," Eurie reassured her. "He hasn't figured out how to fly his machine...not yet. He appears to be working under very limited Earth One ideas about the laws of motion. Flight is not achieved here like it is on other...what did you call it...Earth One...planets."

Didn't Eurie already say she knew about Earth One and Ensea? Rella thought. *Why was she having trouble remembering this all of a sudden?*

All the same, Rella felt a touch of relief, although her mind continued to sizzle with questions.

"So, what is this Wall of Wandering Waves?" Rella shouted as they took another dive.

Before Eurie said another word, Rella noticed that some of the dust clouds and mists across the sky started to brighten immensely, although no sun was actually visible.

Rella was brimming with excitement. She would finally get to see Hleo in the light.

And from an aerial view, she thought, *this is going to be spectacular.*

"You mean that wall beyond those cliffs?" Eurie replied, twisting herself around to watch Rella's expression as she received her first aerial view of Hleo's landscape.

The view of Hleo in the dreams was always distorted through the ideas of the dreamer's own mind. This view, on the other hand, was limitless.

A song began to stir in Rella's mind. Vibrations, like the highest notes of a violin dancing on the breeze, enveloped her.

The wall was steep and grandiose. All Rella could think of was how this must have been what it was like for a fly perching itself on the ledge of one of the great peaks of the mountains diving Eastcon and Westcon.

The sight of the mountains brought back a memory of baking a cake with her mother, Winter. Rella looked at the car-sized jewels covering the mountains and remembered how her mother had given her a bag of oversized candy jewels to place all over the giant cake.

Winter also gave Rella bags of colored sugar powder to pour over the frosting. When she had finished decorating, there were innumerable shades of blue, orange, green, purple, and silver covering the cake, the kitchen floor, and a neighborhood cat that liked to climb in through the kitchen window from time to time. The cat's name, believe it or not, was Jewel.

Hleo's mountainous Wall of Wandering Waves curved and rolled as far as Rella could stretch her eyes, to the east and west (at least based on her sense of Earthly directions).

The Wall was so wide she couldn't see across the northern side to know what, if anything, might exist beyond it.

Thalas lowered herself onto the precipice and allowed the girls to dismount. Rella finally got a good look at Thalas's head.

She thought it most resembled a falcon or a hawk. There was strength and purpose in its sharp eyes.

The two girls stood on the ledge facing the southern coast, and The Dark Waters. As the sky brightened, Rella tried again to make sense of all the mysterious life before her. Most of the shoreline was bursting with texture and layers of color: white sand, orange mists, blue and yellow clusters of leaves, and a few small critters weaving themselves through the branches. Rella tried to spot her chipmunk friend.

The dark water touching the shore, however, showed no traces of blue or green like shorelines back home. Instead, there were expanding patches of black and gray extending out towards a distant island, the island inhabited by, Rella knew, 'the one who calls himself' Archimago. She now had a clear memory of this island from the dream.

Out over The Dark Waters, jagged clouds swirled and thrashed against each other.

Strangely, though, nothing flashed. *Isn't there lightening here?* Rella wondered, unable to recall seeing any, despite hearing plenty of thunder.

Rella's eyes returned to the splendor of the shoreline. She spotted more plants with pinkish and bluish leaves and a variety of tall bright yellow grasses wavering like flames. Still, she found it odd that there was no actual smoke on the shore, or anywhere else in sight.

Rella then watched The Wondercurrent winding its way from the mist-covered stone wall, directly below them, and all the way down to the shore.

"To the southwest," Eurie said, "are grasslands. Not many of us have ever ventured in that direction. There is something mys-

terious about the soil out there, which I hardly understand myself, but I'll show you as soon as I can. Quinn said he barely escaped when the soil nearly pulled him under when he first arrived here."

Rella thought about the note and wondered when she'd
meet Quinn.

Unlike the pastels and vivid colors of the shoreline, the grasslands were chalky and gray, completely without color, and yet,
not exactly the dead white color of bones. They were much more
like the white of a coloring page, waiting to be filled in.

Just beyond the pale grasslands, another forest and a mountain appeared, but it was wrapped in a shimmering blue and silver mist.

"On this side of The Wondercurrent," Eurie said as she pointed down and to the left, we have miles and miles of dense forest
and endless tunnel systems. We don't know who built them, but
they reminded Quinn of some cave systems he had seen in the
mountains near his home in Westcon."

"What about the area beyond those caves?" Rella asked.

"Beyond those, if you look way over to the northeast, you
can see another set of hills leading upwards again, though no one
has told me what might be over there. Some call it the unfolding
ledge, and it has been said that no matter how you try to navigate
your way up through it, you end up where you started."

When Eurie said the word *unfolding*, Rella immediately
thought of the ball of shadow that seemed to unfold before she
was transported here to Hleo.

"And what about the other side of this wall?" Rella asked,
turning back around and staring off into the blank distance.

"Well...that's where you and the scroll might be able to help us," Eurie replied.

"Me?" Rella asked, reaching for her satchel and checking for the scroll.

A strong wind nearly knocked Rella and Eurie to the ground. They quickly turned their backs to the wind.

Rella rummaged both of her hands through the inside of the satchel, but all she found was a tear and a hole the size of her fist.

There was no trace of the scroll.

Thalas, who had been resting her gigantic body quietly along the ledge, had regained her strength and was about to take flight.

For such a large hawk-beast-thing, Rella thought, *she moves with a lot of grace and power.*

"Where's she going?" Rella asked. "Is she just leaving us up here?"

Rella couldn't see any way down.

"I'm not sure. She's probably just going to find something to eat."

"Oh," Rella said. Her stomach rumbled a little at the mention of food.

"Don't worry," Eurie replied, noticing the strain on Rella's face. "She'll be back...eventually. I can't really predict everything she will do..."

Rella sat down and tears formed in her eyes.

Eurie noticed Rella's hand, still swimming around in the satchel.

"It's gone," Rella whispered. "Gone. Gone."

Eurie sat down beside her and offered a comforting hug.

"I know I closed my satchel," Rella said, "But we were flying so fast..."

Rella looked at Eurie. She had her eyes closed and was whispering something in the same unfamiliar language she had used when speaking and singing to Thalas during the flight.

Rella couldn't shake the idea that Eurie was some kind of ancient goddess, though she knew that was silly. Ancient goddesses didn't inhabit the bodies of ten-year-old girls.

When Eurie finished singing, she opened her eyes and looked at Rella.

"We will get it back," Eurie said. "So don't worry. Right now, we just need to get away from this ledge, and get some rest before any more of these storms start up again."

Rella wiped the tears from her cheeks and forced a smile, although in the back of her mind, she was still trying to puzzle out the dark purpose of the flying shadow she had spotted on the treetops.

All she could come up with was the name Dracula, but she couldn't remember who or what Dracula referred to. Her father would be able to remind her. *If only he were here*, she thought, rubbing her hand over her stomach.

"How about some food?" Rella pleaded, "I'm starving."

The wind picked up and they sprinted over to a large boulder about a hundred yards in from the ledge.

"Help me push," Eurie said.

The rock wasn't as heavy as it looked and they slid it quickly out of the way, revealing a small tunnel.

"How did we do that?" Rella asked. "That has to weigh as much as a car."

"It takes a lot of belief," Eurie replied.

"Belief?" Rella replied, "It doesn't really work that way on Earth One. I've tried. I used to believe I could run through walls..."

"But you never did?" Eurie replied, as though she expected Rella to have the ability to run through walls.

"No matter how hard I ran, I smacked into them every time...brick ones, wooden ones, metal ones," Rella said, laughing. "Splat. Every time."

"Persistence and belief," Eurie said, "are two very different things."

"You sound like one of my teachers," Rella said. The silver curves lining Eurie's pupils seemed especially bright.

"Ok. I'll stop. We better get going. Do you still have that luminous stone?" Eurie asked.

Rella reached into her pocket and fished it out. It was a little like holding a tiny star in her hand, though much cooler than an actual star. She handed it to Eurie to use for guidance as they crawled down through the tunnel to Eurie's secret rooms.

When they reached the first room, Rella stood up, stretched out her arms, and arched her back to loosen up her stiff muscles.

A sweet and delicious aroma filled her nose. In her head, or maybe it was her stomach, a robotic voice starting repeating the phrase: *must eat. must eat. food. now. must. eat. now.*

No smell back home had ever made her so hungry. The flavor starting to form on her tongue was a mix of cherry, vanilla, and warm chocolate with powdered sugar. She felt her stomach churning and her mouth dripping.

"That's my newest recipe," Eurie said. She walked over to a hollowed-out section of the cavern wall and picked up a white box. To Rella, it looked like carved ivory. Eurie lifted off the lid and held the box out to Rella. Rella lowered her nose toward the box and took a long, slow, deep breath. Rella nearly lifted off the ground just smelling it.

Rella spoke: "My father once told me a story about a man who sold chocolate that could make people levitate."

"I believe it!" Eurie said. Chocolate is supreme.

Maybe he wasn't just making that up, Rella thought.

"Go ahead," Eurie said. The box, it appeared, worked as a fireless oven.

Rella reached into it and picked out one of the round cakes. It was so light that she almost tossed it into the air. If she would have let it go, she was certain it would have floated for a few seconds, though she never let it out of her grasp before dropping it directly into her mouth.

She chewed quickly and then let it melt on her tongue.

Eurie smiled and watched eagerly for Rella's reaction.

"Mmmmmmmmmm!" Rella hummed, and then giggled with delight.

"You are only the second person from Earth One to try my desserts," Eurie said. "I'm so glad to know you like it. It seems like, when it comes to tasty food, our worlds aren't so different."

"Not at all," Rella said, licking her fingers. "Though I am going to say your food is much, much sweeter."

Rella swiped another cake from the basket and gobbled it up.

"Who is the other person who has tried your food?" Rella asked.

"Quinn, of course!" Eurie said.

"Oh yes, Quinn!" Rella said. "The boy who wrote me the note on the scroll."

As she thought about the scroll, Rella almost started crying again.

"Yes," Eurie said. "I think we better talk about why you are here."

"Of course," Rella said, now bouncing with energy from the delicious treats.

Eurie retrieved a clean piece of parchment from a shelf on the wall. The shelf was covered in various clay pots, glass bottles, and bowls of pastes made from the leaves.

Rella spotted one of the vials that Eurie had been using back when they met in her dream.

Eurie spread out the parchment on the stone floor and poured some of the dust from the vial.

"Can you remember any images that were on the scroll?" Eurie asked. "Maybe sketch a little of it?"

Rella looked down at the powder coated parchment and squinted. She tried recalling the angles, lines, and assortment of shapes. She traced her fingers in the dust and tried to recreate the picture.

In her mind's eye, the picture from the scroll that she was now re-creating looked a little like a painting her parents once had in their secret library.

When Rella was about three-and-a-half, she used to tell her father that she had painted the artwork herself. He always laughed and agreed with her, even though she couldn't have actually painted something like that.

"Anything?" Eurie asked.

Rella didn't have much to say yet, but she felt like she needed to say something.

"Well...my parents had a painting in our library at home that looked a little like this."

"A little like this? Or exactly? This could be very important," Eurie exclaimed.

"Well, the shapes and the lines are the same, yes, strangely exact, but my parents' painting had many different colors, yellows and a touch of purple and a deep blue. The one on the scroll was all black and gray."

"So you are sure you recognize it?" Eurie asked.

"Absolutely. But what does that have to do with...?" Rella asked, trailing off.

Rella shuddered as she pictured The Architect's lifeless face.

"Thinking of The Architect?" Eurie asked.

"Yes," Rella said, anxiously grinding her teeth.

Chapter 15: Mysterious Languages

THE TWO GIRLS CONTINUED discussing the mysterious inner-workings of Hleo. Rella had many questions and Eurie did her best to answer them. At times, Rella felt like Eurie knew far more than she was sharing, but, then, Eurie was also probably bring careful, since Rella had not really proven her loyalty either. Losing the scroll, after all, was a pretty foolish thing to do. And there was no way Rella could prove to Eurie that she hadn't dropped the scroll on purpose.

"We don't know a lot about the Sisters," Eurie said, "I've only seen one of them, from way up above the trees. Quinn has seen the other one a few times, near the shore, unloading and loading the vessels they are using to transport the captured guardians back to the island. Quinn thought she moved in an odd way, though, and not like other human children."

"Why do you call them the Sisters?" Rella asked, taking another bite of one of Eurie's cherry-vanilla swirl cakes.

Eurie picked up the luminous stone, which they were using to light the room, and walked over to a pile of fractured pieces of bark. Rella recognized it as the same bark covering the massive oak-like trees near the waterfall. Most of the bark chips were about the size of a school lunch tray or a poster you might hang on your bedroom door.

Rella followed Eurie's shadow across the room.

Eurie picked up a few of the wooden pieces and placed one on the table. She flipped it over, revealing a cryptic script. The script covered the bark in a crisscross pattern, as though someone had written words on top of words over and over. Rella remembered seeing a few books like that in a museum once. Her father also had one or two in his secret library. It was hard to decipher the individual characters at first because so many words and symbols had been written over each other.

As Rella stared at it, however, a pattern did emerge, and if someone concentrated really hard, they could read the sentences, even though the words swirled all around on the surface.

"Is this a language from here?" Rella asked.

Eurie smiled. "Well, you know how in your world... a sound makes waves?"

"Yes. I learned a little about that in school. It's how things get recorded, so we can play them back on our audio players," Rella replied.

"Exactly. Well, sound, here in this place, makes a wave that gets recorded too. How do I explain this? It becomes shapes on the insides of the trees."

Rella looked at the script and searched her mind for any similar sets of symbols. She had looked at so many books in so many languages, there had to be a similar one somewhere in her memory.

Eurie continued: "So, what you are looking at here is not my language or any language from your world, but at the languages of...well, of...I know this sounds funny...of the trees. Or maybe something that lives in the trees...or something that wants to use the trees as its own private notepad."

"So, you're saying the trees keep a living record of spoken words?" Rella asked.

"Yes. The trees, or like I said, something living inside of the trees, I'm not sure. But they seem to have created languages for each of us...outsiders," Eurie said.

Rella had never heard Eurie refer to herself as an outsider. *Wasn't this Eurie's world?*

"So, how do you know what the words mean? How do we crack the code?" Rella asked.

"Well, that's complicated and I haven't really figured it all out yet. Basically, Quinn and I each grabbed bark samples from the trees near where The Sisters had been standing and talking. And we compared these samples. And, as far as we can tell, the trees have recorded the Sister's words in such a way that we think they are speaking a language created by Archimago. Their speech patterns and word choices do not show that they have come from one natural family unit."

Still trying to make sense of Eurie's complicated explanation, Rella asked a clarifying question: "So, in short, the trees can write things down."

Eurie smiled with relief. "Yes. That's all I was trying to say..."

"Do they talk, too?" Rella asked.

"Sorry for making it so complicated. No, they don't make audible sounds," Eurie said.

Rella looked at her with sleepy eyes, yawned, stretched her arms, and smiled, "Sometimes, you remind me of one of my school teachers or something. Anyways...figuring this out has to be helpful for your mission."

"For our mission," Eurie said.

Rella paused. "Yes, for our mission," she said.

Rella watched as Eurie concentrated her eyes on the hard piece of bark in her hands. Rella sensed deep concern in Eurie's face. She knew that look because it was the same look everyone had in their eyes back home when they gathered around Uncle J's car after the memorial service, before she and Uncle J left Ensea.

Chapter 16: Eurie's Discovery

EURIE COVERED RELLA with a leaf blanket and crawled back through the dark tunnels. As she exited the hideout, she called her guardian, Thalas, from the ledge of the wall. Within a few minutes, they were soaring high and scouting out the best routes back through the forest. The needed to get back to Quinn and to try to begin tracking down the lost scroll.

Eurie considered trying to make it all the way to Quinn's hideout on the shoreline in a single flight, but she knew there was a great risk of being spotted by The Sisters or The Architect.

As she scouted the area, she spotted some commotion along The Wondercurrent. She was about three miles south of the cave and the waterfall.

An animal, perhaps a guardian, appeared to be in distress. She tried to get a closer look, but all she could tell from its movements was that it was likely some large type of wildcat, perhaps a cougar or a leopard.

Thalas circled around a few more times, passing in and out of dust clouds and the mists. Eurie then recognized the silhouette. It was not a cougar or a leopard, but a tiger. And it was trapped in a net made of dark ropes. The ropes looked more like shadows than any kind of cord or wire.

Next she saw the black cloak. The boy was tall, but his movements were not as reptilian or ghostly as she had expected. This was actually the first time she had seen him. He was, like Rella said, a bit bony. *How can I know if this is actually The Architect?* she asked herself, worrying also about the Shadowsplitters.

Thalas circled around again, and, this time, The Architect stopped moving. Thalas had to take a sharp dive as Eurie peeked back at him to see if she had been spotted.

Eurie also caught a glimpse of the tiger. She was furious. She felt like rushing right down to confront the poachers. She had to do something, but she didn't want to risk getting captured herself, or risk having Thalas wrangled by those shadowy ropes.

Eurie noticed that The Architect was with someone. This figure was much shorter, probably just a few inches taller than herself, wearing a dark hood and full-length, thick, rust-colored cape. From her obscured line of sight, Eurie thought she saw thin, curly wisps of black, silver and dark purple hair. The hair covered what resembled a human girl's face, but, as Quinn had noted, the girl didn't seem quite human either. Eurie could barely see the girl's eyes, but they had a look that brought only a single word to Eurie's mind: monster.

Those eyes weren't the kind that ever showed a shred of pity, worry, or consideration for anyone else. Eurie had only seen this kind of ruthlessness in the eyes of one other person, but, here in Hleo, she couldn't even fully remember who that was. She had a feeling, though, that this girl and the pitiless one she couldn't remember had a connection, and they had had contact from the time before she had first arrived.

A Sister, right? Eurie thought. *She's handing the tiger over to The Architect. He's going to take the tiger back to Archimago's Is-*

land. I've got to get to Quinn. This could be our last chance to find a path through The Dark Waters.

As The Architect and this Sister left with the tiger, Eurie knew she would need to collect script samples from the bark. The samples would give her a chance to decipher their conversation, and hopefully pick up some clues to their next move. First, she had to go back and check on Rella.

As she started making her way back to the hideout, she also remembered seeing the watercraft Rella had described. *But would they return to the island without the scroll?* Eurie wondered. *Why did they need to take that tiger?*

Eurie steered Thalas around the treetops on one final loop to make sure she did not overlook any other details or clues, and then, just east of where Rella might have dropped the scroll, she spotted another figure.

This figure was sprinting so quickly along a trail below that Eurie couldn't tell if the figure was actually running, floating, or using some kind of enchanted, floating shoes. *Was she new?*

One thing Eurie recognized right away was that the figure, whoever she was, was carrying Rella's scroll.

Eurie squeezed Thalas's feathers and steered her about a half mile east of the trail, above the trees. Thalas hovered above the largest branch she could find. Eurie leapt down onto the branch to get a closer look at the figure. She knew it would be difficult to see the figure's face from up in the shadowy branches, but the shadows provided good cover for Thalas. She didn't want to risk having the figure, especially if she was one of Archimago's servants, see Thalas.

While Thalas continued to hover, Eurie climbed nearly fifty feet down from the perch and positioned herself so she could see most of what was behind, above, and below her.

Her next focus was setting a trap, in case the figure was the other one of The Sisters. If she *was* carrying Rella's scroll, Eurie was not going to let her get away without a fight.

Based on the figure's speed though, Eurie worried she wouldn't have time to set a safe trap. She didn't want to hurt the girl, but she couldn't let her go.

Eurie continued to watch the trail below for any other signs of motion. The trail did not look familiar at all and Eurie was surprised she had not yet scouted this one out. Of course, the landscape here was so vast that, even with years to explore, it would be difficult to find every hidden path.

This trail appeared to lead deep into the Eastern Forests, the thickest and darkest forested area of Hleo. It was truly the darkest forest Eurie had ever seen. *The trail*, she thought, *might cut entirely through the forest to the foothills of the eastern mountains, but I've never attempted to take Thalas out that far.* The mists in the east were simply too thick, and the branches seemed to lash out at them, like the tentacles of a kraken, any time they approached their borders.

The figure emerged from the shadows below. She was dressed like the one who had been helping the Architect capture the tiger. She was wearing a rust-colored cape as well, and also had uniquely colored hair. Instead of dark purple, like the other girl, her hair was red, like the feathers of a cardinal, but with black tips.

Unlike the other girl's empty-looking eyes, Eurie noticed a completely different, concerned expression in this one's face. Her expression was much more human, sincere, and genuine.

Eurie peered down at the cardinal-haired girl's hand and spotted the scroll. She wondered if the redness in the girl's hair was a protective dye, and if it had anything to do with her interactions with the Shadowsplitters.

Eurie dropped quickly from of the tree branches and landed directly in front of the girl.

Startled, but without slowing down, the girl dashed around Eurie's right side, brushing Eurie's legs with the edge of her cape. Eurie lunged at her, but missed.

The girl then continued sprinting towards the entrance to the thick, dark forest ahead.

The entrance consisted of two gigantic wooden doors that didn't quite touch in the middle. They weren't wide enough for a person to slip through, though they weren't locked, and might be fairly easy to pry apart. Yet they clearly marked an important boundary.

At one time, they might have been used for some kind of protection, although Eurie couldn't think of a specific reason why someone would have needed to block this trail. The darkness within the wood was enough to scare anyone.

Eurie chased after the girl and yelled: "Wait? Wait? Where are you going?"

The girl just ran harder. In another five seconds, Eurie knew, the girl would vanish into the shadows beyond the gate. And then they might never retrieve the scroll.

Eurie was not prepared to enter those gates without knowing what or who might live beyond them. If it was a region where

Archimago and his Shadowsplitters hadn't gone, it was probably still safe. If *he* had broken into that area, though, it was possible she would never make it back out without becoming his prisoner.

Eurie caught up to the girl and reached for her arm. She shouted: "Stop. That's not your scroll. That's Rella's. Stop...please!"

Just before the girl pushed her way through the doors and vanished into the shadows, she stopped and turned around: "Rella...you...are?" she asked.

The reverse question. Eurie knew then that this was an agent of Archimago. Her theory about their speech was correct! She didn't want to risk letting the girl know that Rella was in Hleo, so she didn't answer. She decided to pretend she hadn't said Rella's name.

"Rella you are?" she repeated louder, looking hopeful, and not in any way malicious.

Eurie didn't move.

"Coming are they. Hide must you. Coming are they. Safe be will scroll the..."

The girl then turned and ran into the forest.

Eurie ran up to the two wooden doors. She considered passing through the entrance to the dark forest. But the girl was already barely a speck.

As Eurie peered into the forest, she noticed that the girl was dropping small, luminous pebbles along the path.

Is she leaving me...us...a trail? Eurie wondered. *Or is that just something she needs to help her find her way out?*

Eurie had to return and wake Rella now. They had a big decision to make: to follow the path into the forest and retrieve the scroll, or to try and find Quinn, tell him about the captured tiger, and then explain that they had lost the scroll.

As Eurie climbed back up into the trees to call on Thalas, a series of earthquakes nearly knocked her out of the tree.

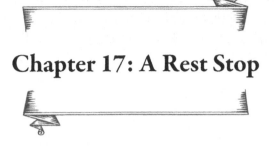

Chapter 17: A Rest Stop

"RELLA, RELLA. REST stop," Uncle J announced in a sing-song voice.

Rella pulled the quilt off of her head. She was stretched awkwardly across the back seat with her seatbelt unfastened.

Rella rubbed her eyes and looked down at the sketchbook in her lap. The surface of the page appeared to be filled with layer upon layer of letters, codes, and symbols. She recognized the three languages she knew how to write, but she also noticed other letters she did not know. Sentences had been written over and around other sentences and entire poems were squeezed inside of individual letters. *I don't remember drawing this*, Rella thought, trying to gather her thoughts. There was also a very thin layer of powder on the paper, which she brushed off and onto the floor of the car.

"I'm ok. I don't really need anything," she told her Uncle J.

"Well, at least get out. Stretch your legs. The sun is coming up and there's a magnificent view of a valley and a lake I want you to see."

Uncle J waited for her to move. She was still trying to orient herself.

"Not a single power line or commercial building in sight," Uncle J. said. "You've never seen anything like it, trust me."

Oh I doubt that, Rella thought, as she stepped out of the car and felt the solid pavement below her feet. It was comforting to feel solid ground again. She took a deep, clean breath and, as a precaution, swiped her forehead to make sure there wasn't any more of that gray-blue powder.

The open air was much warmer compared to the last place they stopped.

Rella followed her Uncle to the overlook and climbed up on a picnic table. The warmth of the sunrise kissed her back as she gazed out at the valley below.

He was right. She had never seen such a clear view in Eastcon. She didn't really believe views like this could exist here on their side of the continent, and especially not less than a day's journey by car.

How far have we traveled? Rella wondered.

A mixed flock of birds and mod-birds hovered and swooped out over the lake. A cluster of trees on the far side of the lake looked like a family or a group of friends all holding hands. Rella expected the trees to glow, but then realized that glowing trees were mainly found in Hleo, not here.

There were two very tall trees. *Those are the parents,* Rella thought. And four smaller trees whose branches seemed to be reaching up and grabbing for the hands of the parents. *And those are the children,* Rella said to herself.

A few more birds in the trees next to Rella welcomed the sun with their own special songs. The mod-birds, however, did not produce any sounds at all. Mod-birds, in case you were curious, are the birds that were made from drone technology and genetic engineering. They were sort of alive, but not actually birds in the usual sense.

Rella was overcome with an urge to go back to the car and grab her notebook for a quick sketching session. *Maybe Eurie would like to see this,* she thought. The memories came back to her like a dream: *The strange letters, the codes. Eurie. The Wall of Wandering Waves. The scroll. The Wondercurrent. Was it a dream?* She was trying to piece it all together.

Uncle J came up behind her with a savory breakfast burrito. She could smell the sausage and eggs and hot sauce, and it woke her stomach immediately.

He held it out in front of her. Without a second thought, she reached out and grabbed it.

"Got another great deal," he said. "Buy one get two free before sunrise."

But the sun is up, Rella thought, as she took a gigantic bite.

"I had to argue with the Automa cashier a little about what technically counts as sunrise, and her sensors told her that the people in line behind me were getting upset. So, I threw a little confusion at her programming for service over pricing," Uncle J said with a smile. "She caved."

Rella laughed, not quite fully understanding her uncle's explanation of how he worked out the deal with the robot cashier. She looked around again, trying to adjust her mind back to Earth One.

There were only two other vehicles in the parking lot, but neither of them looked as old as Uncle J's car.

She smiled through her sausage-stuffed mouth, looked at Uncle J and said, "Thank you. I was starving."

Uncle J pulled an extra package from his pocket. It had two luminous gummies in it. He must have seen her eyeing them at the last stop. She swore she would never try anything like that, but now that he gave them to her as a gift, she was going to have to try them. Rella didn't like eating candy right after breakfast though, so she slipped the gummies into her vest pocket.

They watched the birds hovering over the lake for a few more minutes and then returned to the car.

Uncle J took a few big gulps of coffee and then fiddled with the touch screen on the dashboard. He offered to switch the radio programs to audiobooks or music, but Rella told him she was just going to work on her drawings for a while.

"What were you writing?" Uncle J. asked.

Rella had to think quickly. She didn't want him to worry.

"Just sketching..."

"Good for you. Your mom used to do things like that when we were kids too. She tried to teach me some of her own made up alphabets, but I can't really remember any of them right now."

Rella listened eagerly but didn't say anything.

"Yeah. I bet one of the boxes of books in the trunk might even have one of her old notebooks in it. It's funny...the drawing you were making had some symbols that looked strangely familiar to me... are you sure you haven't seen her old sketchbooks?"

Rella had gone through a lot of the books in the library before they packed, but she didn't remember her mom ever talking about making up a language, and she certainly hadn't seen her mother's sketchbooks. She would remember those.

Rella flipped back to the drawing of the luminous wings she had been working on at the beginning of the trip and studied it closely. Then, without thinking too much about it, she added a pencil sketch of Thalas, Eurie's giant falcon, to the background. After that, she started improvising a drawing of a dreamlike landscape, trying to remember anything from the dream of the land of Hleo. As she improvised, she was recreating images from some of the famous paintings she had seen in the art books in her parents' library. She loved the ones with the melting clocks and many-colored shapes floating around each other.

As she continued working on the sketches, she noticed, in the center of page, a piece of bark lying next to the base of the sketch of a tree. She couldn't remember drawing that bark. And every bit of the bark on the sketch of the trunk was intact.

She pulled the quilt over her head. As she did so, she put her hand on the picture and watched as the bark lit up. The light then started threading itself around her finger. A slow tingle passed over her hands, then down her arms. She pulled her hand back off of the page and tossed the quilt aside. "Not yet," she said to herself.

"What was that?" Uncle J asked.

"Nothing," Rella replied.

Uncle J had an audiobook about the history of old forests playing on the speakers and seemed to be distracted by the scenery.

"Did you see that?" Rella asked.

"See what?" Uncle J replied.

Rella was unsure if she should tell him anything about her dream or the drawing that just grabbed her by the arm.

"Oh. I thought I saw some kind of animal running out in that field."

"What did it look like?"

Rella had to think fast. What kind of animal would be in this area of the continent? She tried to recall some of the books her father had read to her about the wildlife in this area. Then the perfect animal popped in her mind.

"Well. It was moving really fast. It sort of looked like a small deer, but it didn't move like a deer. No, it had horns I think. I couldn't see the color."

"Antelope?" he said. "That definitely sounds like an antelope. Are you sure you saw that? You weren't imagining it?"

The way he said 'imagining' reminded her of the way her mother used to ask the same question. When other people said 'imagining,' it seemed like they just meant 'making things up.' But when her mom said it, it seemed like 'imagining' was a much more powerful and less playful thing to be doing.

"No. I'd know if I were imagining it," she said, though she wasn't sure what that meant at the moment.

"Well. They did live out here in large numbers once, but I haven't heard of one living out in the wild in years."

"I did see it. I did," she exclaimed, remaining committed to her story.

"That's fantastic. I think you're going to like where we are going then, because there's a lot more wildlife there."

Rella knew she wasn't supposed to ask too many questions about where they were going, in case someone was listening.

She looked back down at the sketchbook and tried to get the courage to put the quilt back over her head. *Would Uncle J even believe what was happening?* she thought. *I've got to go back. They need me.*

Once she had the quilt completely over her head, she looked down at the picture in her lap. The small sphere of shadow emerged above the page once again. As it burst into color, she felt like she was falling through the air and also coming up out of a lake at the same time. Instantly, she was back in Eurie's hideout.

Chapter 18: The New Mission

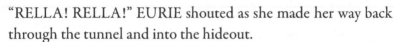

"RELLA! RELLA!" EURIE shouted as she made her way back through the tunnel and into the hideout.

Rella looked around the room. She tried to concentrate on the shadows hovering in the corners. *The luminous stone must have rolled underneath something*, she thought, as she spotted a small sliver of light in a crevice on the dusty stone floor.

Rella reached down and pried the stone out of the crevice with her thumb and index finger. She hadn't noticed all the cracking in the floor when they first came in.

Eurie sat down beside her. She was completely out of breath.

"Is it actually safe in here?" Rella asked, examining all the cracks on the floor.

"I think so, but the quakes have caused some additional cracking lately," Eurie said, catching her breath and fixing her braid.

Rella thought about all the quakes she felt when she last arrived. She also remembered all the crumbling stones she'd seen along the ledges beside the waterfall.

"I think it might be a good time to consider moving," Rella said, as Eurie stood up and began collecting various objects and stuffing them into Rella's satchel.

"We've got a serious decision to make, Rella. Are you rested? Do you need any more to eat?" Eurie asked.

Rella wasn't sure how to answer. *Ready for what?* she thought as she stared at Eurie, trying to understand. "You mean the scroll?" she asked. "Did you find it?"

"Sort of. But there's something more urgent. And it involves this tree bark, possibly one of The Sisters," Eurie replied, continuing to collect vials.

Rella's stomach tightened, but she also felt ready to get out of this cave, which, if her fears were correct, was about to collapse.

Eurie motioned Rella to follow her out of the cavern.

"I spotted The Architect," Eurie said, so quickly that Rella thought she was listening to an audiobook on triple speed. "The boy you described by the waterfall. I saw him. And I also saw one of The Sisters with him. She had silver and purplish hair. She looked really mean. She was wearing a cloak too."

Rella could sense the nervousness in Eurie's voice and tried to prepare for the terrible news.

"Well," Eurie continued, still talking very quickly, "there was also this tiger...she had to be a guardian... and they had her cornered. They were stealing her away..."

Rella interrupted, "We've got to go rescue her...now!"

"Here's the problem," Eurie replied, finally slowing down enough for Rella to understand. "As I started making my way back here to get you, to discuss this exact plan, I spotted another cloaked figure. This time, with red hair, like a cardinal's feathers, and she had your scroll!"

Rella was thrilled to hear that Eurie had found the scroll, but also sensed more dread in Eurie's voice.

"I chased her down and she spoke to me in the backwards phrases. She didn't look angry or scared, but she wouldn't give me the scroll...instead, she asked if I was you. So she seemed to know who you were!"

Was she another dream traveler? Rella wondered.

"Then what happened?" Rella asked, hoping Eurie's story had a happy ending.

"Well, she told me that the scroll would be safer with her, but that didn't make sense to me," Eurie said. "And then she ran through these two massive wooden doors hanging between two wide tree trunks and leading into a dark forest."

"Did you follow her?" Rella asked.

"No. I've never dared to enter that forest alone," Eurie said.

"Oh. I see."

Rella hadn't heard Eurie say much about being afraid to go anywhere before. She didn't like the sound of Eurie's voice when she mentioned this dark forest.

"I did look down the path, though," Eurie said. "And the girl seemed to be dropping luminous stones, similar to the one you have in your hand."

Rella looked down at the stone and wondered if it would stay lit long enough for them to get out of the hideout, before it cracked and crumbled in on them.

"So," Eurie said, "I think she was leaving us a path. What do you think? Should we risk it?"

"But the tiger and the other...," Rella replied.

"Yes. I know. It doesn't feel right not to go after them first, or to try and get a message to Quinn...but we have to act now," Eurie said.

Rella didn't need convincing. She was ready before Eurie had finished her sentence.

"Let's go!" Rella shouted.

"Here," Eurie said, handing Rella her repaired satchel. Eurie had reinforced Rella's satchel with a patch she had made by stitching a fabric she had created herself from extracts of leaves. "I put some of those peach and lemon colored biscuits into the bag. You'll need to keep your hands free to fight, if necessary."

"Fight?" Rella asked.

"Well. I hope not. But...," Eurie replied.

Rella wasn't even very good at flicking bugs off of her clothes. *Fight?* she thought.

"There's one more thing," Eurie said.

"Yes," Rella replied.

"Once we get your scroll back, we *are* going to rescue that tiger!" Eurie said.

"You better believe it!" Rella shouted, slipping the strap of the new satchel over her shoulder and swinging it behind her back.

Rella pictured The Architect and the Sister and remembered something else. There was a blade with a jeweled handle tucked in his belt. Something about the way he looked and moved made her feel a little sad for him, though. She wasn't convinced he really knew how to use that blade, considering how he never seemed to give it any attention during the earthquakes or when he was walking around searching for her or the scroll.

Wouldn't it have made more sense to have his blade out if he was worried about being attacked? she thought. She pushed these thoughts from her mind and raced Eurie out of the tunnels.

Rella stood on the ledge and watched as Eurie pointed her finger out into the vast landscape toward a cluster of trees beside the river.

"There's where the tiger was captured," Eurie said.

Next, Eurie pointed back up near the waterfall where The Architect had once again anchored his transport ship.

Perhaps he was back up there searching for the scroll again? Rella thought.

"There are no signs of The Sisters," Eurie said, "As far as I can tell."

"He's trying to destroy all of it, isn't he?" Rella asked.

Eurie didn't respond. She didn't know what to say.

"He is going to destroy The Wondercurrent, isn't he?"

"Not if we can stop him!" Eurie answered.

Just then, Thalas arrived and they climbed up onto her back. Before long, they spotted the entrance to the shadowy forest where Eurie met the girl with the scroll.

The blue and gray mists above the forest seemed even thicker than Eurie remembered just a few hours earlier.

Just before Thalas made her descent toward the forest, Rella spotted two incandescent wings flicker up over a distant pair of trees. The wings disappeared and then reappeared miles away from where they had just been. The small amount of light in the sky seemed to fade even more, which made the wings in the distance seem even brighter. It reminded Rella of an old film her father had shown her where they put a cartoon character into a live action scene. The animated characters were so vividly illustrated and colored that it made the footage of the real places seem dull. *That movie must be at least 150 years old,* she thought. And then the wings appeared again, glowing briefly in the sky before flickering and disappearing.

Eurie noticed that Rella was distracted.

"Do you see something?" Eurie asked.

"I think so," Rella said. "It looked like a pair of glowing wings."

"Just wings?" Eurie asked.

"Yes. Just a faint outline way out across the sky. They looked mostly clear and white, though there might have been a few shimmers of color." It reminded Rella of a constellation of a butterfly. She could not make out any fully formed body.

"They seem to be disappearing and reappearing in different places," Rella said.

"That's your guardian, Samara" Eurie said.

"My guardian?" Rella replied.

"Yes." Eurie said.

"You haven't met her yet, but Quinn and I and...well...I can't really explain how it works now...but that's her, that's your guardian."

"I feel like I've seen her before."

Rella was thinking of the memorial service and the people bowing their heads to sing the memorial song for the lost members of the Alliance.

"You probably have," Eurie replied. "Usually, the guardian who meets you here has met you in your world first."

Rella continued watching for the wings to sparkle across the sky once again.

"Am I going to meet her?" Rella asked.

The idea of meeting her guardian filled her with warmth, like a fire during the winter holidays.

"Well," Eurie said, "it seems she is trying to communicate something with us, but with The Architect nearby, and The Shadowsplitters, it may be too dangerous for her to come any closer. She is definitely trying to tell you that she's here. And, as soon as she can, I'm sure she'll be ready to meet you."

Thalas paused above the trees. They pulled their hands out from under the grip of her soft, metallic feathers and leapt down quickly to avoid the risk of one of Archimago's servants spotting them.

Eurie spoke to Thalas in a string of commands using their special language, which Rella found even more mesmerizing the second time she heard it. Thalas recognized the seriousness of the moment and quickly launched up into the clouds, spinning and twirling out of sight.

Chapter 19: Deep into the Forest

"RIGHT HERE," EURIE said, "is where she got away from me."

Eurie pointed ahead toward the shady, lush passageway, illuminated by the small stones sprinkled along the path. There were a lot more stones than Eurie remembered seeing before. It appeared as though the stones the girl had dropped were multiplying.

As Eurie walked forward, Rella stopped and looked back at the gigantic wooden doors they had just passed through. Since the doors didn't touch each other, she could still see the mountains and valleys through the opening. Rella felt as though they were leaving Hleo behind completely, though she certainly didn't feel like they were heading anywhere closer to Earth One. *It's like entering an enchanted forest within an enchanted forest,* Rella thought, still facing the doors. The magic, whether for good or evil, would certainly be stronger in here.

Rella turned away from the doors and ran to catch up with Eurie, who was kneeling down and examining a luminous stone on the ground.

"Look, Rella!" Eurie said, pointing at a stone which seemed to be splitting in half.

Rella thought it looked a lot like watching cells divide under a microscope.

"What are these?" Rella asked.

"I don't know. I've never seen these in the forests or any-where else in Hleo," Eurie replied.

Rella reached her hand down and tried to pick up the glow-ing pebble. It felt like it was welded to the soil. She tried to dig her hand into the ground to get a grip beneath it, but all the soil around it was impenetrable. Some kind of reaction was clearly happening when the pebble contacted the soil, but what, they both wondered, was causing this?

"Well, I'm glad the light is multiplying for us. That's a good sign, right?" Rella asked.

"Yes. I agree," Eurie said. "Whether the girl was dropping these for herself or for us to follow, it looks like we're going to have plenty of light as we follow the path...at least for now."

Rella and Eurie continued walking from stone to stone. After an hour of traveling deeper and deeper into the forest within the forest, they noticed that the plants, which were hidden in the shadows when they first entered, were flourishing beyond any-thing they had seen elsewhere, even next to The Wondercurrent. There were hundreds of colored flowers encircling each of the trunks of the trees, which had all of their branches fully intact. The floor of the forest was coated with green plants sprouting from soft, white soil. Red, silver, orange, blue, and yellow stones of different sizes were scattered around the trunks of the trees.

Rella thought they looked like jelly beans. They weren't as bright as the luminous stones though.

The canopy of leaves above was an impenetrable black, but, with all of the glowing stones and thriving plant life around them, they felt safer than they had felt anywhere else in Hleo.

As they wandered off of the path a little, Rella spotted a stone covered in script next to a tree. The stone was square and flat on top. It looked like it might have been used as a table from time to time.

On the front of the stone, Rella also noticed an arrow pointing toward a thicket another hundred yards off the path.

"What does it say?" Eurie asked.

"I'm not sure," Rella said. "Do you recognize it?"

"Some of the script is familiar...but," Eurie replied, "I can't really make sense of it. I do recognize a set of letters across the top. The word translates to something like 'the shelter in the forest.'"

Rella stared at the sign and noticed each successive line was written in a different style. "Perhaps travelers have left messages here?" Rella suggested, just as something sparked in her mind. And then she felt a terrible chill run through her.

"What is it?" Eurie asked, noticing the shock on Rella's face.

"I've seen this!" Rella said.

"What do you mean?" Eurie asked.

"Well, on the scroll. There was writing on the scroll that looked similar to this line here!" She pointed to a large, swirling script with very few breaks between the words.

Chapter 20: Quinn and the Shadowsplitter

QUINN WAS WORRIED WHEN Menagerie didn't return after a few hours. He had felt the quakes about the time she should have been returning, so he thought she might have had to take shelter from falling rocks and branches.

What if she's trapped in the cave? Quinn thought. *She'll have fuel for a while...as long as she listened to my instructions about the elixir on the walls. No...I've got to go after her.*

Quinn was making final adjustments to a retractable arm that would steer his new ship around large rocks jutting out of the water, and he didn't want to leave it unfinished. He was so close to having everything calibrated for the journey.

If Rella could decipher the scroll, he knew they would have a great chance at finding Archimago's Island and freeing the lost guardians.

What if Rella can't do it? What if it's too much pressure for her? Quinn thought.

He tightened up a few of the ropes he had threaded through the retractable arm and inspected all the seams on the sails. He checked their food supply box, which was almost completely full, except for a small space he had left for a few of Eurie's last minute specialties. He couldn't wait to have more of her cherry, lemon, and cinnamon pastries.

Quinn hid the entire ship beneath a blanket of enormous pink and yellow leaves, which rolled and unrolled like cotton blankets, and then tossed a few light branches over them to hold them down. *Any creature passing by will just think it was scrap*, he told himself.

Quinn strapped on his pack, which he had filled with his most important handmade tools, a luminous stone, and a few jars of the elixir, which he planned to refill when he rescued Menagerie from the cave, if she was, in fact, trapped. He would not let himself think about any worse possibilities.

As he trekked north along the river path, he still hoped he would find Menagerie coming in the opposite direction. However, he also kept his eyes open for any signs of The Sisters or The Architect, or any of Archimago's other servants.

Quinn was fairly certain he wouldn't run into The Architect, if he could trust the information he and Eurie had decoded on the bark scripts: the strange collections of symbols and words that only the trees, or whatever things put them there, truly understood.

Although they hadn't deciphered much of it, Quinn used some of his code-breaker training to figure out that there was something in the signs about how The Architect was going to work on a major project along the grasslands in the southeastern region of Hleo, the ones that had recently been drained very quickly of all vegetation.

Quinn thought, for a moment, about his first arrival in Hleo. He had arrived beside an open field of white grasses, with the lights of The Wondercurrent shining in the distance. He also thought about how quickly things seemed to dry up and die in certain areas. Quinn had seen plenty of plants wither and die on Earth One, but seeing a wildflower prematurely plucked from a garden path was nothing when compared to watching two hundred square miles dry up and crumble in an instant.

As far as he knew, and from what Eurie could tell from her flights with Thalas over that area, there weren't any guardians or travelers remaining in the grasslands. Whatever The Architect was supposed to be working on in that area, though, had not been finished yet.

He continued trekking north, picking up his pace. As Quinn looked around, he started thinking about one of the training exercises they used to do at the government school. The trainers, mostly older men and women who were once soldiers themselves, would weigh down their packs and then give the boys a brick to hold in each hand. The boys would have to run circles around a track and then climb up a steep metal staircase. Then, they would make the boys put on earpieces that would simulate the sounds of jets flying overhead.

The trainers told the boys they were preparing for worst-case scenarios. Quinn could think of much worse scenarios than aerial attacks though.

In Quinn's mind, the worst threats always came from inside your own ranks, as he often heard his parents claim. "Be cautious," his father would often say, "Of the ones who claim to be on your side, but seem to hide their true intentions...."

Quinn never enjoyed those training days, but as he rushed to get to Menagerie, his training gave him confidence. The closer he got to the falls, the greater his courage became. He didn't know if it was something in the air around him that gave him this courage or if it was the memory of his home, but he felt ready, if necessary, to take on The Architect.

After a few miles of quiet but rapid hiking up the riverbanks, Quinn decided to climb a tree, one he knew would provide a clearer view of the landscape on the far side of the river.

As he reached the top branches, he saw something flying off in the distance to the south. It looked like a pair of wings, shimmering mostly white and blue with yellow flecks. They would disappear and then reappear, sometimes jumping across the sky fifty and then five hundred yards at a time. Was it some kind of Hlean creature he hadn't met yet?

He had gone over all the taxonomies with Eurie for weeks. She had covered just about every native creature and guardian they knew had come into the lands, at least from the Wall of Waves to the bay. The flecks of white, blue, and yellow reminded him of something he had seen when he was dream traveling in Rella's dreamscape.

A voice echoed from a nearby branch.

"Psst!"

Quinn crouched into a fighting stance on the branch and flipped his staff around in front of his chest.

"Boy, Hello. Here up doing you are what?"

It was unlike any voice or speech pattern he'd ever heard. It was convincingly Earthly, yet seemed to be masking itself. It sounded like an old woman, but then also a young girl at the same time. The more Quinn thought it over, it echoed in a way that almost sounded like two people at once.

Quinn kept his eyes locked on a shadowy figure on a branch in the next tree. He could see the outline of a cloak, then two figures, but the shadow around the figure or figures was so thick he could not see the color. This was not a natural shadow at all. The angles of light were all wrong. *A Shadowsplitter*, he thought, as sharp pins prickled down his spine.

Chapter 21: The Carved Castle

"CAN YOU REMEMBER ANYTHING else about the writing?" Eurie asked, running her hand over the inscription on the stone.

"Well, it's a little blurry, but I remember those symbols. The one that looks like the wings of an eagle as it swoops for a fish, and the one that looks like a canoe, and the one that looks like the profile of a pointy-faced man..."

Rella was disappointed she couldn't remember anything else.

"Don't worry," Eurie said, "we're going to get the scroll back. And I'm sure you'll be able to tell me a lot more about these images. After all, that's what Quinn said in the letter, right? You are the *only one* who can decipher the images. I have always believed that."

Rella nodded graciously.

After walking the path for another hour, Rella felt like she was going to black out.

"Eurie," she said, "I know we have to keep moving, but I really need to take another break. My head feels dizzy and I'm thirsty."

"Oh," Eurie said, "We're in luck! I know exactly where we can get you just the energy you need."

Rella was surprised by Eurie's quick response. It reminded her of how her father often seemed to know she was going to ask for something right before she did.

"Actually," Rella said, reaching her hand into her satchel, "I have already eaten the cakes I brought with me...I'm...just...so...starved."

Eurie laughed. "Oh, Rella. Those cakes were just a small treat. They won't revive you like this stuff."

"Where do we get it?" Rella asked, excited about trying it.

"Well, there's some back at the cave that you might have seen without even knowing it, but we're a little too far away from there."

Rella continued wobbling, looking like she might drop at any moment.

Eurie grabbed Rella's arm and propped her up as best as she could.

They crossed a bare patch of ground and limped through another cluster of smaller trees. The area between the trees reminded Rella of a flower garden she and her mother had planted in a forest near her old home. They picked out packets of every natural seed they could find, avoiding any of the bioengineered colors, and created small explosions of color in the forest.

Her mother was always careful to point out you could create a lot of beauty from what occurred naturally, and that, although the engineered plants from Westcon were pretty, they always lost their luster much sooner than the natural ones.

Rella couldn't walk another step. She sat down on the closest chair-like object she could find, which was a spongy, white blob that looked like a giant marshmallow. She started sinking into the sponge and it nearly swallowed her.

Eurie quickly pulled her back up out of it, but eased her back down when she realized that Rella had already drifted off to sleep. Rella started snoring, which made Eurie giggle.

Eurie searched the area, turning over rocks of all shapes and sizes until she found what she was looking for. She walked back to the marshmallow seat and grabbed Rella's limp hand. She guided it into a small opening in the rock she had picked up.

Rella started to stir as she felt a cool sap dripping onto her fingers. She slowly pulled her hand back out of the opening.

"Taste it, but not too quickly!" Eurie whispered.

Rella put her fingers to her lips and took a taste. Her eyes popped open. Waves of refreshment and a surge of energy lifted her back to her feet.

"Wow! Weeee! Wooo! Zing!" Rella shouted. "More...more...mooooore!"

"Shhhhh!" Eurie said, smiling wide but trying to remind Rella they were in an unexplored area. "Archimago's spies could be watching."

Rella thought nothing could top Eurie's treats, but this sap was the almighty elixir of life.

"How. Did. You. Discover. Thissssss?" Rella asked, bouncing with energy.

"Actually, you did!" Eurie said.

Rella was confused. *What did Eurie mean when she said 'you did'?* Rella thought.

Rella had an odd feeling Eurie was hiding something very important, something about a past journey Rella had made into Hleo, but one Rella couldn't remember clearly.

As she tried to form the words to ask Eurie to explain, she had a strange image flash through her mind. It was a memory of a visit to Hleo. Rella saw herself tasting this elixir inside of the cave. It was just as delicious and energizing. But then, as she tried focus on the memory, it faded out.

She thought she should tell Eurie about what had just happened, that she had this strange image flash through her mind. But she was enjoying this delicious syrup so much, and Eurie was enjoying it so much now too, that she didn't want to ruin the fun.

Following their feast, the revived companions continued on their way.

A warm breeze blew through the glowing jellybean forest, and a soft chime rang in the distance.

"Did you hear that?" Eurie asked.

"Yes. But...what do you think caused it? Should we take cover?" Rella thought of her mother's wind chimes, which hung in the lone cottonwood tree outside of her house in Ensea.

Unlike most trees, this one was what they called an 'original,' which meant it had come from a seed that came from a seed that came from a seed and so on, all the way back to the first forests to ever appear in the Eastcon Territory.

"You know, I feel like we're supposed to keep following these lights, but what do you think?" Eurie asked.

Rella peered down at an arrow carved into the front of a stone and then, making the shape of binoculars with her hands, followed the invisible line toward a distant thicket.

"I don't see how we're going to get the scroll back going any other way," Rella said.

As they passed through the drifting shadows, the light across the path faded just a bit. They noticed that the canopy above was thinning out and that a faint, reddish-orange light was starting to come through the openings.

Rella wondered if this was, finally, a sunrise. In the distance, between the trees, they spotted a lake. They started racing toward the shore.

The red-orange glow filtering in through the canopy melted into the steamy, sparkling surface of the water. The shoreline formed a perfect circle, surrounded by trees with an endless variety of rounded and pointed leaves. At the center of the lake, a magnificent castle stretched higher than the tallest skyscrapers ever constructed on Earth One. This castle was not, however, built from stone, but carved completely from the trunk of an ancient tree. The trunk of that tree, Rella observed, had to be at least five hundred feet wide.

Rella thought of the floating arch and the gigantic, invisible hands again, and began imagining a carver's hands reaching out of the sky and delicately forming this wooden palace. She remembered something her mother used to say about artists who carved sculptures and how they could always see the angel or monster in their heads, and to find it, they just had to chip away everything that was not part of the figure. While she didn't know if her mother was serious, she thought that whoever or whatever had carved this royal dwelling must have practiced for a hundred lifetimes. She wished she'd had her sketchbook, but she understood that they had to keep moving forward.

"How are we going to get over there?" Rella asked, with her eyes still locked on the intricate lines carved into the ramparts and up the tower walls.

"We could take that..." Eurie said, pointing to a small canoe gliding directly toward them.

"Yes," Rella said, surprised she felt no hesitation at all, since boats usually made her nervous. She loved to swim, but she hated being seasick.

Rella adjusted her satchel and followed Eurie into the canoe. At first, it didn't move.

"Shouldn't we find an oar?" Rella asked.

Eurie laughed. "Yes, that would make sense."

Rella looked down towards her feet, to see if any oars might have been left in the boat, but found none. Just as she started climbing back out of the boat to find a branch they might use, the boat started to move, knocking Rella off balance and back into her seat.

Rella reached her arm across the boat and grabbed Eurie's hands to steady her. Then, they waited for the boat to carry them toward the castle.

The boat moved slowly through the water. As Rella looked out over the side, she could see soft, colorful lights and shapes shining up from the depths of the lake. A few small, spinning disks beneath the water seemed to follow alongside them, but it was hard to tell if they were simply fish or if they were some other type of plant life. Rella thought they might be tadpoles of some kind, but certainly not the kind that grew into normal frogs. *More likely, they are tadpoles that can grow into just about anything*, she thought.

Rella watched as Eurie reached her hand down into the water and scooped up a handful, lifted it to her nose, took a sniff, and then drank some.

She followed Eurie's lead and scooped a couple handfuls into her dry mouth as well. Unlike the silent water in The Wonder-current, this water was full of sound. If someone dipped a finger into the lake and ran it in a circle, it would produce harmonies resembling the sound of a harp or a cello. When you drink it, it swirls around on your tongue and then vibrates its way down into your stomach. For Rella, it wasn't too different from the feeling of eating her favorite cake back on Earth One. She always felt that delicious sweets made a song as they traveled down into her tummy.

Eurie started splashing at Rella, creating a brief, but fantastic symphony. If she spit the water out and dispersed it too quickly, she noticed that the sound changed to cymbal crashes, which was not very pleasant.

Rella thought that spitting cymbals was just as fun as making the harmonies. Back home, she would probably get in trouble for spitting, but for musical water, there had to be a different set of rules.

As the boat continued drifting toward the castle, the chimes sounded again, very softly. Once they approached the shore, Rella counted hundreds of stairs leading up to the door. It was going to take some time to get into the castle.

Rella stepped off the boat and followed Eurie up the stairs until they reached a platform leading them toward a grand arch. The arch reminded Rella of the half-crumbled one she had seen near the waterfall, the one that should have collapsed on her head but didn't.

Before passing under the arch, Rella turned and looked back across the water to the trail. It was now only a speck. Everywhere she looked, a dark red and silver mist encircled the island.

"Do you think the scroll is in there?" Rella asked.

"I do," Eurie replied, still taking in all the mesmerizing contours of the castle walls.

"Well, do you think *anyone* is in there? The red-haired girl you were chasing?" Rella asked.

"Maybe..." Eurie said, though she was distracted by all the letters carved into the walls.

"Should we just go in, or should we..?"

"Hello!" Eurie shouted, and then again and again, in about ten different languages, five of which Rella didn't recognize.

The chimes rang again, but no one answered.

"Let's go in," Eurie said.

As they passed through the doorway, they entered a great hall. The floor was lined with glowing stones. They seemed dimmer than the ones out in the forest.

They had enough light to find their way to a staircase, but everything else remained disguised by the shadows. Rella desperately wished there was a way to brighten the room because she started imagining hideous monsters lurking nearby.

"Something is not right," Eurie said.

"What do you mean? Like this place is haunted?" Rella asked, still thinking about the invisible monsters.

"No. Not haunted. It seems safe here. But...like there's someone here who needs our help...like someone is calling for us."

"I think," Rella said. "Well, then we should probably try to help them?"

Rella stood next to Eurie at the bottom of the stairwell and looked back over the darkened hall. There were three other stairwells visible in the corners of the room, but this was the only one lit up enough for them to safely see where they were going.

"Whatever we find here," Eurie said, still looking out over the hall for any sign of an inhabitant, "we must..."

Rella didn't hear Eurie, though, because she had already dashed up one of the staircases and into a small room where she had discovered something unbelievable: her scroll was lying unrolled on a large, wooden table.

Chapter 22: Inside Shelterwood Castle

EVERY WALL IN THE WOODEN room was lined, from floor to ceiling, with Red Notebooks. The bindings were made of a variety of materials: thick leather, thin cardboard, metallic glass, and fabrics of all kinds. The image of her parents' attic library flashed through Rella's mind. She half-expected to see her father coming around the shelf. But this library was a thousand times larger than the attic.

Some of the notebooks were hundreds of years old, yet they carried almost no signs of wear. They all looked like they could have been made that very day. In contrast to the ones with the ancient designs, others were made of materials so bright and pristine one might believe they had been delivered from the future. The shades of red varied, and some books were as thick as a cinder block, while the thinnest ones were barely the width of a fingernail.

"No. Get out. Out. No. No," a muffled voice exclaimed from an adjoining room.

Rella and Eurie jumped. Rella grabbed the scroll and the girls linked arms.

"Hello? Who's there?" Rella shouted.

"No. No. Get out. Please." The panicked voice screamed once more. Rella thought it sounded familiar, like it was an Earth One accent, and also like a young boy's voice.

"What do we do?" Rella shouted. She stared at Eurie, who seemed to be trying to calculate a hundred math problems in her head at once.

"I think we've got to help that person, whoever he is."

"What if it's a trap?"

"I know. But, remember, you said this place wasn't haunted," Rella exclaimed, panicking.

"Ok. No. I think it is a safe place. Let's just stay together," Eurie replied.

The two girls tip-toed quickly back through the door and out into a passageway. They spotted another staircase ahead.

"The sound came from up there," Eurie said, unlinking her arm from Rella's and pointing up at the entrance to a room on the next floor.

The staircase led only to this one room, which had a very low entrance, as though it was meant specifically for children. Most adults would have to squat very low to get through it. The staircase leading up to the room reminded Rella of the fire escape outside of her Uncle J's old apartment building, only it was on the inside of the house and, of course, made of wood instead of iron.

When they reached the room, they heard the voice again.

"He sounds a lot like a boy from Earth One," Rella said.

The voice cried out, "Please. I can't get through...help, please."

As they entered, they saw the shape of a boy lying still on a wooden bed. The boy, much like everything else in the wooden castle, seemed to be carved out of the wood.

Rella's heart thumped so loudly she had to put her hand over her chest to hold it in place. Eurie could sense Rella's growing fear and tried to calm her by gently squeezing her hand.

"What...do...we...do?" Rella asked, trembling.

"Well," Eurie said, "I think I know what's happening here..."

"What do you mean?" Rella asked. She had never witnessed a surfacing.

"Well, you see, one of the ways you can get into Hleo is through the nature portals...specifically, trees, rocky cliffs, and The Wondercurrent...but, typically this is only possible for animals...you know, how the animal guardians like Thalas and Alister arrived. The way that a human enters is still a much more mysterious process."

Rella hadn't met Alister yet, but she remembered reading about him in the note from Quinn.

Eurie thought about when she first learned of the animal portals. It was the day Thalas arrived. She couldn't tell if Thalas was some kind of monster or a real animal, but after helping guide Thalas to safety, Eurie realized Thalas was just a regular Earth One hawk, ready to help Eurie in any way possible.

"Ok. So, what's going on with this boy?" Rella asked, still panicking.

"Well, I can't be sure, but it seems like he might have tried to follow someone, or perhaps an animal guardian might have tried to lead him or bring him here," Eurie said.

"So why is he stuck in the wood? He kind of makes me think of Pinocchio," Rella said.

"Who is that?" Eurie asked.

"Well, it's a story my dad used to tell me. There was a puppeteer named Geppetto who wanted to have a child. So he carved a boy out of wood and then the boy became real. But when the boy started telling lies, his nose would grow...," Rella said, pointing at her own nose and pretending like she was stretching it out.

The boy carved into the bed seemed to be trying to move, and, for a split second, Rella thought she saw the wood changing shape just a little, as if the boy was turning his head.

They both looked at the shape of the boy struggling to surface from the wood. Every part of his body was precisely where it should have been, just as if the boy were really there. Even the small lines on his knuckles and the hairs on his eyebrows were delicately carved into the wood, although the mouth didn't move and the eyes didn't blink.

Eurie closed her eyes and took a few seconds to think. Rella let go of Eurie's hand and unrolled the scroll, desperate to see if a clue for helping this boy might be written somewhere.

As she unrolled it, the boy made another agonizing sound, which caused Rella's stomach to churn. She looked down at the scroll but couldn't make any more sense of it than she had before.

Aside from the wooden boy in the bed, the room had a small coat rack in the corner, which held a variety of long, fuzzy-looking cloaks with various animal prints on them. The cloaks didn't seem useful at the moment, but they were worth investigating.

Rella wondered if they might be some kind of disguise.

Eurie dashed over and examined the cloaks quickly.

"I've seen this one!" Eurie said. "The girl I was chasing, the Sister. She was wearing this! It must be hers."

Eurie rifled through the pockets and checked for any slips of paper or other small artifacts that might help them understand what was happening. She also dropped to the floor and looked under the bed, careful not to miss anything.

"Why would she need those disguises?" Rella asked, looking down at Eurie who was halfway under the bed.

"Maybe she's trying to hide something from Archimago?" Eurie said, crawling backwards out from underneath the bed. "These cloaks would certainly make it difficult to be found, at least from an aerial view, which is one of the main ways I've seen Archimago's other spies working here."

"What does this girl want with this trapped boy then? Do you think she trapped him here? And what was she doing with those books and my scroll?" Rella asked.

"Hmmm..." Eurie continued trying to put all the pieces together.

Rella spoke aloud: "If the girl was trying to hide from Archimago, she might be some kind of spy, which is why she needs the cloaks. That means she's on our side. Thank Heavens! Maybe the boy here is her friend, or maybe even her brother?"

"Wait. Why her brother?" Eurie asked.

"If you had a little brother and you went through a portal, don't you think he'd try to follow you?" Rella replied.

"Oh, yes. So then he got trapped coming in after her..." Eurie said.

"Well, what about this place? Why would she lead us back here?" Rella asked.

"And then disappear so quickly?" Eurie added.

"Wait...I just had another thought," Rella said, "In the note Quinn left, he told me he *found* the scroll...that he thought it might belong to Archimago. But, what if it belonged to someone else?"

Rella opened the scroll back up and looked at it with the purpose of trying to decode a process, like a recipe book of some kind, or a formula. She looked for something indicating steps. Could the scroll contain directions on how to open a portal?

Just then, two feet appeared in the shadowy doorway behind them. The footsteps were not the light, quick footsteps of a child, but the slow, heavy footsteps of a full-grown man.

Rella grabbed Eurie's hand. They were still facing the supine carving of the wooden boy. They were too terrified to turn around.

Chapter 23: The Storykeeper's Son

RELLA AND EURIE GASPED at the sound of every footstep. He was right behind them. They were frozen in place. They felt just as wooden as the boy in the bed.

"I think you're onto something," the voice in the shadows replied. The voice was not, as they expected, an evil voice, dark or full of hisses and whispers. It was not how they imagined Archimago would sound.

"Sorry to surprise you like this," the old man continued. "May we talk?"

The man placed a square stone into a small opening on the wall. Instantly, the room brightened up. The stone, apparently, sent some kind of pulse into the walls, lighting everything at once.

Rella and Eurie stood shoulder-to-shoulder. Eurie spoke first.

"How do we know you aren't going to put us in a cage, or turn us into wood, like the boy here?"

Rella stared in shock.

"Well," he replied, "you said yourselves that this boy here was probably trapped in the surfacing process...if I heard you correctly?"

"Yes. That is what I suggested," Eurie replied. "But maybe you are simply repeating my words..."

"Where do you think we are right now?" the man asked, in a gentle tone. Rella thought that he sounded like a very kind teacher or a kind librarian who wants to help you find a book, even though you can't remember what it is called.

They were pretty certain now that he was not Archimago. But they were still cautious.

"Well...I think we're still in Hleo, but it's an older part, something Archimago's clan has not yet corrupted...," Eurie answered, watching his eyes closely.

"You are on track...what else?" the old man asked, with a gentle smile.

Rella turned her eyes back to the luminous scroll. New patterns had appeared on the surface.

Eurie was still focused on the old man's fluffy beard, trying to detect any hint of suspicion in his eyes. The man continued standing still, waiting patiently.

"Well," Eurie said, "I know we're on a small island, and we're in a castle. So, maybe this is the home of some great, royal family of the forest?"

Rella was watching the scroll closely.

The old man laughed. "Oh..no. No royalty here. Just me and this...boy, and..."

The man teared up a little and tried to clear his throat.

"But..I didn't know adults were permitted to enter Hleo," Eurie said.

"Into Hleo? No. Well...they don't...normally," the old man replied, wiping a tear from his eye and looking over at the boy.

"But...you're in Hleo," Eurie said. "How?"

"Well, you see, I wasn't supposed to stay. None of us were," the old man replied, turning his attention back to Eurie.

"There are more of you?" Eurie asked, looking around for more people to appear. But there was no one else, at least no one visible, in the castle.

Rella looked up from the scroll and over towards the bed. The boy had started making noises again.

Rella gasped and stood up on her tiptoes.

Eurie was still so absorbed in her conversation with the old man she didn't realize the spectacle happening behind her.

Rella stepped closer to the wooden boy and put her hand on the bed.

"No," the old man replied, ignoring the boy's sounds. "Not here."

"So, can you explain then?" Eurie asked.

"Well...I'm sure you've heard of the Storykeepers?"

The boy continued getting louder.

Eurie paused and then spoke a little louder: "You aren't supposed to be...in here...but.."

The man made a gesture with his hands that communicated something so clearly and directly to Eurie that she knew they were safe. Eurie relaxed.

"When we found out what Archimago was doing...some of us had to make a choice...," the old man said.

"But," Eurie replied, "if a Storykeeper comes here, in their adult form, they can't go back...isn't that right? How did you...."

"Yes. It's really true..." the old man said.

Eurie knew he was telling the truth.

"But, then who is going to be back there, to guide the others? Aren't you worried about what happens back there?" Eurie asked.

"Possibly...I had no choice." The old man lost his composure. Eurie saw tears forming in his eyes.

"What do you mean?" Eurie asked.

"The boy in that bed..." the old man said, turning to face the bed again and stunned by what he saw.

"Yes," Eurie said, turning around.

"He's my son," the man said, standing up and trying to steady himself on his cane.

Rella looked at the other two from her place next to the bed. She opened her mouth and tried to scream, but no sound came out. It was just like the time she had discovered a giant rat in her desk at school.

"He tried to follow you here?" Eurie asked, beginning to notice what was happening on the bed.

"Well...," the old man continued, moving as quickly as he could toward the bedside. He placed his hands on the wooden figure in the bed and continued answering Euire's questions. "I was trying to leave, to gather my things to come here. He and his older sister were sneaking around my library, and..."

"And they followed you," Eurie said.

Rella's voice finally broke through and she cried out: "He's moving...!"

Eurie watched the old man lunge forward. He nearly knocked into Rella.

Rella, Eurie, and the old man stared in awe as the boy emerged.

First, he moved his his head slowly to the left, and then to the right.

Back and forth.

Back and forth.

The three onlookers waited to see if the boy would speak.

"Sebastian! Oh Sebastian!" the old man said, tearful, as he reached for the boy.

"Father?" Sebastian said.

Rella's father had read her many books about people emerging in new worlds from strange places, but she couldn't recall any stories where the person who emerged was made of the exact materials of the thing they came out of. She wished she'd had a notebook so she could write all of this down. She wanted to capture every single detail.

As the old man put his arms around his son, Rella noticed that he hesitated, like he had touched something infected with a deadly disease.

But then, just as quickly, he wrapped his arms around his son and laughed with delight.

Rella missed her father's hugs.

The boy, Sebastian, was moving and talking like a regular boy, yet he was completely made out of wood.

"What's happened to me father?" Sebastian asked.

"Son. My precious boy. Don't worry about that right now," the old man said.

"But what's happened to me? I feel so strange. It was so dark in there..."

The old man cradled his son and continued to alternate between laughing and weeping.

"It's ok. Father. I'm ok...right?" Sebastian asked.

"Well...," the old man paused.

"What father? What is it?" Sebastian asked.

"Well..." he said, trying to find the right words to explain what he had just realized.

Rella burst out: "You are...hmmm...you're sort of...Pinocchio!"

"Wooden," Sebastian exclaimed, "I'm wooden!"

He spoke without an ounce of terror or worry in his voice.

Rella expected him to be terrified and was astonished at what happened next.

Sebastian held out his arms and slowly examined them. He knocked his fists against each other and raised them to his wooden ear. They made a clock, clock, clock sound.

"Yes! This is unbelievable. What would the other kids back in Eastcon think about this?" Sebastian shouted, giddy with excitement.

Drying his tears on his sleeve, the old man started to chuckle.

"That's my Sebastian!" he said, looking at Rella. "Always making the best of a situation no matter how tough or strange."

"Oh father," Sebastian said, "Think about it...I can just use my arm for a baseball bat!" Sebastian moved into a batting stance, bent his knees, and swung his arm through the air like he was hitting a grand slam.

Rella giggled. Eurie was unsure of what 'baseball' was, but she laughed too.

Sebastian's energy was a relief after so many tense moments.

They needed Sebastian. Hleo needed Sebastian.

The old man still had a touch of worry in his eyes, though his smile also showed his relief at having his son with him again—even if his son was made entirely of wood.

"Well...let's go down to the kitchen and get something to eat, shall we?" the old man suggested.

"Fantastic," Rella said as her stomach rumbled aloud. "I'm starving!"

Rella tucked the scroll into her satchel. She wondered if any of them had noticed that her scroll was actually the thing that helped pull Sebastian through.

The entire group walked down the long, winding stairs and into the kitchen. On the way down, Rella noticed a variety of symbols carved into the walls and on the curved stair rails. One image, she thought, looked a lot like the quill pen insignia for the Storykeeper's Alliance. Another image resembled something she had just seen on the scroll.

All of the new information and images felt strange inside of her head. It was like she was starting to understand a new language but she didn't quite know what it was yet. It reminded her of when she was learning to read Earth Two English, and she kept mixing up the sounds of the letters from the different alphabets. Earth Two had this letter that looked like a P, but it was pronounced like E and then Earth One English (her third language) had this letter that looked like an X, pronounced fuh, and this other letter that looked just like F but was pronounced ex. For the moment, she kept all of these new observations to herself.

As they waited for this kind man to cook their meal, Rella decided to try and find out if he might know anything about her parents.

Sebastian, meanwhile, walked around the main foyer of the castle, testing out the strength and stability of his wooden limbs.

"Have you ever met my father? Julius Deveraux-PenSword? Or my mother? Winter Deveraux-PenSword?" Rella asked.

"Those names sound a little familiar..." the man replied, flipping a pancake.

"My mother was a member of the Storykeeper's Alliance in Ensea..."

"No...I don't think I've met them," the old man replied quickly. "Well, maybe your father...I'm not sure..."

Eurie sat listening, unsure of whether Rella should be telling this man so much. While he seemed safe, she hadn't ruled out the possibility that he, or maybe his daughter, the spy, was working under the control of Archimago.

"Is there any way my father could make it into Hleo?" Rella asked.

"I don't think so," the man said. "I'm not sure...there could be a way...but."

Rella started to tear up.

"It's ok, Rella," Eurie said calmly, "It's ok. Just sit here...you look terribly famished...here, take this."

Eurie stabbed a piece of pancake with a sparkling silver fork and put the fork into Rella's hand. Rella took a large bite. And another. And another. She felt her body relax and begin to warm up inside. She hadn't felt so calm since the last time her father had cooked her pancakes.

"Thank you, Mister...uh...King, Sire...?" Eurie said as she guzzled down a large glass of syrupy, cherry-flavored juice.

"Oh..no. This might look like a castle, but I'm not actually a king. That's just my last name. King. I guess, perhaps somewhere down the line, we might have been related to a king," he said.

"Well, Mr. King," Rella piped up. "It is an honor to meet you. I can't wait to learn more about this castle. It seems so familiar to me."

King looked at a pile of Red Notebooks stacked on a counter nearby and paused, but didn't reply to Rella's comment.

Just then, Sebastian walked in and reached for a pancake. Everyone gave him a strange look. They were all wondering whether he could actually eat food.

He opened his mouth, placed the pancake in, and slowly started to chew.

"How about that?" King said. "Even though he's made of wood, he's still got an appetite!"

Sebastian swallowed, smiled, and joined in on the feast.

Eurie and Rella tried to figure out how King had managed to warm the pancakes and bake the bread, since there was no fire in Hleo.

"Sir," Rella asked. "How did you heat this up?"

"Chemistry," he said. "There are many ways, besides fire, to create heat..."

"How do you do it?" Eurie asked, still a bit suspicious.

Sensing her skepticism, King offered to show Eurie the precise combination of particles and crushed stones needed to create the heat reaction.

King's offering helped Eurie relax her suspicions a bit, which was a relief to Rella.

Rella knew that they would all have to trust each other to move forward with the mission.

King then explained to Rella and Eurie that his daughter, Scarlett, had told him that two girls, about her age, would possibly be coming and that she, Scarlett, had left a trail of luminous stones to lead them to Shelterwood Castle.

Scarlett had told him that if Sebastian was able to surface before she returned that King should also allow Sebastian to return with the girls. He argued with his daughter about this, but she persuaded her father that it was the only way to help him recover from being trapped in the Channels. She had seen other survivors and had helped them find medicines and restoration in the plants growing along the banks.

King couldn't explain how his daughter knew Rella had arrived in Hleo, but he tried to reassure Rella and Eurie that Scarlett had a plan and that she was not working for Archimago, like it may have appeared. Scarlett, he told the girls, had shown one of the prime instincts of a Storykeeper, the ability to keep a secret, from her earliest days.

As a Storykeeper himself, King knew a lot about Hleo, and other places like it, but Archimago's sudden appearance a few years earlier, when the Dreambridge had been breached, was still a mystery. No one really understood what he was after.

King then took Rella, Eurie and Sebastian on a tour of the castle and showed them all the Red Notebooks in the castle library. He explained that he had been searching them one by one, trying to locate stories from the past when someone like Archimago had appeared in order to learn how Archimago might have tried to close the portals and take over the Hleo.

He still had no leads.

When King explained this to Eurie and Rella, and to his son, they all wanted to know why he couldn't go with them.

"Well, first of all, I don't move very quickly," he told them. King had lost part of his foot in an accident when he was a child and could not run.

"And I'm very heavy," he said as he made a series of gestures with his hands that looked like an elephant climbing onto the back of a giant bird that then came crashing to the ground.

The kids all laughed at his puppet show.

Eurie knew that the bird he had made with his hand gestures was in reference to her guardian, Thalas, which surprised Eurie because she hadn't considered who else might be watching her.

Eurie considered whether Thalas could bear the weight of all four of them, and whether she would make it to the banks of The Wondercurrent to meet up with Scarlett. She agreed with King that his weight would be too much for Thalas.

"And finally," King said, pointing to the piles of books, which seemed to be multiplying throughout the castle every time they looked around, "I've got to read through the rest of these notebooks. Children, we don't have any time to lose. If there are more boys and girls trapped, just like Sebastian, we have to figure out how to open the portals and stop this madman...whatever he is..."

King now had a book in his hand and was pointing to a drawing of a shadowy figure in a book that looked five hundred years old. The heading at the top said something about a queen, but the word was spelled with an extra "e" (Queene).

This spelling looked a little strange to Rella, but she had so many words and symbols floating through her head at the moment she wasn't sure if the word queen was spelled, in Earth One English, with an "e" at the end or not.

Rella thought she recognized the book from her father's library, but didn't say anything.

King wished them luck and whispered a special message into Sebastian's ear. "Son," he said, "you must bring your sister back here safe and sound."

Sebastian nodded and the three companions waved good-bye.

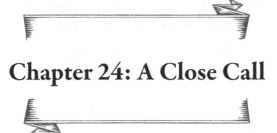

Chapter 24: A Close Call

FOLLOWING ANOTHER DELICIOUS snack of warm, chocolate-cherry scones, the three children all hiked along the trail back out of the forest within the forest. When they reached a clearing, they found Thalas waiting to pick them up.

As they soared along on Thalas's feathery, soft-metallic back, watching the landscape unfold, they discussed the excitement to of the last few hours.

Hleo had so many secrets and Rella had so much to learn.

Thalas swooped as close as possible to the tree line where Menagerie had been captured. Rella listened closely as Eurie told about how she had uncovered an untouched passage along the tree line a few days earlier. And, if the bark samples with the recorded codes were accurate, none of Archimago's servants had ever passed through those passages.

If anyone had come through, Eurie explained, their speech would have left traces on the bark. But all the bark was smooth. Of course, Rella noted, as they continued soaring above the mists, speaking creatures could have passed through the area silently. Sebastian even suggested that it was possible that the bark also recorded people's thoughts.

While they were still at the castle, King had explained what he knew about the bark and why it might be important to learn to use sign language to avoid being recorded, but it still didn't answer all of Eurie's questions.

When they arrived at the drop off point, Sebastian climbed down onto the tree limb first. Even though he didn't have ordinary flesh, his outer layers of wooden 'skin' were very sensitive. His wooden fingers actually felt more sensitive than his human fingers.

When he wrapped his hand around a branch of a tree, he also felt a signal pass from the tree into his arm, sort of like the way a whisper hits your eardrum.

When he reached the ground, Sebastian sensed even more signals passing into him. As he brushed against a large leaf or scraped the ground with his wooden toes, his entire body seemed to try and send back a response signal.

"Are we close?" Sebastian asked Eurie as they walked along the shady trail.

"We've got a long way to go, but this route is our best chance of making it through unseen," Eurie replied.

"And we also have to check on another guardian who has been trapped," Rella added.

"What happened?" Sebastian asked. "Is he like I was? Waiting to surface?"

Rella pointed to her satchel.

"You remember the scroll?" Rella asked.

"Yes. The one you were reading that you said helped you pull me through?" Sebastian replied.

"Yes. Well, Quinn, who we are going to meet, and this guardian...well, she was the one who delivered this scroll for me...," Rella said.

"Unfortunately," Eurie added, "she was captured on her way back to meet with Quinn."

"Oh, I see," Sebastian added.

Rella sensed Sebastian's confusion, and started thinking about her own recent surfacing. She knew Sebastian needed time to orient himself to Hleo's mysterious environment.

"Will Menagerie know we are on her side when we try to set her free?" Rella asked.

"I'm not sure," Eurie replied, "Sometimes, they understand our language clearly. Sometimes, they seem so confused they just run away, like most animals might do on Earth One. I've only actually met a few guardians from Earth One, though, and they were mostly tiny birds."

Eurie stopped and looked back at Sebastian, who had slowed down at the base of a tree and was speaking to it as though it could hear him.

"Are you ok, Sebastian?" Eurie shouted.

Sebastian looked back in their direction, like he had been woken from a dream. He didn't seem to realize he was communicating with the tree.

"Oh...sorry. I'll try to keep up," he said.

They reached a narrow bridge. Rella was amazed. It was built entirely out of woven vines. The bridge was only wide enough for one child to cross at a time, so they would have to go single file. It seemed like it had not been used in ages.

They walked up to the ledge separating their side of the forest from the other side.

It was more than thirty feet across and the canyon below had no visible floor.

A faint glow shined up from the bottom of the canyon. Rella thought it might be water, but she didn't want to find out.

Sebastian stepped up behind Rella and Euire, who were still peering over the ledge and trying to decide whether to try and cross the bridge.

"The trees told me not to take the bridge," Sebastian said.

"What?" Rella answered.

"Yeah...I know. This sounds strange. But, I guess being made of Hleo wood comes with its advantages...."

"Are they speaking to you?" Eurie asked.

"Not with words, exactly, but it's kind of like a whisper...hard to explain," Sebastian said, in a spirited, happy-go-lucky tone.

"Sebastian," Eurie asked, more seriously, "do you remember anything from before you passed through?"

"Not really...just flashes of things. It was like I was standing in a tunnel, but it was too blurry to see anything clearly. I was too afraid to move. Every few minutes, or a bit longer, I don't really remember, I'd see a shadow fly by or a flicker of light spiral down the tunnel...."

"Fascinating," Eurie said. It was the first time she'd heard anyone describe an extended stay in the Channels. She knew they were there...and she knew of at least one other creature who had been able to go into them on command.

Eurie turned her attention back to Rella, who was now halfway out across the bridge.

"No! Wait!" Eurie shouted.

"Why?" Rella replied. "It looks secure to me."

Sebastian ran up to the edge of the bridge and shouted: "It's a trap, Rella...wait." It was too late. Rella heard him just as the bridge of vines broke away from the far side of the ravine.

She grabbed onto the vines and braced for impact as the bridge swung toward the opposite ledge. Her body slammed against the wall, ten feet below where Eurie and Sebastian were standing. Luckily, she had tangled her arms in the vines and didn't drop into the ravine.

"Don't let go! Don't let go!" Eurie shouted. "We'll pull you up!"

Eurie and Sebastian tried grabbing the vine, but it was too heavy to pull up.

"I think I can climb up," Rella called out, still shaken.

"Are you sure?" Eurie asked, worried Rella might lose her grip.

"Wait," Sebastian said. "I have an idea!"

Sebastian ran back towards a tree where some large vines were hanging and reached out his wooden hand. He closed his eyes and, instantly, a vine from the tree moved toward him, lengthening out until it reached his wooden hand. Sebastian grabbed the vine, which was still attached in the upper branches of the trees (too high to see from the ground) and fed it down to Rella, still clutching the bridge.

The vine gently wrapped itself around Rella, pulled her slowly up to the ledge, and set her down.

As Sebastian let go of the vine, it recoiled back up into the misty canopy.

Rella smiled with embarrassment and looked at her companions.

"Oops!" she said. "I guess that was a really bad idea."

Sebastian chuckled. "Good thing I can talk to the trees."

Rella was in awe of Sebastian's new connection to the natural environment. She was as eager as he was to discover what other powers he might have gained as a result of his mysterious arrival.

"Maybe," Sebastian said to Rella, "I can turn myself into a wooden plane and just fly up into the clouds."

Rella laughed as she reached up and grabbed onto Eurie's hand.

"We're going south! It's not worth the risk!" Eurie said firmly as she began marching.

Rella and Sebastian didn't understand why Eurie had become so serious. They were enjoying the adventure. Still, they quickly followed behind and continued scanning the trees and openings between the branches.

Every ten or fifteen feet, a new plant or flower they had never seen appeared. Rella and Sebastian wanted to stop and smell them, touch them, and, particularly for Sebastian, to listen to them to see if they said anything. The companions continued pressing forward, however, for they still had quite a distance to go.

Chapter 25: The Chase Begins

AFTER HOURS OF HIKING along the ledges, Rella's legs felt wobbly. She suggested they all stop and take a break.

"Shouldn't we be getting closer?" Rella asked. "I feel like the road is lengthening out even as we move forward, like every time I take a few steps, the entire road gets longer."

"You noticed?" Eurie replied, motioning Rella to follow her up into the branches of a tree with a wide limb where they could stretch out and also catch a glimpse of The Wondercurrent beyond some distant hills.

"Wait. That really is what is happening? Then we might have to walk ten miles even when it appears to be only a mile," Rella said, putting her hand to her forehead like a wandering sailor searching for any sign of land.

Sebastian was skipping and humming a tune from an Earth One song about a sailor lost at sea.

"Doesn't that happen in your world?" Eurie asked in her familiar schoolmaster's tone.

"Not exactly," Rella said.

"Tell me more about children in your world," Eurie said, as they dangled their feet from a branch among the shadows in the thick leaves. "Children in your world seem to have a very unique experience of...what do you call them...*time* and *space*."

Eurie was such a puzzle to Rella. Sometimes, she seemed to understand Earth One so well and then she asked these odd questions about space and time, like Rella was some kind of scientist who understood all the complexities of the universe.

Suddenly, a nearby branch snapped, shaking the ground violently. The girls froze in place. Another branch snapped and caused half-buried boulders to pop up into the air as if they were weightless.

Rella and Eurie leapt up to their feet and then crouched into parallel fighting stances. Rella seemed to be imitating Eurie's stance, almost like a shadow. Sebastian was impressed with Rella's ability to imitate Eurie's motion.

Eurie and Rella stared ahead and could see the outline of a cloak. And, for a split second, Rella thought she saw a few strands of red hair, though it could have been light brown or even yellow.

Is it a person? Is it Archimago? Rella wondered.

Sebastian looked around for a rock or a twig he might use as a weapon if he had to defend himself. The figure, however, did not seem to notice them, or it was ignoring them on purpose.

They decided to follow the figure, but keep a distance. Sebastian, the optimist, suggested that the cloaked one might lead them to a safer place to cross.

Eurie and Rella were not quite ready to follow Sebastian's suggestion, though they appreciated his attempt to see the more positive possibilities.

For Rella, at this moment, time slowed tremendously. She was not scared, probably because Eurie and Sebastian were with her, but also because Eurie seemed to know so much about this area. And, even if Eurie didn't know something specifically, Rella believed that Eurie would never lead them into danger.

Although it was shaped like a human, the figure wound its way through the high branches and over the trunks of the trees more like a panther.

Eurie and Rella both agreed this creature was not any normal guardian or ward of Hleo.

They looked over at Sebastian, who seemed to have both a human form and was also something like a little tree. They knew all living things in Hleo could transform quickly.

"Sebastian?" Rella asked. "Could that possibly be your sister, Scarlett, up ahead?"

"I don't know. Maybe?" Sebastian replied.

"Could you send a signal to the trees and ask them to give you any more information about who that is?" Eurie asked, knowing Sebastian was only just discovering his new abilities.

"I've been trying to listen, but the signals seem all mixed up here," Sebastian said.

"Yes. I think we might be getting into an area that has been heavily infiltrated by Archimago's Shadowsplitters," Eurie replied.

"Well, we've got to follow that cloak!" Rella said. "If she's Sebastian's sister, then she might be keeping us at a distance on purpose. If not, well..."

Sebastian interrupted her. "I think we should follow her."

Just then, the earth beneath their feet started to rumble and a strong wind swirled around them. Colorful powder, like cooking flour from Earth One, drifted down from the high branches. The three companions huddled together as they waited for the tremors to pass.

When the shaking finally stopped and the silence returned among the leaves, they looked around for any signs of the shadowy figure.

The powder from the trees, luckily, revealed footprints, which allowed them to continue their pursuit.

As they looked around, the girl in the cloak appeared in the branches far up above them. The branches were so wide and tightly interwoven that it was really no different than running on the ground, although there were small gaps where one might slip a foot through.

They continued the chase.

Chapter 26: Samara

MEANWHILE, RELLA'S guardian, Samara, who had assumed her winged form, was eager to make contact. She had so much to explain to Rella about why she chose her. While the typical process was for the children who crossed over to call on their guardians first, for Rella, the calling had happened in reverse.

Samara swooped over the forest, sending a colorful flash of light through the canopy, and hoping to catch a glimpse of the children below. She knew they were on their way to find Menagerie and she wanted to try and get a clear signal to Rella.

When Samara first spotted Rella staring in her direction, from Thalas's back, she didn't believe it. She wanted to be hopeful, but so much was no longer predictable. Entire habitats here in Hleo were rapidly disappearing. New children from Rella's world had stopped coming, and before long, Archimago was going to have this beautiful land turned into a heap of ashes.

"Beautiful destruction," she had heard one of them chanting. "Beautiful disaster."

Any time she heard that phrase, she felt like weeping and her wings seemed to lose strength. But now, with Rella almost in sight, her hope was renewed. She decided to risk exposure and let out the brightest flashes she could summon as she soared over the canopy toward the waterfall.

Rella saw the flash of light coming through the canopy. She began thinking about Samara. But as she approached the banks of The Wondercurrent, her thoughts returned to the rescue mission.

Chapter 27: The Bear in the Tree

"SHE STOPPED AGAIN!" Eurie said.

"Maybe she's finally going to let us catch up?" Rella asked.

"Maybe. It's hard to say. It's still possible she's leading us into a trap," Eurie said.

"Then why are we all following her?" Sebastian asked.

Sebastian had been thinking about his sister and was getting more upset with himself for suggesting that this figure might be Scarlett.

"Maybe she's run into something," Eurie said, not really answering Sebastian's question. "There aren't many other humans from your world left who know how to find this place," Eurie said, "and the ones who might be able to get here, well...."

"Then she's run into someone?" Rella interrupted.

"Likely. But who?" Eurie asked, considering all the possibilities.

"What about Alister, the bear?" Rella asked. "Quinn wrote something about a bear in a tree."

"Yes, Rella. I hadn't thought about him. But I've only met him briefly," Eurie said.

"Well. Quinn seemed to think he would be an important help for me in finding you, but I found you first," Rella said.

Suddenly, the cloaked figure took off at triple speed.

Rella, Sebastian, and Eurie leapt up and tried to start following, but then, it appeared as though the figure was actually moving in two directions. It looked like she had gone one direction and her shadow had run off in another direction.

"Ok," Sebastian shouted, "That's definitely not my sister. She doesn't split herself in half!"

As Sebastian worried more intensely about his sister, the nearby trees started to shake.

"How many are there?" Rella asked, bracing herself against a nearby trunk.

"It's a Shadowsplitter," Eurie said.

"Not one of the Sisters?" Rella asked.

"That thing...the thing we've been following has definitely been sent here by Arch..." Eurie hesitated to even say his name aloud.

One of the nearby trees crashed hard to the ground. Sebastian let out a scream, as though someone had twisted his arm. Rella covered her mouth with both hands and muffled a scream.

Sebastian knocked his wooden fist into his wooden palm and shouted angrily towards the Shadowsplitter that no longer resembled his sister.

"If you've done anything to my sister, you will pay for it!" Sebastian shouted, sending vibrations through the branches of all the nearby trees.

The creature had already slipped out of sight.

"Was it spying on us?" Rella asked.

"Will it hurt us?" Sebastian asked, collecting himself.

"No. I don't think they actually think on their own. They're controlled somehow...I haven't been able to get close enough to see who or what might be directing their movements," Eurie replied.

"Now what?" Rella asked.

"The Shadowsplitter is gone for now," Eurie said, "but the other figure we saw must be Scarlett..." Eurie said, looking at Sebastian, who was still wincing in pain.

"Why do you think the real figure might still be my sister?" Sebastian asked.

"Well, she might have known she was being tracked by the Shadowsplitter," Eurie replied. "That's why she didn't let us get too close," Rella interrupted.

Rella felt something urge her to get out the scroll, so she pulled it out of her satchel and examined the surface.

Eurie and Sebastian watched silently.

At first, no messages appeared. Nothing lit up, no triangles or circles or trapezoids swirled around.

"I can't see anything!" Rella said.

"Keep trying," Eurie whispered.

"I don't even know what I'm looking for?" Rella said.

"Have you tried asking it a question?" Sebastian asked softly.

"I guess I could try that? But what do I ask it?" Rella replied, concentrating on the scroll. She felt a little funny asking the scroll a question, but she had to try something.

"Try it," Eurie said. "You never know until you try?"

"Who was that in front of us? Who were we following?" Rella asked.

For a minute, nothing happened. Rella stared at the scroll and, for just a second, thought she saw something flash across the surface.

"Did you see that?" Rella asked.

Eurie and Sebastian shook their heads from side to side. They hadn't seen anything, but Rella's reaction told them that she most certainly had.

Rella tried again.

"Who are we following? What is in front of us?" Rella asked.

This time, the scroll flashed a combination of shapes and letters in a variety of languages and colors.

"Anything?" Eurie asked.

Rella was so busy trying to translate the information that she didn't hear her friend.

Rella lifted the scroll up in front of her and it became almost transparent. There were lines and arrows indicating a specific path and then the name appeared on the scroll.

"What is it?" Sebastian asked. "I don't see anything!"

"Scarlett!" Rella shouted. "It says that Scarlett was in front of us. And that other thing...it was exactly what you said, Eurie. It was a Shadowsplitter. Scarlett was trying to outrun it...and it seems like we might have confused it...it was definitely tracking her."

"But now," Sebastian said, "it's gone."

Rella tried to wrap her mind around this information and the appearance of the phantom. She knew there were more confrontations to come.

Rella took a deep breath, put the scroll back into her satchel, and picked up a luminous stone from the ground. It was a little dim, but it gave off enough light for Rella to try an experiment.

Eurie and Sebastian continued to watch Rella with absolute wonder. She seemed to be almost in a trance.

She made a small shadow puppet, just to make sure she still had control of her own shadow. She did a few walking-man moves with her fingers. Sebastian walked up next to her to get a closer view of the puppet show.

"What are you doing?" Eurie asked, as she walked towards Rella.

Rella was working out an important idea.

"There's something about the way that light moves and reflects here," Rella said, "and it has something to do with the specific composition of the materials that the light touches."

"I think we should keep moving," Sebastian said. "The trees..."

"Yes," Eurie said. "Should we keep going?"

Rella nodded. She picked up the stone and put it in her pocket.

Before they continued, the three companions looked out at the small, round spheres bobbing down The Wondercurrent. They hadn't even realized that they had reached the banks.

Suddenly, a deep, hollow, beastly growl echoed above them.

Sebastian screamed. Rella jumped. Eurie smiled.

"Who's there?" Rella shouted.

"I think I know!" Eurie replied, suppressing a giggle.

The growling creature sent back a friendly, though still intimidating, grunt in reply.

About fifty feet above the children, the face and head of a gigantic Earth One black bear pushed through the bark in the trunk.

The fur and face were larger than any bear Rella or Sebastian had seen back home.

"I can't...It's...Is it...Hi there!" Rella screamed.

Rella was so awestruck that she could barely get another word out.

Eurie bowed down and offered a formal greeting to the honorable guardian.

"Hail Guardian Bear. I am Eurie, a protector of this land. Do not fear. We are friends."

The bear made another inquisitive and slightly confused moan. It couldn't actually move its head at all, so, if they wanted to look it in the eyes, they would have to climb up into the high limbs.

Rella looked wide-eyed at Eurie.

"Can it talk?" Rella asked.

"The bear?" Eurie replied. "Well...if he's the guardian I think he is, he'll start speaking to us...once he hears our voices."

Eurie explained to Rella that each guardian had a unique way of communicating with their wards, which was the reason she had been sensing those signals from Samara.

Some guardians used traditional spoken word patterns, but many times, the communication was carried out in a combination of vocal patterns created exclusively for the guardian and the ward. The guardian, unless it had previous exposure to Hleo, needed to hear its ward's voice first to begin developing their communication.

While they waited for Alister to speak, Eurie continued on to point out that one of the reasons the guardians and wards developed their special codes was so that impersonators or imposters could easily be identified. Of course, the guardians could also learn to speak with other children if needed, and could shift between communication forms quickly, but the special language between the child and guardian could never actually be duplicated.

"So why did Quinn tell me to talk to Alister then? Is it because Quinn and I are from the same place? Would he already know my language? And how do you know this language I'm speaking right now?" Rella asked.

"Well," Eurie said, "There was another time, or there will be another time when we've already met...let me just say that Quinn was a major help in setting up our meeting."

Rella thought of the strange memories that had flashed through her mind over the last few hours. She hadn't said anything yet, but she was continuing to have flashes of images of walking through this exact forest, only in the flashes a small, blinking blue orb was following her. She kept the image of the orb creature to herself.

"But what about Quinn's language?" Rella asked.

"Quinn speaks a similar tongue to you. The patterns are the same for the most part, but not exact," Eurie said.

"City language, I bet," Rella said.

"City language?" Eurie asked.

"Well, if Quinn is a soldier, like you say, then he has to have come from the military school in Westcon where they train..." Rella said.

"Oh. I see," Eurie said. "So, you speak the same language, but you use different sets of words and patterns?"

"Yes. That makes sense to me," Sebastian said. Because when I heard Rella's voice on my way out of the tunnel, I recognized it as Eastcon, like mine."

"Yes. That's right," Rella said. "I hadn't even thought about asking you what village you were from, Sebastian. Sorry."

Rella turned to Eurie, "We call them dialects, and depending on how we pronounce words, some people from one place might say the people from the other place are speaking with an accent because the sounds are a little different. But really, there is no real standard for the language, so everyone has some kind of accent."

"Ah. But what about when you moved the words in prettier ways, like the winds that vibrate over the water?" Eurie asked.

"You mean singing?" Rella said, puzzled by Eurie's strange question.

"Oh, yes, that's exactly what Quinn called it. Sometimes I forget the simplest words. Yes, what is singing again? Is that a different language or an accent?" Eurie asked.

"Oh. Singing is not an accent, but we do put the words into different patterns to make them rhyme or sound prettier with the notes."

"Notes?" Eurie asked.

They could hear the bear above them taking large, slumberous breaths.

"Is he sleeping?" Rella asked.

"Yes. I think so," Eurie said.

"How do we wake him?" Rella asked.

"Well, you could try to sing some of those really high notes to him," Eurie said.

"Really? Like what?" Rella giggled, picturing herself singing a song to the head of a sleeping bear protruding from the bark of a gigantic tree. She had a small teddy bear at home that she would sing to at times, but she never thought about singing to a full-sized tree-bear.

"Oh. Do you have any wake-up songs? I'm sure he'll love whatever you sing. He just seems to have trouble staying awake."

Sometimes, as it happened, a guardian might not necessarily take on a role because it was perfectly qualified for the job. Really, there were no perfectly qualified guardians at all. The most overlooked animals, the ones pushed aside, were often the ones who were chosen. And, often, those who had the strongest gifts or abilities in one area faced challenges in another area. In Alister's case, one of his challenges was that he struggled to keep himself awake. That should not, however, be held against him.

On the bright side, because he never completely surfaced into Hleo, he also had no belly and never got hungry. But, music, yes, he loved to hear music. He would often travel the Channels just hoping to catch someone singing.

Rella didn't like singing out loud. She loved music and songs, but she couldn't make notes do the kinds of things some kids did. She would try to make the sounds match the other kids at school, but she could never seem to get the notes to come out very loudly. No one ever heard her sing loudly enough to know if she had a pretty voice or not.

"Go on," Eurie said. "Sing something from your world. And then I'll sing something from mine."

"No," Rella said, "I'm not really good at singing."

Sebastian, distracted by something rustling in the bushes below, climbed down out of the tree.

"But I don't even know what good singing is in your world. Everything you say sounds beautiful and fascinating to me, because I had never even heard your language before you and Quinn arrived," Eurie said.

Rella looked at Alister's sleeping face and thought this was as good a time as any to overcome her fear of singing aloud in front of people (or bears) that she had never met. She reached her hand into her satchel and ran her fingers over the scroll. She thought about how they had to defeat Archimago. She had to try, because they had to talk to this bear.

"If it helps," Eurie said, "I can climb down and let you sing by yourself..."

"No," Rella replied, "You don't have to. I just can't seem to remember any tunes. I'm trying, but all I can think of is this silly song I used to sing to my teddy bear to wake him up," Rella said.

"Well, try. You've got to try," Eurie said, smiling and encouraging Rella with her bright, metallic green eyes.

"Well, first I'd cover him with my blanket. Then, I'd stroke his fur a few times. And then, I'd sing:

It's time, it's time, it's time
To gather up your things
Clear the foggies
From your brain
And say farewell
To last night's dreams
It's time, yes time, yes time
To come and join our table
Grab a bowl
And fill it up
with nuts and jam
and flaky rolls
and gobble all you're able

Eurie smiled and clapped. They both then looked at the bear, but he barely twitched his nose.

"Well...I think we're just going to have to wait until he wakes up," Eurie said.

The two girls curled up together and drifted off to sleep while Sebastian rummaged around in the underbrush.

Chapter 28: A Song and a Memory

RELLA, STILL CURLED up with Eurie, opened her eyes. The sky was silver and dark. The air was cool. Eurie was quietly singing to herself. The elegant notes of the song reminded Rella of the sorrow of the Remembrance Day ceremony, but they also soothed her like her mother's fingers running gently through her hair.

Eurie's voice lifted and lowered through a series of notes and patterns and rhythms unlike anything Rella had heard before, including the magnificent songs of the live street performers from the oldest cities of Eastcon.

In one of those cities, when she was traveling with her father, Rella met a man with a violin. He was about the age of Sebastian's father, King, and he played and sang to his violin. He sang to that violin like it was his best friend in the whole world. Some people judged him. Some said he had lost his mind.

Rella visited him every night during the time she and her father were visiting the old city. While her father was in secret meetings for the Alliance, she would slip out of the apartment to go listen to him play and sing.

The man would stand out on the same corner every morning and every night, and he would sing stories about his life, about the history of Earth One, and all that had happened even before

205

her mother's mother's mother was born. He would sing about hopeful times and the sad times.

The violin, Rella found out, had belonged to the man's best friend, a woman. For some reason, she had to leave the old city, and he didn't know when she would return. She left him the violin and said she would return when she was able. She asked him to play it every day out on the corner, so she could hear it and find him. He didn't really understand why she had to go. Even though he was very sad sometimes, he played that violin every single night, to keep her memory alive and with the hope that she would return.

Rella had to leave before she ever found out if this man's best friend had returned, but she believed that she would, as long as he kept playing the song.

Rella imagined that man's music as she listened to Eurie's song.

Rella closed her eyes and took a deep breath as Eurie finished her song. Eurie had not even noticed that Rella was listening.

Next Rella looked across the branch and saw that Alister's gigantic eyelids were opening. They were about the size of a bedroom window.

Rella looked over at Eurie and both girls watched Alister awaken.

But before he could get out a word, Rella let out a thunderous sneeze and almost dropped right off the branch.

"Ahhhhhchoooooooooooooooooooooooooo!"

"Wow! That was the most amazing sneeze I've ever heard!" Eurie exclaimed.

"I don't know what came over me," Rella replied. "There must be something in these trees that is tickling the inside of my—"

Before she could get out another word she sneezed again, even louder. It was so loud it made Sebastian, who was way down below on the ground, jump.

Rella had to grab Eurie's hand to keep her from falling down out of the high branches.

Holding hands, Rella and Eurie faced Alister and looked him directly in his giant sleepy eyes. When they saw the seriousness on his face, they quickly straightened out their own faces and waited for him to speak.

"Quinn...Quinn?" Alister asked.

"He's not here. He's preparing the ship," Eurie answered.

Rella had not heard about this ship yet.

"And who is this little warrior?" Alister smiled at Rella, revealing a massive set of teeth.

"I'm Rella. I come from Ensea, in Eastcon, Earth One. Are you from there? You look like the bears from Earth One...though I've never actually seen an Earth One bear like you in person." Rella was nervous.

"Rella....Rella?" Alister replied, with some confusion. "Can't be...You are too small to be Rella."

"What do you mean? I'm above average for a seven-year-old, thank you very much."

"No...I mean...when we last met." Alister seemed a bit confused.

Eurie interrupted them and tried to direct the discussion back to Quinn and the mission.

Rella, however, had been piecing together the flashes from the dreams she had been having since they left the carved castle. She felt like she was getting closer to solving the mystery of her previous and also future visit to Hleo.

"What do you know about this scroll?" Rella asked. "Have you seen anyone else carrying one?" Rella held up the glassy parchment as high as she could. It was about the size of one of Alister's teeth.

Sebastian, who just appeared on a nearby branch, yelled out: "Wow! A bear!" His wooden eyes nearly popped out of his head. His wooden jaw nearly fell off of his face.

Eurie turned around, smiled at Sebastian, and then put her finger to her lips.

Sebastian put his hand over his mouth.

As Rella put up the scroll, Alister spoke:

"I saw that scroll recently. A tiger was carrying it through here a few days ago. Her name was Menagerie...or was it hours ago, I can't really remember. It was, perhaps, three naps ago, though I don't know how many hours those naps lasted..."

"Yes," Eurie replied. "Did you speak to the tiger...to Menagerie?"

"She looked at me, and we exchanged a brief greeting, enough so I knew she was on a mission from Quinn, but it was clear that Menagerie was very new to this place and that she had not been here more than a few hours. Therefore, she had not learned the ways of communicating with our languages yet."

"What else have you seen in this region of the forest lately? Eurie asked.

Rella and Eurie sat down and listened to Alister explain that he had spotted one of The Sisters, Prisma.

"A few hours after I first met Menagerie, I saw this girl, though she didn't seem quite human, standing along the riverbank. She had trapped something in a shadow net. As I watched the trapped creature struggling to get free, I realized that it was Menagerie. But she was no longer carrying the scroll. Then I heard another boy's voice. This was The Architect. He was discussing how to get Menagerie to calm down and stay in the trap, but then he kept saying he needed to go 'back for something' and that he 'left something at the cave'"

"Did he say anything about a key?" Eurie asked.

"Sorry," Alister replied, "I was getting sleepy by the end of their conversation."

Why is Eurie asking about a key? Rella wondered. *What does a key have to do with the scroll? What kind of key?*

Chapter 29: Quinn and the Shadowsplitter

A SHADOWSPLITTER. Quinn remembered Eurie talking about these malevolent beings created by Archimago and sent to Hleo to be used as part of the plan to rid the land of the guardians. He also remembered overhearing his parents mention something about them once when he was listening outside of their bedroom door. They were discussing something called The Red Notebooks and then his father said something about how it was all still just speculation. *Well*, Quinn thought, *it isn't speculation anymore.*

Quinn had never seen one in person, but he had thought plenty about what he might do if he ever had to fight one, if fight was the right word. He didn't really know if he could defeat one, since they didn't seem to have a material body like he did. However, he knew he would have to outfox it.

As it approached, Quinn could tell that The Shadowsplitter was trying to disorient him, to infiltrate his thoughts. He knew it would be smart to avoid looking directly at it. Just as his mother always told him not to look directly at the sun, because it could damage his eyes, he figured that a similar rule applied when looking into too much darkness.

Yet, he also knew if he tried to go around it, it might lead him exactly where it wanted him to go. He had to work quickly. He had to get to Menagerie. He didn't want her to become the newest captive in Archimago's collection of guardians.

If I go right, it could shift the light and shadows to make me believe I'm going left, or in some other direction altogether, even backwards, Quinn thought. *How do I move if I cannot tell real light or real shadow from false light and false shadow?*

He knew the Shadowsplitter was most likely there to stall him, but The Sisters and The Architect couldn't possibly know he would be in this exact spot. The Shadowsplitter, Quinn reasoned, must have been sent to find someone else.

Quinn thought it over some more and continued watching the figure split apart, come back together, and then stretch itself all around the leaves and branches, always remaining dark, but also reflecting some of the color of nearby objects.

Quinn thought it was like watching thin clouds passing over a moonlit sky back home in Westcon. He would often sit up in the Oakmod tree that grew up through the middle of the two-hundred story apartment building. Quinn loved sitting in the branches of that lone gigantic tree in the courtyard. He thought, for a few moments, about that day he saw the writing on the bark slate as he fell from the branches, and somehow, mysteriously ended up here. He still had the bark piece with the script in his pocket. He tapped it for good luck and then realized he might be able to use it to help him work his way around the Shadowsplitter.

He pulled the bark piece from his pocket, and just as he suspected, it started to glow. It was communicating with the nearby trees. He couldn't tell whether the communication was some kind of radio or electromagnetic signal or something that belonged exclusively to the special physics of Hleo.

Quinn looked at the bark. It continued to blink and light up. There were small explosions of light and color and then more sporadic blinking. When it stopped blinking, he put the bark back into his pocket and slid down out of the branches. He peeled another loose piece of bark from around the base of the tree.

He was in luck. A pattern of signals had recently been recorded. He placed his hand on a giant root and thanked the trees, and Hleo, for the help.

Quinn looked at the shapes in the bark and noticed they were giving him some kind of equation to calculate distance, though there was no time to for calculations of this complexity. Even if he could devise a functional calculator to process Hleo's mathematical structures, its multidimensional shapes and gravitation was always, he thought, always in flux.

Even though the light was changing, Quinn knew he might be able to verify his direction by measuring distance. But variations in light, especially to the degree that this Shadowsplitter was playing with the light, could also skew his perception of the distance. He looked over the equations again. The script on the freshly peeled bark continued to swirl and rearrange itself.

After a few more seconds, the flickering of the lights stopped. The Shadowsplitter up above thinned out and stretched across the space in front of him, turning itself into a wall.

Quinn tried to look beyond the wall of shadow in front of him, but he couldn't move at all. He looked down at the bark in his hand and read a new message. This time, no calculations were needed. The solution was right in front of him.

Chapter 30: Rella and the Shadowsplitter

RELLA TRIED TO REMEMBER if The Architect had spotted her when she first arrived. She couldn't recall if there were any signs in The Architect's movements or facial expressions that would prove that he knew she was watching him. *Were there other ways that he might have sensed my presence?* she wondered.

She could not stop thinking about the Shadowsplitters. No, thinking was not the right word. It was more like the Shadowsplitter had stirred something inside of her. It felt like seeing, looked like feeling, and sounded like memory, if memory was only sound and nothing more.

Watching this creature come apart and move was unlike anything she had seen, even in the horror movies and the scientific documentaries her uncle obsessed over and watched constantly. To understand what was happening, you'd have to imagine that Earth One had become a two-dimensional space, and the Shadowsplitter was a three-dimensional object. He was like a drawing that was ripping through or leaping off of a flat sheet of paper.

Rella often tried to draw objects in a way that made them look like they were leaping off of a page too, but to watch the Shadowsplitter move through the space in front of her was far more intense than she had imagined. Suddenly, she felt much, much older than seven.

The name Shadowsplitter, Rella thought, was not quite an accurate translation. She knew Quinn and Eurie had come up with that word together, using the only language they mutually understood, but Rella thought there was something much more complicated than just splitting its material form away from its shadow form. This thing was rearranging light and space itself so that shadows no longer revealed the positions of the things around them.

But how will I explain this to Eurie? Rella thought. *Will Eurie understand this?* Rella felt like she only really understood this because the scroll had somehow unlocked it for her. If they could somehow catch up to that thing, perhaps Rella could make better sense of it.

She knew that hoping to encounter the Shadowsplitter again was probably not something to hope for. She could hear her mother's warning voice loud and clear: "Be careful what you wish for, or you just might..."

"Get it...," Alister growled, pulling Rella out of her deep trance. They were still up in the branches.

"Rella," Eurie said, "did you get it?"

"Get what?" Rella asked, trying to focus back on Eurie and the Bear.

"Did you get the brush Quinn left with the scroll?" Eurie asked.

"A brush? No. What did it look like?" Rella asked.

"Well, Alister and I have been discussing every detail of the interaction he had with Menagerie, and he thinks he might have seen a brush, something like what you, in your English language, call a paintbrush, tied around her neck. Alister and I thought that it might be possible that Quinn may have left a brush...for something."

"Or," Alister interrupted, "that this brush has something even more important to do with Menagerie's role as a guardian."

"I'm sure," Rella answered, "that when I awoke surrounded by the blue light of the cave, the scroll was rolled up and...oh, wait, the string...the string wasn't actually wrapped around the scroll. I found it lying next to it... but no, there was no paintbrush on it."

"Is it possible," Eurie asked, "that the paintbrush could have been lying nearby...but with all the flying debris and the ground shaking, you might not have seen it...or you didn't realize what it was?"

Rella tried to concentrate on every detail of that moment when she surfaced in Hleo, but she could not remember the paintbrush. She continued to picture The Architect's dreadful eyes, and she remembered his cloak swirling in the wind as he exited the cave.

He *was* carrying a small object. It glinted for a brief moment. She thought that flicker of light was strange. The Architect, however, hadn't seemed to notice the glint.

As Rella thought more about it, it seemed like she might have been the one who caused the object to glint, like it recognized her presence, sort of the way a book cover sometimes did that to her back on Earth One. She would peruse her parents' library, and then she would find a book staring right at her. She had never seen the book before, but she knew that it was exactly the book she was supposed to read.

Now, though, the stakes were much higher, because this glinting object, possibly a brush, may very well have the power to stop the destruction of not only a single book, but countless books, dreams, and entire lives.

Eurie read the grave expression on Rella's face and asked Rella to share what she was thinking, even though she already knew the awful news.

"The Architect found it, didn't he?" Eurie asked.

"I think so," Rella quietly replied, her stomach bubbling up with fear.

"But what could it be used for?" Eurie asked, not sounding as dreadful as Rella thought she should have. Eurie's confidence comforted Rella. If Eurie was not too worried, then Rella would not be either.

"There are a few possibilities," Alister interrupted, speaking slowly and sleepily, but trying to concentrate despite his tiredness.

"Yes?" Eurie and Rella replied together. Eurie was holding Rella's hand again to comfort her.

Rella looked down at the scroll peeking out of her satchel, released Eurie's hand, and unrolled it. She checked it over again for any new messages. As she scanned the shapes and vectors, shaded areas, and various circles and triangles that had appeared on the scroll, she noticed something new.

Reading the surprise on Rella's face, Eurie said: "At first, I thought these were blueprints for...oh, I don't know, for a ship he was working on, one he might use to attack Hleo from the across The Dark Waters...but somehow, I guessed, they were written in a code that only people from Earth One, like you and Quinn, could read."

"But Quinn didn't know what the drawings were meant for," Rella said, examining the exact words on the note again: *Dear Rella: Whatever you do, don't let The Architect find these blueprints— if they are blueprints? Let me know, will you? He's going to be looking for you.*

Eurie repeated the lines from the letter. "The line 'Let me know, will you?'...yes, it's pretty clear Quinn thinks you alone will be able to tell us all what they are."

A new thought formed in the back of Rella's mind, like puzzle pieces moving slowly together. She thought again of the Shadowsplitter, of her parents' library, and of The Architect. But she really could not say that she understood this scroll as any type of blueprint for a cathedral of evil, or a warship, or a city—where books and beauty would be eternally banned.

And then her mind shifted over to the light emitted from Samara's wings. The more she thought about the luminous glint on that brush in The Architect's hand, she felt certain that it was all connected.

Chapter 31: The Architect and the Paintbrush

AFTER LEAVING PRISMA to wrangle the tiger, The Architect returned to the cave below the falls. Draped in his silver cape, he searched frantically through the rubble outside of the cave. He noticed a few of the girl's footprints, but he couldn't be certain whether she had been crushed by an avalanche or had escaped. He didn't seem too worried about being crushed himself, in the event that another set of quakes occurred. But that was because his silver cape was made from a material fabricated on Archimago's island. The metallic material was stronger than titanium, though it moved like soft leather. Archimago had given him the cape as a reward for all the devastation he had already accomplished since joining the mission.

He leaned over and picked up the paintbrush. He then tied it to a string and put it around his neck. As he fastened the loop, he noticed something spectacular about the transparent bristles. Each thin bristle glowed a different color, and there were thousands of them. When he tried to touch them, they created a strange sensation in his bony fingers. It felt like a pair of cold teeth gnawing on the bones in his hand. He quickly ripped the string from his neck and threw the paintbrush to the ground. As it hit the ground, it continued to glow but also started sinking into the white soil.

Terrified to touch it, The Architect grabbed the sword with the red jeweled handle, which he'd been using to sift through the rocks, and tried to pick up the brush. He now treated it as though it was some kind of infected or poisonous bug. As he dug the tip of the sword into the soil, the brush started cutting through the soil and heading toward The Wondercurrent.

A tug of war ensued between The Architect and The Wondercurrent. There was really no way The Architect could have overpowered The Wondercurrent, so another force must have been working nearby.

After a few minutes of struggle, The Architect knew he was not going to win this fight without some reinforcements. *Someone, much stronger than Archimago, is trying to get this paintbrush back*, he thought.

He lifted the sword into the air and, from the tip, launched a sequence of signals into the dark, silver sky. He didn't understand completely how Archimago's sword worked. But he really wasn't sure if he wanted to know either.

Chapter 32: Eurie Departs and Rella Investigates the Scroll

"DID YOU SEE THAT?" Rella asked, as they stood up in the branches above Alister's head to figure out the distance they still had to travel to reach Mena.

"Yes. At the falls by the cave," Eurie said. "That's got to be The Architect. I've seen that signal before...it's the sword."

"So he did travel back up looking for the scroll?" Rella asked.

"I don't know...but he's in trouble," Eurie said.

"What do you think is happening?" Rella asked.

"Well, I've only seen the signal when he was capturing a guardian and needed back up...."

They watched the flares dissolve into the mists like dying stars.

"We've got to split up," Eurie said. "He could also be trying to lure us into a trap. There's also a chance he might have that paintbrush, and we've got to get it back."

"Can you tell me more about this paintbrush? What do you mean?" Rella replied. "Shouldn't we be trying to avoid The Architect?"

"I'm sorry, Rella, but Sebastian and Alister will be with you. I have to go..." Eurie said.

"So what do I do?" Rella said. "You can't leave me. What if I...?"

"Sebastian will stay close by," Eurie said, looking around. Sebastian had wandered into a thicket of thorns and branches and was now out of sight.

"Sebastian!" the girls shouted together. "Sebastian! Where are you?"

"Over here!" he yelled as he crawled out from between the branches.

"Please don't wander off like that," Eurie said.

"Sorry. I thought I saw something," Sebastian said.

"What was it?" Rella asked.

"It sort of looked like a blue blob...well, more like a ball, I guess, than a blob...but it rolled away," Sebastian said, frowning like a sad puppy.

Rella felt like she should recognize what he was describing. Like it was something she should have seen and been able to describe herself. Another lost memory she couldn't quite bring back.

"It might be best to leave it alone, whatever it was," Eurie said, turning back to Rella.

"It's okay," Rella said, tearing up but looking directly into Eurie's eyes with her father's confidence. "I understand. I'll stay here with Sebastian and Alister."

"One more thing," Eurie explained, "As you may have realized, Alister can't fully surface from the tree to protect you, but he can roar loud enough to rattle the brains out of any living thing. Trust me, I've heard the roar."

"Yes," Alister interrupted, "but my roar is also guaranteed to give away our location, so I would have to retreat back into the Channels if *they* came after me." Alister growled at the thought of Archimago and his servants.

Eurie assured Rella that she would return soon. Rella desperately wanted to go along with Eurie, but she understood. Eurie didn't want to put her in danger before she was ready.

Rella's mother often had the same approach when she was teaching Rella something new, like swimming or bike riding. She could remember her mother's voice exactly: "When you're ready, Rella. There's no hurry. I will wait."

Rella unrolled the scroll and looked it over. If this scroll is so powerful, she thought, maybe it can get a message to other people out there...or in here.

"Mom!" she whispered, as she stared at the colorful, pulsing images on the scroll, "Are you there? Is dad with you?"

Sebastian continued wandering around at the base of the tree, trying to find the little blue blob. He even started calling for it, like it was a pet. "Come here, blobby, blobby...come here, boy."

Rella, seated up on a wide branch, unrolled the scroll and examined the images, all while trying not to think about the kind of danger Eurie was heading into. Ever since she saw the Shadowsplitter, she felt a bit strange, especially when she looked into shadowy spaces, like the branches laced together right below her.

She looked into the space above her, right over Alister's head. It was almost like the shadows were the clear things and the colored and textured objects around her were blurry, or at least no more vivid or detailed than the empty space.

She wondered if this was how some people who had to wear glasses felt sometimes. She remembered seeing pictures of people with glasses in old photos in the books. Of course, the bioengineers in Westcon had nearly eradicated the need for glasses in her world. Everyone could have that revised with gene editing before birth, or treated with implants, medications, and surgeries quickly afterward. Every once in a while, a person with glasses might be seen walking around a rural village in Eastcon. Never in Westcon.

As she looked at the map, she also started reimagining the various intersecting lines, colors, and geometric shapes in relation to the possible movement of lights and shadows. And then, certain angles she had never seen before appeared. She remembered a book of optical illusions her dad kept on a shelf in the secret library. She would press her nose into the picture and slowly pull it away to reveal a three-dimensional image of a chair or a bird in flight.

With these drawings, however, she did not seem to need to press her nose into it or pull it away. The images just seemed to change as she shifted her thoughts from color and lines to imagining what was hidden behind these shapes or what kinds of shadows these shapes might cast if they were meant to represent real objects, like trees or hills or mountains.

She pressed her finger into the purplish sphere in the upper left corner of the page. As she ran her palm across the page, the sphere suddenly appeared on the back of her hand, like someone was projecting this image onto the paper from above.

She stopped for a moment and looked back up over her shoulder. Her heart fluttered. She continued to concentrate on the image and ran her fingers along a slanted line that was floating in midair above the surface of the scroll. The line connected the purple sphere to a slightly smaller triangle. The triangle was outlined in yellow and colored in with green.

This time, unlike when Sebastian surfaced, the line hardened and she could almost wrap her fingers around it, like the shaft of an arrow. Though, when she tried to actually lift it or move it, it didn't budge, and her hand simply dropped back into the scroll's surface.

She continued trying to use her hands to manipulate the shapes and lines in different ways. She could push certain shapes around a little, to peak behind them, but they always moved back to their spots before dissolving back into the flat plane of the page. She wanted to stick her nose into it, to see if it had a smell or a taste, but she did not want to get sucked into the picture either. She had seen that happen enough in old movies. Plus, she had already had a difficult enough experience adjusting to this new world.

Rella had read enough of the forbidden books to know how children could easily fall into and through pictures, and she was not interested in that kind of journey right now. She rolled the scroll back up and tucked it back into the satchel. Her heart continued pounding and fluttering with shock at what the picture had enabled her to do and see.

She hadn't stopped worrying about Eurie either. Because her head was too crowded with other things, she spoke her thoughts: "If I can climb to the branches above Alister's big sleepy head, I might be able to get a glimpse of the washout around the waterfall."

Next, Rella started climbing through the shadows with cautious awareness. She spoke aloud again: "Who knows what other beings or creatures might be trying to track me." She looked around.

As she reached the top, the sparkling waterfall appeared in the distance. However, she could not see what was happening at the bottom, where she knew Eurie was headed to try and track down The Architect.

As she stared at the rushing falls, watching the glowing, colorful orbs drop down over the crest and down through the curtains of liquid, she spotted the wings drifting back and forth, like a child's hands weaving gently and carelessly through the air. They were the exact ones she had been sketching in the car. And for the first time in a while, she thought about her Uncle J.

Chapter 33: Scarlett and Prisma

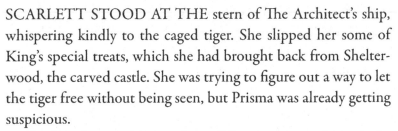

SCARLETT STOOD AT THE stern of The Architect's ship, whispering kindly to the caged tiger. She slipped her some of King's special treats, which she had brought back from Shelterwood, the carved castle. She was trying to figure out a way to let the tiger free without being seen, but Prisma was already getting suspicious.

"Where have you been...Sister?" Prisma spat as she poked a jagged stick into Menagerie's cage.

"Just looking for berries, fruits, gifts to bring back...for him, for our master," Scarlett said, trying to divert the conversation away from herself and back to their mission.

"Yes. I think he's going to be the most pleased with me though," Prisma said, looking through the cage at Menagerie and hissing at her again. "I've captured the biggest prize of all."

Prisma hissed at Menagerie and rattled the stick against the cage.

Scarlett could feel her insides boiling. She didn't want to get into another pointless squabble with Prisma. Archimago, she knew, wouldn't care what either of them brought back. He didn't really care for anyone. But he did demand that his servants complete their missions thoroughly. And, the mission this time was to release the Shadowsplitters, destroy The Wondercurrent, and retrieve his lost scroll.

Scarlett still couldn't believe The Architect had talked her into stealing it and helping him smuggle it off of the island. *What was he planning anyway?* she wondered. Of course, The Architect had always been kinder to her than anyone else, and she could sense that there was something different about him, despite his flawless execution of so many of Archimago's plans.

Scarlett always took his precision as a sign of loyalty. *Perhaps I was wrong,* Scarlett thought. *Perhaps there's something I don't know about him. After all, haven't I been hiding my real identity? Could he, too, be a spy of another kind? Did he have someone to protect, like she had to protect Sebastian?*

Scarlett needed to stall Prisma. She had to give Eurie and Rella, and hopefully her brother Sebastian, a chance to make it to the bay before Prisma and The Architect unleashed the Shadowsplitters.

Chapter 34: Samara

SAMARA...MY GUARDIAN, Rella thought, as she peered through the leaves and across the quilt of green, orange, and blue treetops out in front of her. *She's hiding right inside of that waterfall.* Rella didn't know if Samara was visible to anyone else at that moment. If she hadn't studied the wings so closely herself earlier, and if Eurie hadn't pointed them out, Rella wouldn't have seen any outlines. It was like the trick with the book of optical illusions again. She had to concentrate in a certain way, like sliding a delicate switch in her mind. Only then would she be able to see the hiddenness of things in the landscapes and beneath the water: the scroll in her hands suddenly felt much, much heavier.

Rella watched the majestic wings flutter beneath the sparkling water. Though she knew it was much too far away to catch Samara's eyes, she still tried to signal to her by waving both hands above her head.

At this distance, for any creature with typical, Earth One vision, Rella knew she would seem no bigger than a mouse. But here in Hleo, everything seemed possible.

Rella continued to watch the wings move slowly in the current. It seemed that her guardian's attention was fully focused on something happening below the falls. As she watched the wings, Rella felt waves of warmth and then ice coursing through her chest and stomach. She knew her guardian was working to help her, even at that moment, even from across this great expanse.

Rella remembered how her mother would often tell her that nearness wasn't always an issue of physical distance. Being close, and sensing each other's concern, was a matter of concentration. Her mother would tell her that, if she was missing her touch, she just needed to quiet her mind and meditate on the most beautiful thoughts she could find.

Rella closed her eyes and took a deep breath. She tried her very best to listen and imagine.

Sebastian, meanwhile, continued leaping around in the underbrush, searching for the blue orb.

Chapter 35: Sebastian's Risk

"MR. ALISTER?" SEBASTIAN asked.

"What is it little wooden human?" Alister replied, lethargically.

"Do you remember seeing me in there?" Sebastian asked.

"I'm not sure. What do you mean?" Alister asked.

"Before I surfaced, when I was trapped in the Channels...I saw flashes...images of children and animals from Earth One and maybe elsewhere passing by me...and I was wondering if, maybe, you were one of the ones I saw?" Sebastian asked.

The Channels, to Sebastian, felt like being stuck at the top of the inside of a large pipe, except there was no gravitational force pulling him down. You might think of it as being inside of a plane in the exosphere, the outer edges of the sky of Earth One, or any earthlike planet, where gravity is extremely weak.

"Let me think about it," Alister said, closing his eyes. Sebastian laughed aloud as he watched the bear's face scrunching and twisting. He had forgotten that his own wooden face probably looked just as funny as it moved around.

"You know," Sebastian said to the bear, "I know how lonely it can feel in there. How long ago did you first try to surface?"

Alister opened his eyes. He couldn't recall ever seeing Sebastian in the Channels.

"I've tried to surface here for a while...," he replied, "not sure how long...but I can move around from place to place as needed."

"Are you only able to move through the Channels connected to the roots and the trees?" Sebastian asked.

"Yes, that's all I've been able to channel into. Why?" Alister asked.

"Well, I had this thought. You see...I think I might have a way to try and get you out."

Alister's eyes widened and he listened intently as Sebastian explained how Rella had helped him cross into the world.

"First," Sebastian said, "she started reading from her scroll. I don't know if she was actually reading aloud, but her thoughts or her voice created a vibration...and I was able to grab onto that vibration like a rope. It was so strange, but, as long as she was reading the scroll, I could hold onto the rope...and, then, I was pulled through into a bed...in a room in the castle. And my father greeted me. And Rella was there..."

"What happened next?" Alister asked, eager to know more.

"Pretty soon, I started getting these sensations...a little like the rope-sensation I got from Rella...but I also realized I could send messages back through the forest...and I was communicating..."

"With the trees?" Alister said, finishing Sebastian's sentence.

"Yes. I think that I could help you...my father and I...we could help you get through too. I know it!" Sebastian said.

"Well," Alister said. "It would be nice to not have to pop in and out of trees...to feel my legs beneath me again...but I'm really not much in control of where I end up when I move from one tree to another...and there are hundreds of thousands of trees here...How will I find one close enough to the castle for you to help me?"

"You might have noticed something about me," Sebastian said.

"Yes. You seem to have a different kind of fur...hide...I mean, skin, no?"

"I'm completely made of wood!" Sebastian said.

"Oh..yes. That's it," Alister replied, laughing.

"I'm not ordinary wood though. I'm Hleo-wood, I think."

"I see. And what exactly does that mean?"

"This might sound looney, but I think I might be able to let you, in a way, ride somewhere on...in...this little area here...on my back, maybe my shoulder?" Sebastian reached his hand behind his back and pointed to the area below his shoulder, known in a human body as the scapula.

"But, well...you are wood, but you're not actually a tree," Alister said.

"Not exactly a tree, no," Sebastian replied. "However, when I plant my toes down into the soil...I am connected to the Channels."

"So, you want me to transport myself onto your back?" Alister asked, laughing. "I'm a bit large, no?" Alister thought it sounded a little risky, but he really wanted to be able to surface into Hleo, to feel his legs and his body move on their own, and to eat a meal, or maybe three, or four.

"It's fine. I think your size is dependent on where you channel. Please...try it!" Sebastian said, as he dug the tips of his toes into the surface of the soil. "I'm ready!"

As Alister's massive muzzle retreated back below the surface of the bark, Sebastian planted his wooden feet further into the soft ground, burying himself to his ankles.

With his eyes shut tight, like a child waiting for a vaccine, he waited for Alister to pop into and out of his shoulder.

As Alister retreated back beneath the bark of the tree, the tree shook violently. The tremors disrupted Rella's deep meditation. Rella woke, disoriented, and had no idea what Alister and Sebastian were trying to do.

Her tongue felt dry and she was suddenly craving more of the blue elixir, which Eurie had left for her in a small, glass bottle with a red cork plugging the top.

She pulled the bottle out of her satchel. As she prepared to drink it, Alister roared so forcefully it nearly knocked her off of the branch. She dropped the small bottle and watched it descend and bounce with a clink...clink...clink...from branch to branch, almost hitting Sebastian on his round, wooden head.

To Rella, it appeared that Sebastian had merely fallen asleep at the base of the tree. She didn't realize that Sebastian was in the process of channeling to bring Alister directly onto the surface of his scapula for transport.

When Sebastian started moving, the roaring stopped. The forest grew quiet.

Rella quickly climbed down out of the tree and let out a blood curdling scream. At the sight of Alister's now tiny head emerging from Sebastian's back, like a three-dimensional tattoo, she fainted.

Chapter 36: Experimental Chemistry

EURIE SCRAMBLED TO her feet from behind the rubble and spotted The Architect. She thought he would be older. He looked famished and a bit pale.

The Architect was using the tip of the blade to pin something in place on the surface of the soil. The way he held the object in place without pressing down too hard showed Eurie that he knew the risk of pushing anything too far into the soil. Though Eurie had not recently tested any samples of The Wondercurrent lately, she remembered one element that she could use to create a diversion. If she could just catch one of the yellow glowing orbs, she might be able to get away.

Eurie knew she didn't have much time because The Architect had already sent his signals out, most likely to the Shadowsplitters.

She knew she could not allow The Architect to keep whatever he was pinning down in the soil, especially if it was some kind of animal. Hleo's minks were some of her favorite critters, though she rarely saw them. Unlike the animal guardians, who passed in and out of Hleo, certain species had settled permanently, most likely because their habitats back on their home planets had been destroyed. Eurie always felt a kinship with these creatures because she too was permanently bound to this place. *Oh, if he's hurting one of those minks, he's going to regret it!* she thought.

Eurie knew she would have to move unseen to the bank of The Wondercurrent and scoop up one of the orbs. She had only recently tested reactions with the yellow and red ones, and the red ones did not seem to respond to any type of prodding. The yellow, however, shot off flashes that had the potential to temporarily blind most sighted creatures. She was still unsure of whether these flashes were a sign of distress from the yellow orbs, or if they were simply playfully chatting with her. When she prodded a bright yellow one she had scooped out of the river a few weeks ago, it didn't seem to have suffered any shock or degeneration after being triggered. It just shut off after a few minutes. Hopefully, this would be the case this time. She didn't want to risk hurting any part of Hleo's intricate ecosystem.

Eurie traced a route with her eyes. It reminded her of one of the stories she had quickly scanned while she was at the carved castle. The story was called "El jardín de senderos que se bifurcan," which Rella translated for her as "The Garden of Forking Paths." She didn't have time to read it all, but it made her think of a labyrinth in a garden with unlimited possibilities for exploration and discovery. As she mapped her route between the underbrush, the boulders and fallen limbs, she thought of the forking paths.

She planned to follow this route to sneak as close to The Architect as she could before rolling the yellow orb directly at him. Then, she would set it off at just the right moment to shock and confuse him. This would let her rescue whatever he was awkwardly pinning down with that terrifying-looking sword.

As she crept toward The Wondercurrent, watching his cloaked back all the way, she was surprised at how still and statue-like he seemed to be. The more she studied him, she thought he might actually be frozen in place, temporarily stunned or magnetized by something in the area. She had to be careful that the forces didn't lock her in place as well.

She waited beside the bank of The Wondercurrent for about two minutes before a yellow orb blinked within arm's reach. She leaned over the ledge and reached down into the dry liquid to pick it up. The liquid dropped off of her hands with no trace of actual moisture.

On Earth One, people might say it just evaporated, but, in Hleo, nothing evaporated. The drops thickened and hardened as they mixed with the soil or merged with the mists in the air.

As she pulled the orb out of The Wondercurrent, it immediately stopped blinking, like a toy whose batteries had just run out.

She could hear the pounding in her chest, but almost no other sound. She pulled a small vial from inside of her belt and poured a pasty liquid into her hands. She rubbed her fingers together, closed her eyes, and wiped the liquid over her eyelids and around her eye sockets. The paste, which she had created from a combination of flower and stone extracts, would protect her eyes from the flashes. It didn't last long, but it was strong enough to prevent the blindness from an exploding orb.

Suddenly, the branches over Eurie's head began to rustle and snap. She looked up and examined the gaps between the limbs, but saw nothing but crossed limbs. Seeing nothing, though, didn't mean something wasn't snaking its way through the branches, waiting to strike. Did it see her though?

She fixed her eyes on The Architect's cloak. He was about thirty yards away. He was no longer a statue, though he still pinned the sword firmly against the ground.

The snapping in the branches increased and became more rhythmic, like rain on a tin roof. A dark string of light twisted through the trees above, thickening itself by pulling the colors off of the surface of the leaves.

Eurie was so focused on The Architect, she didn't see the Shadowsplitter weaving into the space above her.

"Now I've got you!" she yelled, as she sprinted towards him with the yellow orb. She threw it as hard as she could in his direction.

The orb flickered off of the blade of the sword and The Architect took his concentration off of the half-buried paintbrush. As he lifted the sword, the brush continued to slip down into the soil and quickly disappeared. As the orb rolled back towards the water, it flashed more erratically than Eurie had anticipated.

The Architect crouched down and covered himself with the cloak, counting on it to protect him from whatever powers were now closing in around him.

The flashing orb triggered a tremendous earthquake along the banks of the water. The mountains trembled, sending three massive boulders rolling down the edge of the waterfall and directly at The Architect, who was still encased in the cloak. The jewel on the hilt of the sword gave off a red glow inside of the cloak that shined through its thick material.

He remained crouched and covered, but he could no longer control his mind.

Archimago had channeled in.

Through the film of the eye-paint, Eurie caught a brief glimpse of the glowing paintbrush. The Architect lifted the sword and allowed the brush to sink into the soil. She had seen the soil take things many times before. Sometimes those things returned other places in the land, and sometimes they never reappeared. *Hadn't King mentioned something about a paintbrush back at Shelterwood Castle?* Eurie wondered.

As the lights continued to flash, the Shadowsplitter that had woven itself through the leaves of the nearby trees was now floating behind her, waiting to strike.

Amidst the flashing lights, the shape-shifting figure had divided rapidly into a multitude of colorful shapes, like a stained-glass window shattering in the updraft of a tornado. The orb-light was also now expanding and breaking into pieces, and piercing directly into the luminous chards of the Shadowsplitter.

Eurie had never considered the orbs as potential weapons, but, she wondered, *would the power of the light actually keep this dark material from closing around me and stealing my color? And, if it is stolen, what would happen to me? Will I become invisible? Will I die?*

Eurie knew the flashes interfering with the Shadowsplitter would stop soon and that her protective paste was wearing off. She had only a few options: head back to The Wondercurrent and try to find some debris she could use as a getaway raft, or head into the caves. There was no guarantee of a tunnel that would lead her back out of the caves, which meant she could easily be trapped in. Falling into The Wondercurrent was also a major risk. If she stayed submerged too long, she could run the risk of being permanently caught in someone else's dream or even another world with no way to return to Hleo.

She ran for the cave.

As she ran, Eurie glanced back at The Architect. The flashing lights slowed down and The Architect, now uncovered, looked skyward, trying to focus his eyes on the terrifying chards of color and shadow swarming above and around him. The broken pieces of the Shadowsplitter seemed to be trying to attach themselves to him while other pieces tried to reassemble themselves back into a singular form.

The Architect made several attempts to swing his sword through the pieces of shadow, but he failed to hit any of them. Eurie, now standing at the entrance to the cave, felt unexpected sympathy for this boy. He was clearly incapable of wielding the sword. In fact, he seemed just as terrified of the sword as he was of the shadows.

He's being controlled! Eurie realized.

He glanced back in her direction. He looked helpless. An unexpected desire overwhelmed her. She felt compelled to help him like she would a friend or even a brother.

But she couldn't possibly want to help *him*. He was a part of Archimago's destructive clan, and he deserved whatever pain or punishment befell him.

As Eurie entered the cave, a force, like a pair of gigantic, invisible hands, pulled her back. She could not let this thin, pale boy continue to suffer. She rushed back toward the river and grabbed another yellow orb, hoping to finish off whatever pieces of the dying Shadowsplitter were still swarming, bat-like, around The Architect's body.

She hurled the orb directly at the ground in front of The Architect's boots and it flashed again, dissolving the colored pieces around him into a stream of steam.

Without turning back around to see if The Architect had survived the explosion, she rushed deep into the cave. Eurie didn't know how deep the tunnels in the cave might go, but if she stayed out in the open, she knew she would be far too vulnerable to any other evil thing that might be on its way toward the falls.

Chapter 37: The Finger Trap

THE FINAL FLASH DIED down and The Architect lifted himself back up onto his knees. The red light on the sword had stopped glowing. He had now regained control of his own thoughts. He immediately tried to find the paintbrush, but it had vanished.

The further he tried to dig down into the soil, the tighter it griped his fingers. It reminded him of a finger-trap toy he had once owned as a small boy. He couldn't remember who had given it to him, but the memory of the pressure on his fingers as he tried to pull them out was still vivid.

Behind him, spread over the ground, was the fractured outline of the Shadowsplitter. He thought of a cracked piece of ice he'd seen in a puddle on Archimago's island, back when he was first captured, before he assumed his position as The Architect, before he'd lost his name.

The Architect had never seen a Shadowsplitter destroyed before. He did not really know they could be destroyed. Archimago had not given any written explanations about where they had come from, how they were created, or how he had come to control them.

As the nearby trees and rocks settled, The Architect peered up at the falls and down into The Wondercurrent. The colored orbs flickered as far down as he could see. As they passed over and under each other, their lights would mingle and then separate. Part of him wanted to dive in and see how far down he could swim. He even hoped that, somehow, he might find some kind of city or world hidden beneath. He wanted to escape.

Now that he no longer had that paintbrush, The Architect knew he would not have leverage to arrange a peaceful meeting with Rella, Eurie, and Quinn, who needed to know why he had given them the scroll.

He sat down at the base of the waterfall to rest and think. He could have chased the girl, Eurie, into the cave, but he didn't want to get too far from the ship. His eyes grew heavy, so he took off the cloak, rolled it into a pillow and placed it under his head.

As he drifted off to sleep, he kept thinking of the finger trap toy, and, then, the image of a woman appeared before him. She was trying to help him remove the finger trap, but he was too hysterical to let her remove it. He was much younger in the dream. The woman, he remembered, had very mysterious eyes, with a silver sliver along the edge of her pupils. He must have been three or four years old. There was also a girl in the room, about his age. She had braids in her hair and she was lying on the floor, flipping through a Red Notebook that had fallen off of a shelf.

When he woke up, The Architect decided to return to his vessel, to Scarlett and Prisma, and turned his attention back to his master's mission: preparing to open the path into The Wondercurrent.

Prisma was supposed to summon the army of Shadowsplitters at the mouth of the river. They would divide the army in half and begin destroying the trees on each side of the bank until they reached the falls. Once they reached the falls, they would stand guard and capture or destroy any orbs that came over the falls while The Dark Waters flowed up the current.

When Archimago had formulated this plan, however, he didn't know that his miscreations could be destroyed. The Architect, however, couldn't say for sure that what he had just witnessed was actually the destruction of a Shadowsplitter or not, and he didn't want to give any false report back to his master. He had other motives as well.

He decided to proceed with the plan.

Meanwhile, Eurie rushed further into the cave, hoping to find a tunnel that might lead out to a clearing where she could meet up with Thalas. As she twisted and turned through the tunnels, she reached into the top of her shirt and pulled a metallic feather from a string around her neck, squeezing it tightly between her thumb and forefinger. She was summoning. Eurie began to worry. *Will the signal make it through the walls of the cave? Will Thalas find me?*

Eurie had never experienced doubt like this before.

Chapter 38: Reunion

AS QUINN RUSHED THROUGH the underbrush, he looked for signs that Menagerie had passed through the area. At first, he only spotted a few colorless leaves that had fallen from the trees above, which indicated that a Shadowsplitter had likely come through. He scanned the trees for any additional movement, and, then, he spotted one of Menagerie's paw prints. The strange thing was that the paw prints indicated a tense physical struggle. They went in circles, in various directions—and then vanished. Menagerie had clearly been captured, and now Quinn would have to find her.

Suddenly, a familiar, powerful roar echoed nearby. *Alister*, Quinn thought, *Oh, let it be him! Let it be him!* He sprinted like wind towards the sound.

As he reached the bottom of the tree, Quinn found a half-empty bottle of blue elixir. *Eurie?* he thought. *No...oh...It's Rella!*

He looked up in the branches above and saw only the smooth surface of bark. Then, at the base of tree, behind a twisted pile of roots, he saw the feet of a small girl.

She was lying flat on the ground, unconscious. Standing right over her, was a boy who appeared to be made entirely of wood. He had seen many fascinating things in Hleo, and during his brief time as a dream traveler, but he had never imagined meeting a fully proportioned wooden boy. He looked down, ter-rified, at the motionless body of the girl.

It's too late, Quinn thought.

Quinn knew it was too risky to send the scroll to Rella, and now he was regretting it. Now this tiny wooden creature, surely another evil creation of Archimago, had killed Rella.

Quinn reached down to the ground, picked up a sharp stone, held it up over his head, shouting a deadly warning at the wood-en boy.

"Get back! Get away! You will pay for this!"

Sebastian looked at Quinn pleadingly, but Quinn found it difficult to read his emotions. *Was the boy actually asking for help?* Quinn was startled.

Quinn recognized the desperation and took a risk. He knew Archimago's deceivers could easily be made to pretend to care, in order to trick innocent children, but Quinn didn't want to be rash. *The boy could, after all, just be trying to wake Rella*, he thought.

"Can you help us?" the boy shouted. "Please, can you help us?"

Quinn walked carefully over the bed of leaves covering the ground and looked down at Rella. "What happened?" Quinn asked.

A lot of questions about the boy's peculiar appearance popped into Quinn's head, but he had to focus on reviving Rella.

"I think...I hope she just passed out," Sebastian said.

"Why?" Quinn asked.

"Well...." Sebastian wasn't sure how to explain what Rella had seen, so he just turned around, lifted his shirt, and pointed one of his wooden fingers at the figure on his back

Alister appeared and let out a low growl and then smiled and let out a big "Hello there!"

Quinn nearly jumped out of his own skin.

"Alister! But...no...fascinating...but...how?" Quinn wanted to reach out and touch the tiny bear's head protruding from the boy's back.

Alister explained as quickly as he could while Quinn looked down at Rella's motionless body. He felt his heart pound in his throat. No amount of training could have prepared him for this. He knelt down and lowered his head over her mouth to check for breathing. There was a faint breath, but no other motion. They all sat beside her and waited for her to move, to say something.

Quinn asked Sebastian a lot of questions and tried to explain what they were all doing in Hleo: they discussed the mission to rescue the guardians from Archimago's island and the plan to stop The Dark Waters from infiltrating The Wondercurrent.

Sebastian shared that he was on a mission to find his sister, Scarlett, but, before he could get too far into the details, Rella began to move.

First, she wiggled her feet. Then, she lifted her hands in the air.

Quinn immediately grabbed Rella's hands. The touch was familiar, but Rella still couldn't place it. She knew these hands, she had been rescued by them before...in a dream.

She opened her eyes.

"Rella?" Quinn asked.

"Yes!" Rella said.

"Did you...do you have...the scroll?

"Yes. I've got the scroll. But where's Eurie?"

Rella continued looking at Quinn, trying to remember his face, but it didn't seem like the same face from the dream. That was true with Eurie too, though. The dream travelers don't appear quite the same way in the dream as they do when you actually meet them.

Quinn was a few inches taller than Rella and she noted that his posture was superb, like you'd expect of a boy from the military training schools in Westcon.

"I have so, so, so many questions," Rella said, still finding her breath.

"Yes. I know. Me too. I'm so glad you're here!" he replied. "We've got to get moving. We can talk on the way."

"Where are we going?" Sebastian asked.

"Back to my hideout, near the bay where The Wondercurrent opens out into The Dark Waters," Quinn said. "We've got to regroup there."

"But where's Eurie?" Rella asked.

"I was going to ask you that," Quinn replied.

"Well, last I knew, she went back to the cave at the falls," Rella said.

"Why would she do that?" Quinn asked.

"The Architect sent out a signal," Rella replied. "Eurie had to leave to find out what happened to the paintbrush, the one you left with Menagerie?"

"Paintbrush?" he replied. "I didn't leave a paintbrush. What are you talking about?"

"Well...when I found the scroll, I also saw a string lying next to it and then Eurie, no, Alister mentioned something about seeing a paintbrush tied around Mena's neck, but then not seeing it the next time...oh I don't know."

Quinn touched his chest as though searching for something beneath his shirt. It was his guardian's key, a single bear claw.

"Why would Menagerie have a paintbrush?" he wondered aloud.

"That's what we are trying to figure out," Rella said.

Quinn then explained that both he and Eurie had special keys. They weren't actually keys like they used in locks back home, but more like transmitters that would allow them to communicate with their guardians. His key, however, only partially functioned because Alister had never been able to channel all the way into this world, though Alister was his guardian. Eurie's key, a metallic feather, allowed her to communicate with Thalas, when she could actually get her attention. Thalas, though, had a very strong will of her own, and Eurie was still trying to get her to come on command, which she didn't always do.

"So, if the paintbrush wasn't from you, who might have put it on Menagerie's neck? And why?" Rella asked.

Rella thought more about her own guardian. *Is the brush meant for me?* she thought. *Could my guardian have passed it along to Mena so that she would find it? Or there is another child out here and she's lost?*

Rella looked at Quinn and spoke aloud: "Could it have been for me?"

"That's what I'm trying to sort out," Quinn said.

Rella felt more at ease with Quinn now. Even though they had just met in person, it was clear he knew her. Though she didn't remember all the details of the other dreams she had before she arrived, she was starting to remember him. Quinn was a dream traveler, just like Eurie. But he was also from Earth One. They had met many times before.

Quinn was now tracking again, trying to find signs of where Menagerie might have been taken.

"Did you say The Architect was up at the falls?" Quinn asked.

"Yes, we think he went back to look for the scroll. He doesn't know that I have it because I slipped away without him seeing me. So, he might still think the scroll was there," Rella replied.

They stood at the edge of the banks of The Wondercurrent. Quinn looked upstream.

"Did he have a ship?" Quinn asked.

"Yes. It was quite a machine, an ominous machine..." Rella replied. She then described the sharp angles, sleek design, and cage on the back.

"It wasn't just made for traveling on The Wondercurrent, was it?" Sebastian asked.

"Oh no," Quinn replied. "It was created by Archimago to cross The Dark Waters, that mysterious labyrinth of waterways and mists between Archimago's Island and the shore of Hleo." *I would love to have the plans to that ship*, Quinn thought.

They continued walking along the banks, counting the colorful orbs that flicked and spun in The Wondercurrent. Rella could tell Quinn was working out a plan for what they would do when they reached the falls and how they would approach and confront The Architect.

"What can you tell me about the drawings on the scroll?" Quinn asked.

"Oh," Rella said. "Well, I don't know exactly. At first, they seemed to be some kind of diagram or some instructions, but then the shapes seemed to move around, like someone was sending a message. When I looked at them..." Rella paused. She thought she'd heard the sound of an engine.

She continued: "There's more power in these images...something...I really need to show you...." Just as Rella started to pull the scroll from her satchel, the mechanical sound grew louder and she and Quinn knew that it must be the sound of The Architect's ship.

"There it is!" Rella shouted, pointing through an opening in the trees.

Quinn stood in awe, trying to take note of every angle and dimension of the ship.

He also saw, off the back of the ship and trapped in a cage, the shivering body of Menagerie.

"He's got Menagerie!" Quinn said.

"And there's my sister!" Sebastian shouted. "Scarlett!"

Sebastian waved his wooden arms so rapidly they created a rush of wind. Being wooden had not diminished Sebastian's ability to wave his arms like propellers.

"But what about Eurie?" Rella shouted, nearly bursting into tears. "What do we do? We've got to chase him down, now."

"No," Quinn said. "He doesn't have Eurie."

"How do you know?" Rella asked, still panicking.

"Because she's over there, up above those trees!"

Just then, Eurie appeared out of a cloud of white mist riding Thalas. Thalas's metallic feathers clanged as she swooped down as close as possible to the riverbank. With no clear landing space, she had to climb back up through the mist, finally landing in a clearing behind a line of trees on the opposite side of the river.

Boulders, scattered in the river, made a bridge to the other side, which would only require small jumps to get across. Quinn and Rella raced each other to see who could reach Eurie first.

Meanwhile, Sebastian continued trying to get his sister's attention, but he couldn't tell if she had noticed him. For a half second, he thought he saw her looking in his direction.

The expression on her face told him she had seen him and he knew that she was holding back strong emotions. He also saw the other girl, or whatever she was, Prisma, standing on the back of the ship as well.

Rella ran over to Eurie and gave her a big hug, like the ones she gave her parents when they would get home from a long trip away. Quinn, Rella, and Eurie all started talking over each other, trying to fill each other in on everything that had happened.

They quickly devised a plan to get back to the delta, where The Wondercurrent spilled into The Dark Waters. They would need to be cautious of running into any more of Archimago's servants or miscreations, but once they reached the hideout, they would begin their plans to stop the Shadowsplitters.

Sebastian, however, was making other plans to reunite with his sister. Without a word, he sprinted off down the shoreline. The others couldn't have stopped him if they tried.

Thalas swooped in and picked up Eurie, Rella, and Quinn and took them on a flight inland and down toward the shore, as close as possible to the hideout. As they swooped over the quilted canopy of the forest, Eurie explained how she had figured out a way to stop the Shadowsplitters. Quinn discussed the mysterious paintbrush, and the different possibilities for how they might find it, once they rescued Menagerie.

Rella, exhausted, sat in silence.

In a small corner of her heart, Rella began worrying about going back home. Her head still felt wobbly and woozy from all the new information, and she didn't feel ready for any more adventures right now. She really, really just craved more rest. But she knew they were counting on her. So she told herself to keep reaching deep down, and, somehow, the strength would be there when she needed it.

As they landed near the shore and disembarked from Thalas, Quinn and Eurie realized Rella was barely moving, practically sleepwalking.

"You miss your home," Quinn said.

"I do," Rella said. "But the scroll," Rella said. "I have to figure it out...but I don't really know how I did what I did, or even if I could do it again."

"Rella, trust me, and trust Eurie, we know you will fulfill the mission...we've already seen what you can do in your dreams, remember?" Quinn replied.

Rella paused for a minute. Another series of images, from the memory of another dream, flashed into her mind. She seemed older, and she was with Quinn and Eurie in Hleo, and they were all walking away from Shelterwood Castle with a huge crowd of children behind them. They were mostly dressed like children from either Eastcon or Westcon, although there were a few, like Eurie, who seemed to be from an earlier time, and to have made their own clothes from the natural elements of Hleo. The memory was so brief she had no time to consider its meaning. She also thought it might have just been something from a story her mother had read to her once. But it was a hopeful memory.

Rella cherished Quinn's confidence in her, and she knew he was right. She had found a way to bring Sebastian through. If they needed more help, she would find a way to use the scroll to help more children enter or get home.

They all had their eyes on Rella, waiting for her to make a decision.

Rella spoke, "Yes. Something happened...something is happening now...and I can't describe it, but I'm seeing things differently, not just in my mind, but even as I look around... and when I look at these shadows or those lights...I feel things coming sharply into focus...."

"There is timing, Rella," Eurie replied. "Just as you arrived here right on time, you'll return home right on time, and you'll find your family right on time as well."

Rella didn't say anything. She just continued staring at the scroll, now unrolled in her hands, thinking about how they still had to save Menagerie. They just couldn't let The Architect steal her away to that dark and dreary island.

Chapter 39: Sebastian and his Sister

SEBASTIAN CONTINUED tracking The Architect's ship as it sped down the river. He leapt through branches and over boulders ten times faster than he was capable of doing back on Earth One. If he had the choice, he decided he'd rather stay wooden and fast than go back to being slow. The ship, it seemed, wasn't rushing toward the bay, so Sebastian was easily able to get ahead of it. *But how can I get Scarlett's attention without putting myself at risk?* he thought. *What would she do?* And then he remembered. *She would use the knocking code.*

He hadn't used it in a while, but he knew it would get Scarlett's attention. As the ship approached, he let out a series of rhythmic knocks by tapping his fists together. He knew that the other girl on the ship, Prisma, and The Architect, might hear him, but he also worked out a way to set a trap for them.

Before he starting sending the signals to Scarlett, he swung through the vines laced along the river and got about a half mile ahead. He then asked Alister, who was comfortably resting in his scapula, if he had any ideas on how to build a quick trap to catch two kids, slightly taller than himself.

"Aren't you the one who can communicate with the trees?" Alister asked.

"Well...I can ask the nearby plants to help, I suppose. But, how do I know they would be okay with me having them help to capture somebody...or, in this case, two somebodies?" Sebastian asked.

After a brief pause, Alister replied: "You'll just have to try, Sebastian. Sometimes, you have to believe before you know how it will all work out...."

Sebastian replied, "But I can't make any mistakes. I've got to save my sister, and these two bad people with her, well, they are more disgusting than abc fungus."

"What is abc fungus?"

"A.B.C. Already been chewed."

"Oh...gross."

"And they might do something terrible to me, and to her, if I don't succeed."

Alister understood the seriousness of the risk, but he tried to encourage Sebastian to follow his instincts.

"Sebastian," Alister said in a kind, sleepy voice, "You must trust in the goodness of everything you have seen here. It is a good place. There is a purpose."

"I'm not sure..." Sebastian replied.

"You have been given a special ability...of understanding and communicating with the environment all around you. I don't know if anyone else here has ever had your particular gift. You must trust that Hleo will understand your needs too," Alister said.

Sebastian closed his eyes and tried to concentrate on whoever or whatever might be listening. He asked the trees for help to rescue his sister, and, then, a very specific plan seemed to drop, like an acorn falling, directly into his wooden brain.

As he shared his plan with Alister, Sebastian suddenly had the urge to eat a whole pile of acorns.

Minutes later, Sebastian was running back up the shoreline, hiding behind trees and boulders, and sending signals directly to his sister. He completed a series of knocks, which Scarlett heard and quickly translated, like Morse code, as: "It's me. Sebastian. Yes, I'm made of wood. And I'm here. I've got a plan. Get them to stop the boat, and then listen up."

"Stop the boat! Stop the boat!" Scarlett shouted, with a malicious tone of voice. She was completely back in character as Archimago's servant. "I saw something! And *he* will want to have it."

"What is it?" Prisma replied, darkly. "What is it?"

"I saw an animal or maybe a child, I don't know. But we've got to check it out. It could be one of those kids *he's* been seeking."

Prisma agreed. The prospect of bringing another captive back to Archimago was too delightfully evil to pass up. Prisma begged The Architect to stop the boat, so they could investigate. Scarlett kept silent.

"Can't the two of you just go looking?" The Architect asked, still nursing his wounds from the battle at the falls.

Scarlett had to think quickly.

"No. You've got to come with us," Scarlett said, pointing to the sword in this belt, "There could be two or three of them, and you've got the only useful weapon."

The Architect couldn't let on how much he hated that sword. He wished they knew that Archimago had given it to him as a way of controlling him and not as a gift. He always knew, when the jewel began to glow, that Archimago was about to break through, and he could do nothing about it. It was never for very long, and his powers were still limited across The Dark Waters, but The Architect knew there would be a time when Archimago would figure out how to channel more fully, and when he did, everyone, whether you were his servant or not, would be subject to all of his evil intentions.

"Fine," The Architect said, "But let's go. You know *he's* going to get impatient. The army is on its way."

The one loyal and the two questionable servants of Archimago climbed out of the boat and ventured into the woods.

Suddenly, they heard a low growl. It reminded Scarlett of an Earth One black bear. The Architect and Prisma did not recognize the sound. Prisma was especially terrified.

"Well," The Architect said, "It seems like you did hear something. But what kind of creature is that?"

"I think it's a bear," Scarlett said.

Sebastian was now up on a tree branch, only a few hundred feet ahead of them.

Alister was doing his best to growl and roar loudly, despite his currently miniscule size. He had never channeled himself into something so small as a boy's scapula and then tried to roar before.

Sebastian climbed higher into the branches and did his best to lie flat and blend into the tree. His wooden complexion made him nearly invisible when he was lying down on the branches.

"Let's climb up," Prisma said, pulling a small, retractable shadow net out of a case attached to her belt. "I'm going to catch this thing. What did you call it? Bear? Is it like a squirrel or something?"

"They can be many sizes," Scarlett said, trying to hide the truth. She knew that Sebastian was trying to play a trick. The bear's roar did sound exactly the same as one she had heard numerous times around Hleo when she was pursuing a bear in the Channels, but she was too distracted at this moment to make a connection. Scarlett was fully convinced this bear sound was simply one of her little brother's pitch-perfect imitations.

Alister growled one more time as Prisma approached. Once Prisma had climbed high enough, and she was out of the sight of The Architect and Scarlett, Sebastian hurled a vine in her direction. On its own (though with a bit of Sebastian's influence), the vine began coiling itself around her like a python. She screamed as the leathery vine tightened around her arms.

Scarlett looked at The Architect and shouted: "Is she screaming? Aren't you going to help her?"

The Architect, of course, would have been happy to leave Prisma up there, but he didn't want her to report back to Archimago that he had left her to be eaten by a bear.

"Why don't *you* go up there?" The Architect replied, trying to keep his villainous demeanor, but considering this as a good opportunity to talk secretly with Scarlett. He wanted to explain that he had seen a Shadowsplitter defeated.

Scarlett heard the false tone in his voice and almost considered spilling her secret right there. It would be a big risk, Scarlett knew, but wasn't it The Architect who had originally stolen the scroll in the first place and sent it here? Was she wrong in thinking that he might actually be on her side? Then again, sometimes there aren't just two sides to a fight. And she didn't want to find out that she was not on his side.

"You have the sword. You go up there," Scarlett said.

"Fine," The Architect replied, climbing up the tree.

Just as the tail of his cloak disappeared from sight, up in the branches, Scarlett heard rustling behind her.

"Pssst!"

Scarlett turned around and nearly screamed.

"It's me!" Sebastian said, leaping towards her with open arms.

She recoiled and he stopped, knocking into her. She reached out her arm and lightly placed her palm on his wooden shoulder.

"You're really made of wood!" she said. "Every part of you, even your eyelashes...yet everything moves...and...." Scarlett lost her words and tears began to flow.

"Let's move!" Sebastian said, grabbing her hand. "We've got to get to the others. Those vines won't be much of a match for that devil's...or whatever he is...sword..."

Scarlett couldn't believe how well the earlier plan had fallen into place.

Eurie actually found the trail to Shelterwood Castle, she thought. *And Rella must have somehow been able to use the scroll to free Sebastian.*

She wouldn't have to pretend to serve Archimago ever again.

Now the real fight was about to begin.

"We can't steal the ship, though," Scarlett told Sebastian. "I'm sure *he* has some way to track it. We've got to go on foot."

Sebastian and Scarlett hurried back to the boat and quickly cracked open the cage. As she exited the cage, Menagerie let out a growl and seemed to instantly triple her normal size.

"It's ok," Alister shouted. "Menagerie wants you to climb on-to her back."

Scarlett wondered how Sebastian knew she was called Menagerie. But, you might remember, reader, she hadn't met Alister yet.

With the children clutching her back, Menagerie bounded over the river like it was a small puddle and headed straight down the tree line towards the bay and Quinn's hideout.

Scarlett shouted to Sebastian, who was sitting in front of her:

"Why were you talking in that funny voice? It sounded like you were talking from the back of your head to…"

Sebastian reached his hand over his back and pointed to his shoulder.

Alister's face appeared out of the wood grain, like one of the moving tattoos often seen on the arms of the citizens of Westcon, and he looked right at Scarlett and roared: "Surprise!"

Scarlett looked at Alister in disbelief and burst out laughing. She was quite accustomed to the wild surprises of Hleo.

"Only you, Sebastian. Only you!" Scarlett shouted back as the wind blew through her long, shimmering red hair.

"Nice to meet you, Mr. Bear!" Scarlett said.

"Nice to meet you!" Alister replied, roaring but then yawning loudly.

Chapter 40: No Going Back

"I'M GOING TO TAKE YOU back to the cave. I think someone might be waiting there to meet you," Eurie said.

"I knew it," Rella whispered, smiling brighter as she spoke. "I saw her from the tree...and what was she...what did she..."

"Well...she will answer all of your questions, and she has a very special gift waiting for you, something the Architect tried to steal, but she was able to hold on to," Eurie said.

"How did you meet her? What was she like? Can you tell me anything?" Rella asked, visibly anxious about meeting Samara.

"Well, when I came back out of the cave, the Shadowsplitter had been destroyed by the light of the yellow orb. I saw The Architect rushing off. I looked up at the falls and she splashed water at me to get my attention. She and I communicated briefly, and she said that your mission, for now, had been fulfilled and you could return home."

Rella felt the tears running over her cheeks but she didn't move. The word 'home' brought so many feelings at once. She wiped her eyes and waited for Eurie to finish speaking.

"She also said she needed to see you before you go, but when the time is right, she will also lead you back to fulfill your next important role."

"When will I return?" Rella asked.

"What is your age?" Eurie asked.

"I'm seven...in Earth One years," Rella said.

"And that is 365 Earth One sunrises, approximately. So...then...by your eighth birthday. Yes, on a late winter morning, you will return."

How could she possibly know that, Rella wondered.

"And by then, you'll have learned the new skills you will need to help us complete the mission," Eurie said.

Rella turned away from Eurie and prepared to say goodbye to Quinn, who was now back to work on the ship, assembling a small engine.

Rella walked over to Quinn and tried to speak, but couldn't get any words out.

"It's ok, Rella," Quinn said, "You've done your part. We can't ask more of you right now. Thank you for trusting me, and my message, even though you didn't know me. You kept the scroll safe for us...even if you *dropped it* briefly."

Quinn smiled at her, trying to reassure her that it was a fortunate mistake, and more than likely, wasn't actually a mistake at all.

Rella handed the scroll to Quinn and asked, "Should I tell you any more about what I've learned?"

Quinn unrolled the scroll again, looked down and contorted his face, trying to make sense of what he was looking at. It still didn't make sense to him at all.

Rella told him about a few of the mysterious things she had seen, the way the scroll would become animated, and what she thought was happening, though she didn't have any clear ideas on how it worked.

"Even if you haven't figured out what the figures and shapes fully mean yet, we know that you can and you will in time," Quinn said, returning the scroll to Rella.

"This is yours now," he continued, "only yours, and you will protect it for us all."

Rella set the scroll down on the worktable. She noticed that it was covered with colorful bits of fabric, metallic rock, and shredded plants.

"You are quite a whiz with this stuff!" she said, and then extended her hand to Quinn.

Quinn met her halfway with his own hand. As the two shook hands, Rella felt a small shock, almost like she had been in two places at once, like she had two bodies and each one was in a different place. The odd sensation, however, left her body just as quickly as it had come on.

Quinn's handshake reminded her exactly of the way her Uncle J shook hands: direct eye contact, a humble smile, and a slight nod of the head.

She was ready to go home.

Quinn then stepped back, offered her a salute, and without lowering his salute, turned towards Eurie. Eurie nodded slowly in his direction. Quinn lowered his hand and nodded back.

As Rella watched the brief exchange between Quinn and Eurie, she sensed an even deeper personal past between them, one she had not yet come to understand, but felt that, in time, she would understand. Rella was now a part of a fellowship, like so many of the books and tales she'd imagined.

Like her mother and her father, she had been chosen to help defend and restore the world of stories, and, conversely, the stories of many worlds.

"Brighter days will come," Rella said aloud, repeating something her father told her whenever she asked about her mother. Quinn and Euire smiled.

Eurie and Rella climbed out of the hideout and walked back on the path toward a clearing on a hill where they would catch a ride from Thalas.

A loud crash echoed in the distance.

"Wait!" Rella shouted, grabbing Eurie's arm and turning her around. "Did you hear that?"

"Yes! It was back along the shore...it sounded like someone screaming," Eurie said.

"And...was that the sound of a ship smashing into the rocks?" Rella asked.

Eurie and Rella turned and rushed back through the tangles of vines and twisted branches. When they entered the hideout, Quinn was already holding weapons and armor.

He handed Eurie and Rella lightweight shields and armor made from a conglomeration of colorful leaves, stones, bark, and various metallic substances that he had been able to forge without any fire.

Quinn had designed the armor based on all the ancient types of armor he had either studied at the youth military training school, or seen in museums, including armor from samurai, sub-Saharan African tribes, and late medieval Europe.

"Where did you get these?" Eurie asked. Rella was already clasping hers on. The blend of metal, bright colors, and stone reminded Rella of camouflage.

As she put on the armor, Rella asked Quinn what to do with the scroll. She didn't want to lose it. He handed her a secure puzzle box that he had crafted.

Quinn quickly demonstrated the combination of moves to get the box to open. It was exactly like a toy they used in her school to test to see who had the skills to be chosen for the special military program for youth. She always pretended she didn't know how to solve it because she didn't want to get put in with that group.

"I was working on a new form of armor for the exterior of my ship, and I realized that this material would also make great personal armor," Quinn said, as he continued to tighten the straps.

"It's really amazing. It's so flexible and comfortable!" Rella said.

"I've been engineering the material to respond to various conditions and environmental factors here along The Wondercurrent," Quinn said.

Eurie adjusted her braid and tightened the headpiece Quinn had made especially for her.

"It still needs a few adjustments," Quinn said. "I didn't think we would be jumping in to battle tonight."

"It fits perfectly," Eurie said.

Rella then slid the puzzle box into a special slot Quinn had installed underneath his work table. It was too risky, of course, to bury things in Hleo's soil.

Eurie handed each of them a vial of her special blue elixir. They all took a drink and then huddled together to discuss strategy.

They still didn't know if Menagerie was a prisoner, or if she had broken loose in the crash, or if Sebastian had even caught up to his sister.

Rella hooked the slingshot Quinn had made for her onto a loop on the strap of her satchel and placed it over her chest plate. She stepped confidently forward as they left the hideout.

"We must keep close together and keep our shields right up against us," Quinn said. "They will deflect the false shadows. And they are actually going to help us navigate the darkness along the shoreline."

"Got it," Rella whispered.

"And keep the luminous stones in the black pouches until you are ready to use them," Quinn said.

"Wait," Eurie interrupted, "I think I have something better than the stones!"

"What do you mean?" Quinn replied.

"Well...I think I found something better...you see, there are these yellow orbs...," Eurie explained.

Before Eurie could continue, the soft soil started shaking and thunder pounded down upon them. The black waters began to spit up a thick, dark mist about fifty yards in from the shoreline.

"Stay close," Quinn whispered. "Listen for voices."

The three armor-clad children moved slowly until they they heard the voice. It resembled a girl's voice, but also seemed to have a robotic tone.

The Architect's ship was in pieces near the mouth of The Wondercurrent. Though, as the black waters began moving up the current, it seemed less and less like The Wondercurrent.

Quinn, Eurie, and Rella, covered in darkness, stood on a ledge beside the darkening water.

"What's that sound?" Rella asked.

"The sizzling?" Quinn replied.

"Oh...that sounds terrible...what's the popping?" Rella asked, still trying to concentrate in order to recognize if any Shadowsplitters were in the area.

"The bacon-in-the-frying-pan sound is the current sinking, maybe dissolving, into The Dark Waters. The pops are the orbs being drawn down underneath the surface...," Quinn said, as he pulled a handful of luminous stones, similar to the ones Scarlett left along the trail to Hleo, from his pocket.

"We can't be sure," Eurie said, terrified, "of what is actually happening to the orbs. They don't seem to be blowing up or anything."

"Did you hear that?" Rella whispered. "It sounded like voices..."

Quinn hurled a handful of luminous stones across the river and towards the voices, lighting up the wreckage. Pieces of The Architect's ship were tangled up in vines all along the shore.

Rella spotted the empty cage first. Mena was out. But was she hurt? Was she free?

And what about Sebastian, Scarlett, and Alister? Rella wondered.

"Eurie," Quinn said, "We need to find Menagerie, and we need to do it without allowing The Architect to see us, at least until we know whether he is alone. Prisma might be close by too."

"And Rella...where's Rella?" Quinn exclaimed. "Rella, Rella?"

Rella had vanished.

Did she run back to the hideout? Eurie wondered.

"Rella's gone," Eurie said. "But I think I know where she's going."

Quinn was distracted and not really listening to Eurie at that moment.

He had managed to catch the robot eyes of Prisma, whose purple hair was now twisted in knots. She was scrambling, awkwardly, out of the wreckage. She seemed to have broken limbs, but didn't appear to be in physical pain.

"It's Prisma. I'm going after her. You find Rella," Quinn said.

Quinn heaved his last luminous stones across the river towards Prisma to keep her in view as he rushed to the bank to search for a way across. As he got closer to Prisma, he stopped moving, waiting to see what she would do next.

Prisma had climbed up onto a gigantic rock that jutted out over the river. She looked over at Quinn and then Eurie (now standing behind him). They both aimed their slingshots at Prisma.

Down below, the orbs in the water continued flowing, casting a faint, colorful light onto Prisma's face. She was grasping a long, thin paintbrush in her right hand. The bristles seemed to spark.

Prisma spotted them, lifted the brush over her head, and shouted, "Those little stones aren't going to save you!"

Just as another crash of thunder pounded overhead, Quinn and Eurie released a shower of luminous stones. They were perfectly aimed at Prisma's head and should have put out both of her eyes. But, just as the stones reached Prisma's face, a Shadowsplitter swooped in and knocked them off course. Quinn and Eurie jumped back. The trees along both sides of the river began to fall like toys.

Quinn and Euire looked at the swarm of dark clouds over Prisma's head. The clouds began to move rapidly along both sides of the riverbank. Suddenly, hundreds of dimly colored shadows split off from the dark clouds and swirled above the trees, turning themselves into hoops, like lassos. One by one, they pulled the trees to the ground. As they destroyed each tree, they absorbed every shade of natural color and turned it into pitch.

"You see now!" Prisma shrieked. "I've got hundreds of them. And we are going straight up this path...all the way to your precious waterfall. Hleo will be *his*, once and for all!"

Prisma lifted the paintbrush above her head and swirled it around in the air as though she were conducting an orchestra. The Shadowsplitters continued to glide along.

"Quinn," Euire screamed. "We can defeat them. But we've got to get more yellow orbs."

"I don't know if we can get up the river fast enough."

"I'm going to try to summon Thalas..." Eurie said, backing away from the shore.

"But what about Rella?" Quinn said.

"She's going to get the scroll. She knows what she's doing," Eurie said.

"And where's The Architect?" Quinn said.

"Who cares! Maybe he fell into the current...," Eurie shouted before she started sprinting away from the chaos along the banks of The Wondercurrent. They knew they wouldn't get any closer to Prisma at the moment. Quinn sprinted after Eurie.

It didn't take much time for the army of Shadowsplitters to destroy a single tree, but there were so many ancient, broad trees along the banks that Quinn and Eurie felt they had enough time to put together at least some defense.

But first, they had to retrieve Rella.

Chapter 41: Shadowsight

RELLA, CLAD IN ARMOR, ran through the darkness at full speed. She headed directly back towards Quinn's hideout. She had left the scroll in the workshop. She originally thought it would be safer than keeping with her. Now, she was retrieving it because she realized that it was precisely the tool she needed to help Eurie and Quinn defeat Prisma's army of Shadowsplitters.

She had seen a message on the scroll depicting the entire attack plan, only she didn't realize that that was what she was looking at when had been studying the scroll earlier that day. Prisma was going to lead the Shadowsplitters up The Wondercurrent to hold back the orbs and allow The Dark Waters to seep into and destroy Hleo's defenses. By breaking the defenses, *he*, Archimago, could then, eventually, get into the carved castle of Shelterwood, and destroy The Red Notebooks.

Rella suddenly realized something else, which connected back to the dream of the children walking away from the castle. Sebastian wasn't the only one trapped in a bed. There must have been hundreds of rooms, all the way up the giant tower, where children remained trapped in the Channels.

She sprinted between massive trunks, swerved around wild shrubs, and slipped through the thick vines. What she failed to notice was that she was doing all of it in total darkness. All of a sudden, the darkness appeared no different from the light back on Earth One.

Rella squirmed her way back through the thickly woven leaves and limbs. *Why couldn't Quinn have forged us swords,* she thought. *That would have made it much easier to hack through these vines!*

Once she made it through the entrance of the hideout, she rushed over to Quinn's worktable, pulled out the puzzle box and retrieved the scroll. As she unrolled it, it emitted a faint glow. Rella slowly realized that she had been running completely in darkness over the last few minutes. But this new power, the ability to see in the dark, was not something she could turn off and on. It seemed to work on its own.

She examined the glowing lines and triangular shapes drifting across the scroll. She tried reading the images, looking for a message or a signal. She held it up and tried to look into it, like she did when Sebastian had surfaced.

She shook it and rotated it. *Come on! Come on!* she thought.

Then, suddenly, the scroll became a clear frame. In the center of the frame, a boy's face appeared. She gasped. She had been haunted by that face ever since she saw him near the cave.

"Now I've got you!" The Architect shouted, stepping out from behind Quinn's ship and cornering her.

Rella rolled the scroll, gripped it tightly, and glared at the bony, gaunt face of the tall boy. He looked like he could have been fourteen years old (Earth One), yet also like he had sprung from a drawing of a demon in some ancient book.

This would be a good time for Eurie and Quinn to come looking for me, Rella thought, as her heart continued to pound faster and faster.

"You figured it out, didn't you?" The Architect asked. He spoke without anger or aggression.

Rella was confused. He sounded almost like a friend, and not a fiend.

Rella lowered the scroll and kept her eyes on The Architect. She wondered how he could see her in the dark.

"It's called shadowsight," The Architect said, softening his tone of voice even more. "You are learning how to use one of your gifts," he said.

Rella was still suspicious that this was a trick. She wanted to believe the friendliness in his voice was real. She wished Eurie and Quinn were with her.

Suddenly, however, the friendly tone shifted back to one of threat, almost like another person was controlling him. The jewel on the sword on his belt started to glow red:

"I'm going to make one request," the Architect said threateningly.

This was not the voice of the boy who was speaking just seconds earlier. It was an older voice.

"Hand the scroll over to me, and I won't make you come back to the island. I'll leave you here, and you can go back home, to your world. Refuse, and you, the scroll, and your friends will never see their homes again."

The Architect's voice was now even more aggressive and desperate, though his face looked puzzled and fearful.

Rella stood her ground. She thought about Samara, the wings she had seen, and then just faintly, she thought she heard a whisper, like a spirit, floating through the air: "Just hold on, Rella. Be strong."

The Architect's mouth stopped moving, but the aggressive voice continued to fill the room.

"Give me the brush!" the voice boomed.

She saw confusion and desperation in The Architect's face. He was clinching his teeth.

The red jewel on the sword glowed brighter. The voice continued, now sounding like the cracked-tooth bully from the school bus stop back in Ensea:

"You don't want me to drag you back to my island...it's a terrible, terrible place for a nice girl like you. You wouldn't survive long...."

Rella remembered how close that bully would get his cracked teeth to her face before he would push her down into the mud.

The Architect, who was frozen in place, tried to signal Rella with his eyes.

As she watched his eyes, she sensed that he didn't want her to listen to it, even as the voice continued to threaten her.

The sound of the bully's voice was too much to handle. She began to feel weak. She slowly rolled the scroll and held it out to The Architect.

She lowered her head, tearing up, and said: "Take them. Now."

"Good choice," the voice, which was coming from the sword, intoned.

The Architect limped forward and took the scroll in his hand. The red light from jewel in the handle of the sword surrounded both of them in the darkness.

Rella felt disoriented and could not figure out where the red light had come from, or how it could bend around them in such odd ways.

As The Architect attempted to pull the scroll from Rella's grip, Rella noticed that his clothes were torn and he was bleeding.

"You're hurt," she whispered, still unable to loosen her grip on the scroll.

"It doesn't matter," he said, trying to pull the scroll from her hand.

"Why don't you stay with us?" Rella whispered, trying to talk to the actual boy and not the one under the influence of the jewel.

The Architect laughed with a mix of arrogance and anguish. It was like watching two faces at once.

"You don't, you can't, understand," the double-voices said. "Once you are mine, *his*, you don't, no one can, change sides. Ever."

"But you don't really want to be his servant. I can hear it...," Rella replied, just inches from his pale face.

"No!" The Architect replied through clenched teeth. The hesitation in his voice was gone. "For me there is no going back..."

"Are you from one of the Earths?" Rella asked quickly, trying to catch the Architect's eyes. He would not look at her.

The Architect, under Archimago's control, was now pulling hard on the scroll.

The scroll stayed firmly in Rella's grip. No matter how hard he pulled, he wasn't going to get it.

"I've seen other things in this scroll, you know...," Rella shouted, as the scroll continued to flex and stretch in her hands, trying to pull itself away from The Architect's grip. "Maybe I could help you. We could work together?"

"You've been warned," The Architect said, staring her down. Now Rella didn't know who was speaking.

The jewel in the sword glowed brighter.

Rella knitted her brows and stared determinedly right back at The Architect. As the scroll twisted itself in her hand, she could feel her physical strength and her confidence increasing.

"You're just an innocent little child. You don't know anything girl!" The Architect shouted.

If there was one thing anyone could say to Rella that would make her ears spout hot steam, it was those two phrases: 'You're just a child!' and 'You don't know anything, girl!'

That was exactly what the cracked-tooth bully said every day at the bus stop.

"Can a child do this?" she shouted, as she pulled the scroll loose, raised it above her head and flipped her entire body up onto the roof of Quinn's half-built ship beside them.

The jewel on The Architect's sword went black. The power in the scroll had severed *his* connection with the sword.

The Architect tried to lunge after Rella, but the pain in his legs was too much to bear. It reminded him of the time he fell off the top of a twisty slide when he was four. As he passed out, he thought about the woman again and the girl with the braids. And the finger trap.

Rella rushed out of the hideout, leaving The Architect lying, helpless, in the dark.

Chapter 42: Menagerie Speaks

MOMENTS LATER, RELLA was dashing through the forests, away from The Wondercurrent, and back into the thick fog. In the distance, she spotted the silhouettes of two children riding a large beast.

It's Scarlett and Sebastian, she thought, *and they're riding on Menagerie's back. But she looks so big?*

Menagerie was now a deep shade of orange and was triple the size of any Earth One tiger.

"Rella!" Sebastian shouted. "Hop on!"

Menagerie lowered herself and Rella, still in motion, jumped on and landed right behind Scarlett.

"Where are we going?" Rella asked.

"Back to Shelterwood Castle," Scarlett said. "It's nice to finally meet you Rella! Cool armor!"

Rella looked down and realized that she was still wearing the chest plate from Quinn. She clutched her satchel, where she had once again stored the scroll.

"Great timing!" Rella said.

"For sure!" Sebastian yelled.

"Sebastian...," Rella shouted as they bounded through the forest. "I don't think we have time to go back to the castle right now. Quinn and Eurie are in trouble..."

"What is it?" Sebastian asked.

"The Shadowsplitters!" Scarlett replied, peering off into the distance. "They're moving up The Wondercurrent!"

"What do we do?" Sebastian said. "We can't fight them!"

"I think Eurie might have found a way to stop them," Rella said.

Menagerie had reached a clearing on a hill between two great forests.

"Can you guys make up your minds?" Menagerie said, growling a little.

They all gasped. None of them had heard Menagerie speak until now.

"You do speak!" Sebastian said.

"Yes. When I need to. My mother taught be a listener first," Menagerie replied, making a friendly chuffing sound as she bounded forward.

"My dad says that's called a prusten," Sebastian said.

"What?" Rella said.

"The chuffing sound. When a tiger makes a nonthreatening chuffing sound, it's called a prusten," Sebastian said.

Menagerie continued on for a few more minutes until they reached the top of a large hill. They all looked towards the river, which was now miles below them, and they could see the trees beginning to topple over.

Prisma and the Shadowsplitters had already made it a quarter of the way up the river. They were closing in. There was no sign of Quinn or Eurie.

The children climbed down off of Menagerie as she rolled onto her back and began to change colors again.

"Here's the plan!" Rella said, still gazing up into the sky for any signs of Thalas. "We've got to collect yellow orbs, but it's too dangerous to go back to the falls to find them."

"Sebastian, since you can communicate with..." Rella pointed towards the trees.

Sebastian nodded, but, as he started to speak, he doubled over and appeared to be in intense pain. His eyes closed and he nearly fell to the ground.

Scarlett wrapped her arms around her brother and held him upright.

"What's happening, Rella?" Scarlett asked.

"The trees might be...connecting to him," Rella said. "If the Shadowsplitters are destroying them, they may be trying to get to us..."

"What can I do?" Scarlett said, panicking.

"Leave him here with me," Rella replied. "Maybe we can get him to safety in Eurie's hideout. There's medicine there too."

"You take Menagerie back to the lake around Shelterwood Castle and collect as many yellow orbs as you can...and then come back here."

Scarlett lowered her brother onto a soft stone.

"No," Menagerie interrupted. "We go together!"

Rella could tell that Menagerie wasn't going to back down.

"Ok. But let me check the scroll first," Rella said.

Scarlett lifted her brother onto Menagerie's back and then climbed on behind him.

Rella, standing beside Menagerie, unrolled the scroll and started running her hands over it, waiting for something to appear. A message. A symbol. Anything?

She looked back toward the banks of The Wondercurrent. The trees had started falling even faster.

Chapter 43: Beyond Imagining

AT THE BASE OF A NEARBY tree, just above the roots, Rella saw a few flickers of light.

Small signs and symbols began appearing on the trees all around them. It seemed like someone was using an invisible pen to etch the glowing symbols into the trees.

Sebastian remained fast asleep, but seemed calmer.

As Rella looked out toward the glowing symbols on the trees, the shapes of various animals began to emerge from the trunks of each one. There were too many to count.

It's Sebastian! Rella thought. *He's trying to help the guardians to surface. He's not sleeping. He's connecting to the roots and The Wondercurrent!*

Next thing she knew, an army of guardians was standing in front of her: Black Rhinos, Giant Pandas, Marine Iguanas, Snow Leopards, Jaguars, Artic Foxes, and tiny little Poison Dart Frogs.

Sebastian opened his eyes and took a long, loud, deep breath.

"Alister," Sebastian shouted. "Where's Alister?"

Rella slipped the scroll back into her satchel and turned toward Sebastian.

"You did all that!" Rella said, pointing. "Didn't you, Sebastian?"

"Did what?" Sebastian said.

"You brought them here," Rella said.

"Not me..." Sebastian said. And then, a gentle, deep voice floated up from behind Rella's shoulder.

"He had a little help," the voice said.

Sebastian, Scarlett and Rella all turned around and looked at the man towering above them. It was Julian. Rella's father.

"Father! Father! Father! Father!" Rella said, hugging her father around the waist and bursting into tears.

Julian lowered himself down to eye-level with Rella.

"I haven't got much time, Rella. I don't know how long I can stay," he said.

"No, father. Please don't leave again!" she said.

"I won't be far away, Rella. I promise," he said. "Remember the scroll! Look and you'll find me there. I've been talking with you already. You just didn't know it. You're going to beat them...."

Rella looked toward the army of guardians and back at Sebastian. She didn't know what to say. She wasn't ready.

"For now," Julian said, looking at all of the children and the guardians, "you all need to work together. You must defeat the Shadowsplitters. Your families need you!"

The army of guardians grew larger by the minute.

Julian gave Rella one more big bear hug, looked her in the eyes, and said: "We will be together again soon!"

Rella watched as her father sprinted away and disappeared into the dark forest.

"No! No! No! Wait!" Rella shouted. Scarlett wrapped her arms around Rella from behind.

"We've got to get the orbs," Scarlett said.

"Climb on," Menagerie ordered.

Rella joined Scarlett and Sebastian on Menagerie's back and they took off for the lake beside the castle. The army of guardians followed, marching in formation.

When they reached the lake, the guardians surrounded the entire shoreline and waited for instructions.

The three children climbed into the small boat and rushed over to the castle to find King. *He would have advice, for sure,* Rella thought.

Rella wanted to ask him about her father, if he knew all along that her father was here, or how her father had got through...and if he, King, had anything to do with it.

As the boat ferried the children to the foot of the carved castle, Menagerie order all the guardians to find vines, leaves, bark, and any other materials to make pouches and nets for carrying the yellow orbs back toward The Wondercurrent to battle the Shadowsplitters.

When the three children reached the doors of the castle, they knew something was wrong. The door was open and King had not come out to greet them. Sebastian, now feeling recovered, ran through the halls, shouting for his father. Scarlett searched the kitchen and the bedrooms, but there was no trace. Rella ran up to the room where Sebastian had surfaced, but there were no signs of King. However, Rella did notice that two of the cloaks from the rack were missing.

The army outside, led by Menagerie, had fished hundreds of yellow orbs out of the lake and were ready to move.

The children rushed back out of the castle, jumped into the small boat, and were transported just a few meters from the shore.

Menagerie walked out into the water, which was fairly shallow near the shore, and stood next to the boat. The three children climbed up onto Menagerie's back. Everyone was waiting for Rella to speak. Rella, still thinking of her father, was too shaken. She couldn't get a word out.

Menagerie turned her head back over her shoulder and looked at Scarlett.

"It's your turn," Menagerie said, as she climbed up onto a gigantic boulder next to the shore.

Scarlett gazed out at the rows and rows of guardians and tried to rally them: "You've got an important task. The most important call any guardians have ever known."

The guardians howled, growled, grunted, and cheered back, urging Scarlett to continue with her speech.

"For a thousand years," she continued passionately, "Hleo has been a safe place for children, for all dreamers. When a hungry child needed restoration, Hleo has been here. When a lost child waited to be rescued, Hleo has been here. And your ancestors...all our ancestors, they have been here too. But now, this...darkness...this evil one, who calls himself Archimago, has come to destroy it."

Scarlett paused and took a deep breath. A cloud of sweet fog drifted past her nose. Every strong, beautiful animal, young and old, kept its eyes on Scarlett.

Scarlett shouted: "But he will not destroy it! Not today! Not tomorrow!"

Rella and Sebastian joined in and all three bellowed: "Not Ever!"

The animals howled their response in unison, making waves on the lake and shaking thousands of leaves down from the surrounding trees.

"Because we, the guardians and defenders of Hleo," Scarlett shouted.

"And the dreamers of Earth One..." Rella shouted.

"We will fulfill the promises of our ancestors," Sebastian yelled.

"We will defend it to the end," Scarlett proclaimed.

Suddenly, a strong wind rushed down from above. A gigantic pair of metallic wings swooped over the ranks. Rella looked up and spotted Eurie and Quinn. They were still in their armor and riding on Thalas.

Thalas lowered herself into an open space on the shoreline, right next to a mound of yellow orbs. Rella slid down off of Menagerie's back and ran through the shallow water towards Eurie.

"Grab as many as you can!" Eurie shouted. "And get on!"

A few of the guardians standing nearby, including an Iguana and an Arctic Fox, charged up to Thalas. Rella could see that they knew her. Thalas also let out a joyful cry at seeing her long-lost friends.

Rella took a bottle from Eurie, who had just finished sticking orbs all over Thalas's back. The orbs, Rella figured out, would stick to Thalas's feathers like magnets. They loaded her up with at least a hundred on each wing.

"What's this bottle for?" Rella asked.

"You need to put a little of this ointment over your eyes," Eurie said, "and then get Sebastian, Scarlett, and Menagerie to help you distribute it to all of the guardians. This will protect everyone from the damaging effects of the explosions...when the Shadowsplitters dissolve and break up in the air..."

"How does it work?" Scarlett asked, now standing next to Rella.

"When the light from these orbs slices into the Shadowsplitters, they explode into thousands of pieces...if their reflections get into your eyes, it could distort your ability to see...or worse...so this creates a filter," Eurie answered.

The children ran through the lines of guardians and applied the ointment as quickly as possible. All the smaller animals who could help also took some of the ointment and passed it along. Sebastian tried his best to call on the trees themselves to lend their limbs to assist.

"Are you ready?" Scarlett shouted from Menagerie's back. Menagerie was now five times her regular size and sparkled with red and black stripes.

"Let us charge forth," Sebastian shouted, "and save The Wondercurrent!"

Alister heard Sebastian's shouts and woke up from his temporary home in Sebastian's scapula. He roared so loud that it knocked an entire row of guardians off of their feet. The entire army jumped, howled, and roared in response to Alister's battle cry.

Thalas blasted off into the air with Eurie, Quinn, and Rella clutching her back. Scarlett and Sebastian, riding Menagerie, lead the charge into the forests and all the way down to the banks of The Wondercurrent.

Chapter 44: Believe, Believe

WHEN THE ARMY OF GUARDIANS arrived at the banks of The Wondercurrent, Prisma was stunned. She had assumed that her master's army was invincible. And when the orbs started flying, she was forced to retreat.

Eurie, Quinn and Rella swooped in first, high above the trees, and hurled orbs down from above. Rella was terrified at the chaotic vision. First, the Shadowsplitters dropped into the lower branches. When they went low, though, the teams of guardians below were ready to hurl the orbs and obliterate them all at once.

One thing Quinn didn't account for, however, was how far the chards of Shadowsplitters might be thrown before they dropped to the ground. The pieces that fell into The Wondercurrent dissolved quickly, but the pieces that hit the trees caused terrible damage all over the land.

Once Quinn and Rella had thrown all the yellow orbs from Thalas's back, Eurie, who was navigating, dropped Quinn and Rella safely to the ground. She immediately flew away with Thalas. It was clear that they were going to win the battle soon, but they had to minimize the damage.

Rella and Quinn each had a single orb remaining.

"What do we do now?" Rella asked.

"I think it's almost over," Quinn said, just as something started moving through the trees nearby. "Wait here!"

"What are you doing?" Rella asked.

"I think something is hiding in those trees!" Quinn said.

Another sound echoed on the other side of the forest.

"Why don't you go over behind that rock!" Quinn said, pointing toward the other side of the clearing where a stack of boulders provided shelter.

"Ok," Rella said, holding the orb like a baseball and running for the boulders.

"I'll go after the noise!" Quinn said, running in the opposite direction.

When Rella reached the shelter, she watched Quinn disappear into the forest. And then, behind her, she saw the figure of a man hiding behind a tree.

"Father!" Rella shouted, "Father? Is that you?"

There was no reply.

"Mr. King...is that you?" she yelled again, clutching the orb.

The figure sprinted from one tree to the next. Rella was almost certain it was her father.

"Wait, father! It's me!" Rella shouted, running into the woods.

As she entered the forest, the phantom disappeared and, up above, a Shadowsplitter, darker and more twisted than any she had seen, started to descend. She was ready to throw the orb, but she knew she only had one chance. Rella remembered all those times in her dreams when she could make things appear and disappear.

And then she remembered everything. The first meeting with Eurie, when they were discussing her father's book about

Archimago and the knights. The discovery of the scroll. The storms. Rella knew this wasn't the dream, but something inside of her prompted her to try it. She focused her thoughts: *Believe. Believe.*

And then, up above, through the mists, the dust clouds, and the shadows, a shower of colorful lights broke through. The Shadowsplitter turned toward her. As it attempted to spread around her, Rella hurled the orb up at it, turned, and sprinted back towards the shelter of boulders.

Quinn was waiting at the shelter. He was clutching his side and wincing.

"What happened?" Quinn asked.

"I believed! I believed!" Rella shouted.

Quinn took Rella by the hand and the two companions charged toward the battle scene at the bank of The Wondercurrent. If they had thought to look back, they would had seen the outline of Rella's guardian, Samara, shimmering behind them.

Chapter 45: Victory and Defeat

THE GUARDIANS ON THE ground had formed lines on both sides of The Wondercurrent and worked in teams to squeeze the remaining Shadowsplitters together between the banks.

When the final explosions rang out, Prisma knew it was over. She continued waving her paintbrush in the air, desperately trying to orchestrate the movements of the Shadowsplitters around the tree trunks, but, as the guardians continued press in from both sides of the river, she dropped the brush.

Before anyone could catch her, Prisma scurried off into the shadows. Scarlett and Sebastian saw her slip away, but Menagerie was too exhausted and couldn't carry them any longer. They knew they couldn't keep up with her on land, and it was too dark to try and follower her.

As the quiet began to descend upon them, like a blanket, the army assembled along the banks. The black water creeping up and through The Wondercurrent receded and the beautiful, colored lights returned to the water, illuminating the surrounding forests.

The animals all bedded down along the current, tired and hungry. Suddenly, something dropped out of the sky. Everyone looked up. Rella leaned over and picked up one of the objects.

"Is this a pastry?" Quinn asked.

"Oh look..there's another one!" Rella shouted.

"Here's a blueberry and chocolate one...," Sebastian shouted, stuffing one into his mouth.

They looked up and saw Eurie dropping cakes and desserts from above the trees. It was a medicine and a reward, a healing elixir baked into pastries. The scores of guardians all enjoyed the feast of a hundred lifetimes. Hleo was safe once again.

Chapter 46: After the Battle

"HOW ARE YOU DOING THAT?" Quinn asked, straining his eyes.

"What?" Rella asked, dodging a branch.

"Moving so quickly through the dark," Quinn said.

Rella thought about what The Architect had said, when he wasn't being controlled by Archimago: "It's called shadowsight."

Rella grabbed Quinn's hand. "I'll lead us back," she said.

Quinn grabbed Eurie's hand, Eurie grabbed Scarlett's, and Scarlett locked hands with Sebastian.

Rella pulled them back through the mist and through the vines. As they entered the hideout, Rella ran back to the spot where she had left him. A small shredded piece of his silver cloak lay on the floor. The Architect was gone.

"He was here earlier," Rella said. "He was hurt, limping. There's no way he could have escaped without help."

"Wait...there's something over here," Eurie said, pointing to Quinn's work table, which was covered with various tools, scraps of metal, and handcrafted sprockets.

Rella spotted a piece of the tree bark. It was illuminated with swirling symbols.

Rella and Eurie recognized the scripts from the sign at the path leading to Shelterwood Castle.

"Do you think he dropped it? Or did he leave it for us?" Eurie asked, stroking Menagerie's thick, soft neck. Menagerie had shrunken back down to the size of a regular tiger now. Her fur had settled into a stylish blue and black pattern.

Eurie held the note up toward her face and examined it without saying a word. She then handed the note to Quinn and Quinn handed it quickly back to Rella. He was not even going to attempt to read it. He wasn't in the mood for code breaking.

"Rella," Quinn asked, "What do you see?"

Rella examined it closely. The words started to make sense, though they made no sound in her head, like other words did when she read to herself.

Rella looked up. She could see from their expressions that Quinn, Eurie, Sebastian, and Scarlett were anxious to know whether another threat was on the way.

Despite Eurie's healing pastries, they were all still so tired from the battle.

Rella tried to work out the meaning. She looked it over twice. *Could this be true? Is the Architect trying to help us? Is this another trick? What about my father? And my mother? Can they see me now? How does this fit in with the Dreambridge? Father didn't say much about the Dreambridge.*

Rella thought more about that final confrontation, where she was alone with the Shadowsplitters.

Believe. Believe. Believe.

Had her belief, somehow, affected the connection between the worlds, between Earth One, Hleo, and the dreamworld?

She looked all of her companions in the eyes, one by one, with a blend of surprise and worry.

"What is it?" Quinn asked, shuffling through a pile of objects on the worktable. Scarlett was still holding Sebastian's hand. Eurie had her eyes closed.

"In part, the message is a warning. It says: 'Stay away from the island. *He* knows you're here and *he*'s setting traps. Please wait. Don't rush it. I will help."

Quinn and Eurie gasped and looked at each other. Did The Architect, Archimago's loyal servant, just offer to help them?

Rella would have to explain the sword. At the moment, she continued examining the note. "There's more," she said, reading the note aloud. "'When I first surfaced, I thought I was coming to a magical place. A place of healing...'"

The writing was messy and clearly rushed.

Rella continued reading: "He says...'I was trying to get away from something...And I believed what I was reading. I really did...'"

Eurie looked concerned but didn't speak. Scarlett and Quinn were puzzled.

"I don't believe it?" Rella said.

"What?" Quinn replied.

"He says he met a dream traveler!" Rella answered.

"And?" Scarlett said.

"The dream traveler told him about the guardians...he says he believed the traveler and he was so excited to explore the world of Hleo...The Wondercurrent and the sweet mists...," Rella said, frowning.

"But?" Quinn said.

Rella was thinking about her own surfacing and about Hleo, and Shelterwood Castle, and King's story about The Red Notebooks.

Rella continued reading aloud, translating The Architect's note as quickly as possible:

"'But,' he says...sorry, it's hard to read...'the dream traveler deceived me. He took something from me. I have no choice but to serve *him* now, until I can figure out how to get it back...don't cross The Dark Waters.'"

Everyone sat in silence.

Rella started to remember something from a story her father had once read to her. But she kept reading. A tree limb crashed outside as strong winds rustled the makeshift hideout.

Eurie tried to get her mind around this new information about The Architect. She was certain he was pure evil. But he wasn't at all a bad person. He was a prisoner.

Tears streamed down the side of Rella's face. Everyone agreed that Menagerie would stay with Quinn as a lookout, to help him gather up the parts from the ship to continue working on it, until Rella received a new message from The Architect. Menagerie, shrinking further down to the size of a tiger cub, curled up at his feet and began to chuff.

Chapter 47: Rella Receives A Gift

THALAS HAD BEEN HIT by one of the chards of the Shad-owsplitters, which left her with a scar on her wing, but she could still soar. She whisked Eurie and Rella back toward the waterfall. The orbs were flowing brightly as ever. They flowed all the way to the mouth of the river, and new trees were already beginning to regrow along the banks.

Eurie barely spoke a word to Rella and seemed to be whispering something excitedly under her breath, like she had figured out a brilliant solution to a puzzle and she didn't want to lose her train of thought.

To Rella, it sounded like Eurie might have been saying "Why didn't I see this? How did I miss this?"

Thalas's feather clanged softly as she landed. The girls climbed down and walked toward the edge of the river. Eurie handed Rella a handful of her homemade cakes to enjoy before her journey home. She put her hand on Rella's shoulder and looked confidently into Rella's eyes. She spoke just a few more words, which Rella would have to think about for a while before she really understood them: "Find your name. Watch for us in the light. Dream of us in the colors. Be careful in the shadows."

Rella nodded and Eurie turned and leapt back onto Thalas. Rella repeated the phrase to herself. She thought of the last dream she'd had before she ever came in to Hleo. The conversation where she told Eurie that she would call herself Rella PenSword. Somehow, she had forgotten that her name was actually Rella PenSword.

Rella watched Eurie and Thalas soar away, back toward the caves atop the Wall of Wandering Waves. As Rella's eyes passed over the gigantic trees near the base of the wall, she thought for a moment that she had caught a glimpse of Alister, though she knew he was no longer channeling around, poking his nose out of the trunks. He was still with Sebastian and they were on their own journey.

She thought about the magnificent wooden castle, whose tower was visible from atop the falls. She thought of a picture of a Sphinx she'd seen once in an old printed magazine, or was it a notebook? Perhaps it was in one of her mother's very own sketchbooks?

Rella knew that Sebastian, Scarlett, and King would figure out how to free the children, and Alister. She thought for a moment that she should have gone back to Shelterwood Castle with them, to see if the scroll could help. She really wanted to know more about the books in that library. She knew that her own family's secrets were somehow in there as well. And, if she wasn't just dreaming it, she also remembered seeing Uncle J placing that Red Notebook at the top of a box he had packed into the trunk of his car before they left.

Rella turned her eyes to the twinkling falls and looked at the wings emerging behind the curtains of water. She felt a small tremble in the soft soil beneath her feet. Down to her right, she noticed something sprouting out of the ground. *Was it a flower?*

It looked like a lily on the verge of blooming. It opened up like a toy, like someone had just pulled an invisible string; and then, right in front of her, a paintbrush, her guardian's key, appeared.

She reached her hand in between the petals, plucked it out, and curled her fingers around the handle. The handle was made of carved wood, the same beautiful wood of the castle. It had elaborate symbols all over it, some Rella recognized and some she did not. As she rotated it between her fingers, it sparkled and glowed in an array of colors, many of which she couldn't even name. The bristles were completely transparent. They reminded her of The Wondercurrent. Perhaps, in Hleo, water could even be molded into a solid form., like clay.

Rella pulled a string from her satchel and tied the brush around her neck. Behind her, from within the cave, a bright blue light blinked out over her shoulder and across the water, mingling its light with the transparent lights of Samara's wings. Rella stood in awe of the elaborate assimilation of shapes, vapors, lights, colors, and motions before her.

"Hello?" Rella whispered, gazing at the wings flickering behind the falling water. "Rella... I... am! I...am...." Rella pointed a finger at her chest and then pointed up at the wings.

"Yes, of course," a soothing, motherly voice replied, and then, chuckling, exclaimed, "Know I...I mean, I know."

Rella remembered the reversed language she was told that some of *his* servants once used as a code, and she could tell that her guardian was just making a joke.

"And you have your brush, I see...," Samara said. Her voice was clear and confident and direct, nothing like the mystical, almost spooky voice she was expecting to hear.

Rella looked down and clutched the brush hanging from the string. She bowed her head, too shy to look up, and gazed into the shimmering, silent river.

Red, blue, and orange orbs blinked brightly as they floated slowly downstream. Rella smiled broadly as her eyes continued following the orbs downstream until they disappeared into the mist.

As she thought about her guardian looking down upon her, she felt as though she had become a musical note, suspended in the center of some mighty chord.

She turned her eyes back to the cave one more time, still too nervous to look directly at Samara's wings. The slow bluish blinking in the cave seemed to be signaling her, calling her by name.

Rella adjusted her necklace, checked her satchel for the scroll, and started moving toward it. She couldn't figure out why her guardian didn't try to stop her, yet she also sensed this was not the time for conversation. The blinking sped up, and she had to follow it, like an old friend calling her to play hide and seek.

How could a blinking blue light also be an old friend? she wondered.

She continued walking toward the cave. Her guardian's voice whispered in echoes from behind and above her, urging Rella to return to the cave, to where the journey began.

As she entered the cave, she felt the fabric of her grandmother's quilt fall upon her shoulders.

She was going home.

Chapter 48: Reunited

"FATHER! FATHER!" SCARLETT shouted, as she and Sebastian climbed out of the boat and ran to greet him on the shore. King stretched his arms wide and wrapped them around both children.

"We did it! We did it!" Sebastian shouted.

"What did you do?" King asked.

"We saved the tiger! And..." Sebastian shouted.

"What is that on your back!" King interrupted.

"This is Alister, dad. He's a bear," Sebastian said.

"Well...hello Alister!" King said. Alister was sleeping, however, and did not reply.

"Oh...he sleeps a lot. But I brought him here because I think we can...we need to help him...," Sebastian said.

"I see..." King said, turning his attention to Scarlett, who was fighting back tears.

"And you? My precious daughter," King said, reaching his arms out for a hug.

"Rella's got the scroll now," Scarlett replied as her father squeezed her, "and she's on her way home now."

"That's great news, Scarlett," King replied.

"Yes, but I think there's something...oh, I don't know...something terribly strange happening with The Architect...he knows my secret now, and...," she said, tripping over her own words.

"What is it, dear?" King asked, trying to slow her down by slowly patting her arm.

"I don't think he's working for Archi... (she didn't like saying *his* name, which wasn't really *his* name) ...Archimago. He's not really working for *him*. Or, at least, The Architect is not ...."

Scarlett was struggling to put her thoughts together.

"I am sure we will figure this out very quickly. In fact, I've just found some passages in one of The Red Notebooks that I know we can use to help this boy you call The Architect," King said.

"I wish I could have told him more about us, about this place, so he would know there was somewhere he could go. So that he wouldn't have had to return to...," Scarlett said, tears beginning to stream from her eyes as she collapsed into her father's arms.

"Well...he knew about Eurie and Rella, right? And, *he* was certain to figure out that you were not actually working for *him* soon enough," King said, comforting his daughter. "And what about the other girl, Prisma?"

Scarlett pulled her head back from her father's shoulder, and smiling like a child who had just been caught with an empty bag and a full belly of chocolate chip cookies, replied: "She fled, and oh my, ohhhh my, was she fuming about losing track of that tiger...But I don't know much more about her...she never seemed real to me."

"Yes! Yes! We saved that tiger, dad! It was amazing!" Sebastian interrupted, clapping his wooden hands together.

"Yes, Sebastian?" King replied.

"Dad, I know how we're going to help the other ones," Sebastian said.

After a brief but heavy pause, King replied: "Let's go inside and have some tea then. We have a lot more...I have a lot more to tell all of you."

King, Scarlett, and Sebastian all returned to the dining hall of Shelterwood Castle and began drawing up plans for the next steps they would take to restoring the Red Notebooks and protecting Hleo.

Alister woke from his nap and began answering questions, though he answered them very slowly. They asked him to tell his story, how he had come from Earth One, so they could make notes and gain even more clues to how they would rescue the other guardians. So many were still trapped on Archimago's island.

Until Rella's return, however, they would have to remain hidden in Hleo.

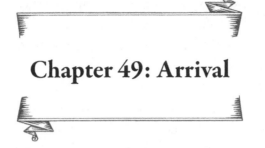

Chapter 49: Arrival

RELLA LIFTED THE HEAVY green quilt off her head. She spotted Uncle J's silhouette. The sun shined brightly behind him as he leaned over into the backseat of the car and gently lifted her up off of the floor. She felt like she hadn't seen sunlight for years.

"Didn't I tell you to stay buckled?" he said, in a fatherly, but only half-serious tone. He was too relieved that the long drive was finished to be worried about Rella's little act of defiance, and he was overdue for some rest. He had driven nearly three thousand miles in just a day and a half.

As she unloaded her boxes from the trunk, Rella spotted the Red Notebook that uncle J had mentioned finding in the hallway before they left. She looked at the cover and her heart began to race.

Uncle J looked at Rella and said: "I know these self-driving vehicles are supposed to have eliminated most of the dangers of the road, and you weren't in any real danger lying on the floor without a seatbelt, but I don't really trust these new technologies. Why can't we just go back to simpler times?"

Rella noticed him, but quickly turned her attention back to the notebook.

"But enough about that," he said, "Are you ready to see our new place? And your new room?"

As Rella stood in front of the tall apartment building, trying to adjust her mind and bring her vision back to earthly angles and dimensions, she felt something small and hard pressing against the middle of her chest. She reached her hand over it and knew it was the paintbrush.

"Yes," Rella said. "I'm ready."

They walked into the new building and headed directly up to bed.

Rella tucked herself into a sleeping bag on the floor of her new room. Uncle J said he would put her bed together as soon as the shipping planes arrived, probably within a week.

Her new room's white walls were barren and flat, like the screen of the Ensea drive-in theater in the middle of a winter storm. She was already getting ideas for decorating them.

Rella then realized that she hadn't even changed clothes since the car ride, but she wasn't planning to go to sleep yet. She wanted to sketch and hang up at least one picture before she drifted off.

She rolled over inside of the bag and propped herself up on her elbows. Something hard poked into her leg from inside her pocket. She reached down and pulled out a luminous stone and set it on the floor in front of her.

She formed a heart with her hands and cast a shadow on the wall. She thought about her parents. She glanced over at the quilt, neatly folded and lying in the corner.

As she started to think about her bedtime routine with her parents, she could hear her father's voice echoing through the room, just as it often sounded when he read from his favorite book. Only, this wasn't the book about the queen of the fairies. It was her very own story:

There once was a castle carved from the trunk of a tree the size of a city block. The castle was surrounded by an enchanted lake in a magical land known as Hleo. Within this castle, there lived a wooden boy named Sebastian, a father named King—who was not actually a king, and a daughter called Scarlett. The castle was filled with mysterious Red Notebooks that magically appeared and sometimes disappeared. One day, an evil force, a shape-shifter who called himself Archimago, appeared...trying to erase them all.

Rella wiped a tear from her eye. She was tired of dreaming.

Suddenly, there was a knock at the door.

"Yes?" Rella said, slinking down into her sleeping bag.

"I'd like you to meet our new neighbor," Uncle J exclaimed, cracking the door.

Rella sat up as the woman, who was carrying a small Red Notebook, entered the room.

As she looked the woman in the eyes, Rella noticed two things: the golden braid in her hair and the silver lines that formed along the outer edges of the woman's pupils. They reminded her of an eclipse.

"Hi, Rella. It's so good to meet you in person. If you aren't too tired, I'd like to read you something. It's about your parents. They have a message for you..."

The End

A Special Thanks To...

JONELLE AND KARTINI, I appreciate your enthusiasm and critical feedback on my drafts. I could not have finished this book without your editorial insights and thoughtful comments. Thank you.

About the Author

Author Jason Parks' earliest experiences with writing involved co-authoring a children's book in his elementary school art class called 'Flying Freddy' and a small collection of poems he wrote in the fifth grade, mostly about flowers. More recently, he has published multiple non-fiction essays on teaching, multilingual modernism, and literary magazines. After becoming a father, and spending nearly a decade reading wonderful books to his four children, he discovered his passion for creating whimsical and fantastic stories. He currently spends his time to teaching English at a liberal arts university in the Midwest (USA) and going on adventures (real and imaginary) with his family.

Read more at www.parkswrites.com.

Made in the USA
Coppell, TX
25 July 2020